The Perfect Everything

by
Jeffrey Allen

ISBN: 0692229361
ISBN 13: 9780692229361

Printed in the United States of America

First Printing, 2014

For more information about the novel, visit:
www.theperfecteverything.net
For media inquiries, feedback or ordering information, email:
mediape@yahoo.com

"I was at this casino minding my own business, and this guy came up to me and said, 'You're gonna have to move, you're blocking a fire exit.' As though if there was a fire, I wasn't gonna run. If you're flammable and have legs, you are never blocking a fire exit."

-Mitch Hedberg

Chapter 1

ELDEN LEWIS, THE GREAT SEER, the Zen master of the human psyche, the perpetual barstool philosopher and my best friend, predicted I will cry three times during a one-third-life crisis this year, and he will be wrong. This is my thought just as Cassandra throws her espresso martini at me across the dinner table in the middle of a busy Manhattan restaurant. The drink nails my linen shirt--an amazing shot actually--and the utter shock and embarrassment of the spectacle must have me blushing, but there's no way I'm crying. I say it just like that too, while looking away from her as though I'm addressing a T.V. audience.

"You don't see me crying, do you?"

The restaurant hushes. I hear the clangs of forks dropping on plates, and I don't look, but I sense that all eyes are suddenly on us--the two 27-year-olds acting like teenagers.

"Excuse me?" My girlfriend can scarcely believe her ears. After all, we almost never fought in our five years together.

"Yeah, sure. You're excused," I say. For a moment, I even conjure up a smug smile. But this isn't me at all. It isn't her either. Call it the irrational by-product of nervousness and confusion, call me a nouveau asshole, call anything whatever; the fact is, we're both in extremely un-chartered waters, flustered, going by what we've only seen in movies, and here in front of a live audience no less. People are always hungriest for drama, even if they do have an excellent meal in front of them.

"You know what," Cassandra says, grabbing her purse. "You've become impossible to love. And I'm leaving." To be honest though, all I hear is her friggin' volume. Suddenly that's the worst part. If she smeared moist cat food in my hair it wouldn't be as bad...just keep it the fuck down. And how did I become that guy in the cliché public shouting match anyway? For the first time I sorta buy into the shock value that Hollywood's selling. Hell, I'll even buy into spontaneous combustion.

"Ssshhh. Can't you keep it down?"

"Fuck you Allen," she yells, standing up.

"I know you want to," I fire back after her. She turns and gives me the finger and scurries off for the exit. Gone. There's nearby laugher--some blatant, some poorly concealed behind cupping hands--but I hate this rebuttal. I know you want to? Why am I insisting on quirky jokes now? I can laugh and cry at the same time. But if I cry, that's only from embarrassment and that doesn't count now, does it Elden?

And why the drink toss? What acts could I possibly have committed monstrous enough to warrant such a proverbially furious response? I'm dazed and as curious to know as anyone. Moments after Cassandra leaves the restaurant, my check is mercifully handed to me. I pay for only drinks since we hadn't ordered food yet, and then tip a make-believe hat to the facetious round of applause I'm getting. Then I gather up my wine buzz and pour out onto Lexington Avenue.

✳✳✳

Sunlight bathed us on the walk to the restaurant, but now a slow May twilight has begun descending on the city, along with a gentle rain shower that coats the streets wet jet black and streaks them with reflections of car lights. I walk slowly despite not having an umbrella because the water washes the espresso from my shirt and helps me blend in with society. After the restaurant episode, I'm thankful that my 15 minutes of negative fame are up and I've never appreciated anonymity more as I walk past the throngs of early Saturday evening pedestrians. I walk in the general direction of uptown because I live downtown with Cassandra. I know it wouldn't be wise to go there straight away. For one thing, it would be awkward, like when you say goodbye to someone and then you realize you both still need to walk in the same direction. More importantly, she needs to cool off. If she goes home, she'll probably use the deadbolt for which I have no key (as I learned in a lesser fight a month ago). Or--worse--if I did manage to get up there, she'd probably slap my face to complete the square.

Above all though, I need to sit down and have a drink and replay and analyze what the hell just happened.

Since I didn't get to eat at the restaurant, I stop at Subway--the sandwich chain--and I have to wait for this one jerk-off who can't make up his mind about what he wants on the terrible sandwich he is ordering. I find I'm always criticizing other people's sandwiches, their choices on toppings and how they get something toasted when it shouldn't be. This gazoon has the works on roast beef with a pound of olives and a sea of ranch drooled all over it. The shittiest sandwich I've ever seen.

The rain shower lets up and there's a warm wind as I approach 60th Street, and it occurs to me that I'm near a place I've always wanted to check out. It's called The Book Bar, which is supposed to be a semi-private cigar lounge. Translation: it's one of the few places in New York that I heard will let you get away with smoking cigarettes. Not that I'm a much of a smoker--I have to stop and buy a pack for this state of disarray--but when I get stressed I can use one, and right now I can use a pack.

So here's the deal: everyone needs to wear a suit jacket at this bar. I guess they get around the no smoking law by posing as some sort of semi-private club with a dress code. I suppose if I don a tux I can light a joint, but any clothes will do now as I'm fairly soaked.

"Well I don't have a jacket on me," I say, half in jest, to the rigid hostess.

"We will be happy to provide you with one at this time," she says. She snaps her fingers the way billionaires must and a man materializes to my left. He pulls out a tape measure and I'm a 40 regular and two minutes later I'm looking sharp. I just love getting all dressed up to defile myself.

"What can I get you sir?" the bartender says before I reach the bar. I can tell this place calls for scotch, which is something Elden got me into.

"Scotch on the rocks. 15 years. Something peaty."

"Would you like to see our menu?"

I say yes only to buy time to decide what to do, where to sit. In light of the rare opportunity to smoke in a public building, I pull out a cigarette and begin fishing for a light while scanning the congested bar area. Three very old men in various checker-patterned sports coats are sitting to my left talking over pipes. Their chatter is of the slow and sullen variety that you might expect from this dark, smoky place, which isn't entirely different from a VFW or Polish-American-type club except that there are leather-bound books instead of the usual collection of color-faded flags. I tune everyone out because I'm too busy trying to dissect my own feelings. I've never been truly in love with anyone before Cassandra--or Cassan as I much prefer. Nor have I been in a lengthy relationship before. I've certainly never been in a fight with a woman like we just had either. If her threats about leaving me were legit, what would happen? How would I react? Is heartbreak really as bad as it's cracked up to be? I should be all devastated, but I'm not. Will I be? I'm just sort of confused and in shock I think. My fingers shake noticeably as I drink, but I'm not sad per se.

✳✳✳

My attention turns to my immediate right, where two attractive and slightly older (30-something) women are seated. A tall brunette and a short blonde, both smoking cigarettes and discussing the cons of the latter's recent date or boyfriend.

"It's just that he's too inconsiderate," the short one says.

"How's that?" The brunette is listening intensely, nearly falling in her lean. She seems to think she's having a drink with Moses as he confides in her that there's actually an 11th Commandment.

"Just like he has no sense of manners. He always walks ahead of me and he never opens doors. Oh, and he never says thank you for anything."

I don't want to interrupt, but all I have in my pocket are wet matches for my own cigarette I've longed for.

"Hey, sorry to bother you. Do either of you have a light?"

I cringe, hoping their anger won't transfer to me. They turn and look me over a second, and the shorter one sticks out a lighter and flicks it. I reach towards the flame until the tip of my cigarette crackles orange and take a long, soothing drag. After I exhale, we all sorta watch the smoke unravel into the air for a moment. Then I look them both in the eyes.

"Thank you," I say, with an added touch of sincerity. They laugh in unison, realizing I overheard them.

"Made up your mind?" the bartender says.

"Another one please. I'm gonna grab a table too."

I give the girls a toast with the remainder of my first drink and they smile back. I trade up for a fresh new snifter glass of scotch and walk away and sit at the last free table in a cozy little nook beside a collection of encyclopedias.

Here's where I can finally gather my thoughts, and they are good thoughts. Memories--as if my relationship is a thing of the past already! And I can see how painful everything could be if we do break up, because five years of dating someone translates to five years worth of sweet and heart-wrenching reminders; Five years worth of favorite shared songs and movie lines and parties and discoveries and trivial experiences of joy together in the city, not to mention the bedroom. There's a photo of a violinist on the wall next to me, and I remember how I was handed tickets to a symphony orchestra once; how Cassan and I reluctantly decided to check it out. We started at a pub and drank too long and had to run to Lincoln Center drunk; at the performance, how we yelled "bravo" far too loud and much too often, and other times quietly jeering or giggling like we did as early as college in the library, and really, as we always do in places we shouldn't. It's nothing to speak of to anyone--just simplistic snapshots in time--but they occupy my mind.

I smile at the thought that if Cassan were here now, I'd call extension 207 to ask her what happened at dinner. By saying "Extension 207," she would know to immediately take a time out from our humor and be serious. Our relentless absurdity requires such a safeguard and we somehow we arrived at Extension 207, which is essentially like verbally dialing the other's sincere attention. She would quickly shut up and be all ears.

Because so much of our relationship was predicated on our mutual sense of humor, the growing arguments of late and especially what just happened are so crazy to fathom. We have always been a bit cocky even about our particular brand of humor, referring to it as "The Humor." If I told her someone was funny, she'd ask, "does he have The Humor?" Invariably the answer was no. Elden has it when he wants too, but nobody else we've met.

I remember one night vividly when Cassan and I first moved in together. We had a small party at the apartment and everyone took turns introducing drinking games.

"Let's play Shit Ass," I yelled. Everyone looked at me puzzled. Everyone except Cassan.

"Yessssss! Great call," she yelled, even though she knew it was something I was just making up on the spot.

"What the hell is shit ass," somebody (rightfully) asked.

"I can't just tell you because it's sort of a puzzle game, but you'll figure it out." The key to messing with anyone is to talk fast and sound distracted. Cassan and I exchanged devious glances, fighting back laughter. We knew the road was paved for levels of ridiculousness normally reserved for when we were alone. The idea of the game was making people think there were actual rules they had to discover and that they had to drink when they screwed up. The only real trick was how long Cassan and I could keep up the charade until we were made.

"I'll start," I said. "Just try to follow along. OK, 1, 2, 3..." I took a sip of beer and slammed my cup down and pointed across the table at a girlfriend of ours, yelling, "shit ass!"

"What do I do," the poor girl asked.

"Just drink," Cassan said. This made me nearly spit out my own drink in laughter. Naturally she was right there with me in this fake new game, her beautiful blue eyes beaming with anticipation.

"My turn." There were about seven of us seated around a long coffee table that was littered with bottles and cups of beer, vodka and wine. "OK, Wild Bill!"

Everyone stared at her perplexed, but I leapt into action as if it was obvious what to do. I jumped up onto the table and air-rode a make-believe horse before throwing an empty red party cup at a guy I didn't know.

"What the fuck," the man yelled.

"Drink Chris," Cassan said.

"What for?" He protested, not happy to have to drink on top of getting hit.

"He got you with Wild Bill. Drink and then you start."

"Start what? How do I start."

"Drink for not knowing."

And on and on like that.

I fast-forward to the changes in Cassan and I; the decline of our witty and goofy conversations and the passion in the things we shared. Then came week-nights on my own chasing my dreams of stand-up comedy while she hung out with new friends she made in the fashion industry. Frustrations and arguments began to mount. The whole turn for the worse has been a slow capitulation that makes it difficult to both see and feel where things started going south. Regardless, I could never imagine that a love built on a mutual sense of humor and creativity and respect could lead to what happened tonight. And so I shake my head suddenly with this thought: Screw her that she threw a fucking drink on me!

My face is buried in my arms. I reach blindly for my glass and swish the ice around with the stirrer. I guess I knew this was coming. Things haven't been right in a while; I realize that now.

✳✳✳

"Are you meeting someone here?"

I look up and the girls from the bar are already placing their jackets and pocketbooks on empty chairs at my table.

"Um...no. Is this a communal seating bar?"

"No, but these are the only free seats at any table, the brunette says.

I don't know how I feel about this. First off, this isn't supposed to be how it works. Women sniff out confidence in men, and if they do initiate things, their motives are typically predicated on that confidence. Me, I'm a bit of a wreck right now. Pounding scotch and smoking with my wavy wet hair tousled about like a flustered Muppet.

"No. I mean, sure. Please."

"Cool. I'm Stacy," the taller brunette says. She sticks out her hand to shake, revealing a large diamond on her married finger in the process. This annoys the hell out of me. Why come over if you are married? I picture cupid as some sleazy dick just above her, cackling in accusation that I botched my own relationship. But in the same nano-second, I know what this all means about the married girl: Stacy is the wingman for her single girlfriend.

"I'm Kate," she says while putting away her phone. She has that sort of hotness that's probably still in place even when she wakes up in the morning sans makeup or while sweating out a fever. With her model nose and turquoise eyes I'm sure she is much more attractive to the general public than Cassan, but not to me. Kate's hair is something out of a conditioner commercial, all long and light and silky smooth, and she has to clear it from her face as she talks.

"Kate Winslet, actually," she says with a laugh. "Like the actress."

It's not funny though, so I just toss her a complimentary smile to be polite.

"Alan Jones, since it's all formal."

"So what brings you two over? Is it the suit?" I tug on my lapel.

"I live around the corner and we like that we can smoke here," Stacy says.

"But otherwise it's boring," Kate adds. She shoots Stacy an obvious set of facial codes that I read as either, "he's cute" or "he seems cool," and then she revs things up.

"Actually, we had a bet. We debated what could bring an attractive young guy to a stuffy bar like this by himself on a Saturday night."

"Attractive huh?"

"Somewhat," Kate snaps back immediately, right on top of my question. Then she smiles at me.

"Is it girl trouble?" Stacy asks.

"Is there any other kind?"

"Actually," she says, "My grandmother just passed away."

There's an awkward silence, but I want to laugh. I'm reminded of Sacha Baron Cohen's Ali G character who fed on awkwardness. And she's right of course. There are plenty of other troubles out there, but the only trouble you can profoundly feel is the kind you have. I take a gargantuan slug of the golden scotch liquor like some down-and-out cowboy in a melodramatic B movie and feel myself slipping into the part seamlessly.

"Well, at least she's peaceful I guess." I can't help letting out a little smile at this--at the comedic value of being out of line. It's the first moment I've felt a bit like myself all night actually.

"So what happened with this girl?" Kate says.

"Well, I just came from this intense, ridiculous fight with my girlfriend and I'm not sure if we broke up."

"Whoa!" She reaches to pull her hair back and I notice for the first time that her breasts are huge--much bigger than they should be for her frame--and there's this uneasy feeling that she might topple over at any moment. They must be fake though, and I'm not a fan of anything fake.

"Yeah, but what I mean is, I'd rather not get into it."

The girls sip at their martinis with boiling curiosities and I think I'm right: I think that I'd rather not talk about it.

"So what do you do Alan," Stacy asks.

"Copywriting for an ad agency."

"Cool. What accounts do you work on?"

"Sports mostly," I say. "Right now I'm working on Major League Baseball."

This is all true. In fact, I'm supposed to hear back Monday on approval for a major campaign I pitched that compares baseball to a soap opera.

"So what about you," I ask Kate.

"I'm a commercial actress. And I'm a Scorpio and I want babies."

And this isn't the conversation I want to have. Not because I don't know birth signs (I do: we did a campaign for the PGA tour that attempted to bring more personality to the sport by defining the best golfers by their horoscopes), but rather because my mind is too fired up in all directions at moment for small talk. Besides, what can I say about Scorpios except that they're all about willpower and optimism and include legendary golfers Fuzzy Zoeller and Gary Player.

"No, not that. Tell me something juicy. Who's smarter out of you two? Who's better in bed?"

I'm really just a ball of apathy now and I feel like some seasoned player.

"I'm better in bed. Stacy's smarter. Where are you from?"

I explain how I grew up in Stamford, CT just 40 minutes by train to Midtown Manhattan. How I had the best of both worlds with the beaches and trees and nice coastal towns that are ideal for growing up. But I bore myself talking about it.

Luckily Kate is already loaded with a different question.

"What's your dream job?"

I pause, letting out my usual breathy laugh that makes me sound like a stoner. Then I tell her how I always dreamed of doing standup comedy.

"Cool. So why don't you?"

"Well I had been doing it for a bit actually. I took a class at Caroline's on Broadway and did open mics and shows at lesser-known comedy clubs."

"Nice. Why did you stop?"

"Well for one, my style doesn't translate to stage. But also my girlfriend didn't like losing me to the shows on Friday and Saturday nights."

"But that was your dream right?"

"Yeah, but I wasn't very good at it. Plus I need to pay the bills and I did the comedy for free."

✳✳✳

The ice has melted into the remainder of my drink, diluting the glorious golden hue of the scotch. We carry on for another 20 minutes about NYC living until I remember that I still have two tickets for a comedy show tonight. Nearby too. The tickets were for the defunct Cassan and myself, so I decide to invite the women to join me and hope we can get a third ticket at the door. What else is there to do now, and why not? Laughs are in order. Laughs are always in order, damn it.

"So who wants to see some comedy over on 82nd?"

"I do!" Kate yells.

But then they exchange the sort of advanced non-verbal communication that only long-time friends can before Stacy stands up, gesturing towards the restroom. Kate indicates one moment to me with her finger and follows her.

As I wait I realize this: I'd prefer to go with Stacy to the show. After all, she's married and so (presumably) she is safe company. As for Kate, the thing I've learned in my distant past about going for attractive women like her is that it will always come back to bite you. There's always some sort of baggage or drama. And not that it matters tonight being that I am presumably still in a relationship, but hot women like her are always being pursued 24/7 and you know that every second you're not with them another man is trying to be. Another thing with Kate is this extremely shallow attraction-personality theory that Elden and I crafted one drunken evening. The basic idea is that terribly unattractive people tend to be less socially skilled thanks to a less engaging social life (i.e. less "practice"). The same goes for those on the other end of the beauty spectrum like models, who are often pretentious and conceded divas and mere reflections of the socially skilled. This means that the average-to-cute-looking people in the middle often have the best personalities. To visualize this, you have to imagine a bell curve with personality on the vertical axis and attraction on the horizontal. Except the curve is slightly skewed so that those who are above average looks-wise but *not* hot fall at the apex of the personality curve, like Cassan. I know, I know: It's a mean and gross generalization and whatever.

My only point is that Kate is too hot to be cool and probably not the sort of laidback fun type I go for. God, maybe I am an asshole.

"I'm in for the comedy," Kate says when they return from the bathroom. "I live in that neighborhood and I like the idea of staying local tonight."

"Just you?"

"I have to meet some other friends downtown soon," Stacy says.

I sigh inwardly, not sure if I buy it, but it does solve the ticket problem. I suppose I'm lucky to have any further company tonight too. Almost like an instant rebound, but without the sex. Just a night to remind me the world is bigger than Cassan. We grab our check and say our goodbyes to Stacy outside on the street, and then Kate and I start walking east towards the show.

Chapter 2

MOST THINGS ARE FUNNY TO ME and throughout my life I've always taken great pains to write them down, whether on my phone or in a bedside notepad or however I can instantly capture a comedic thought. I explain this to Kate as we walk past a bum, recalling one joke I had about how much money bums are saving. I jotted down a whole bit about this on a cocktail napkin and added it to one of the many folders loaded with humorous observations and other comedy material that I have filed away in my apartment.

Comedy has been my passion since the age of 8 when I used to set up mock stages and perform shows for my parents and their friends. I had a wooden stool that I demanded for my birthday one year and a turkey baster for a mic, and I would make my father emcee my shows after dinner parties. I'd push through the country-themed living room drapes replete with images of broken wagons and covered bridges and hop up onto my stool before the brick fireplace that served as my backdrop.

"Get a load of this crew," I began often. Of course, my skills as a fifth-grader were fairly green then so I didn't articulate any further, and simply moved on to my next joke. And that's what they mostly were then: jokes. At college parties I was a hit with my flawless recreations of standup comedy bits from Louis CK (my all-time favorite), Dane Cook, Bill Burr, Eddie Murphy, Jerry Seinfeld and countless others, and when I made my way to New York after college, I put together a few routines of different lengths and started my side career as a comic.

Cassan never really encouraged my pursuits of stand-up. I guess that's because I was much better at copywriting (which is also quite lucrative) even though I always complain about it. We met at Dartmouth College and became best friends, but we didn't start dating until after graduation. Somewhere before the drinking started back at the restaurant tonight though, she carried on about how much we both had changed. Had I grown a bit antsy in life? Sure. Not changed though. If anything, *she's* the one who changed--and for the worse I might add. So much for all those college superlatives I won that seemed to matter to her then. Worthless now are those home-made college certificates praising me for "Best Sense of Humor," "Dorm Partier," "Most Creative," and "Best Eyes." My eyes are brown though, so I never put much stock in that one anyhow.

✳✳✳

Kate and I arrive at the Comic Strip Live late but they held the last table for us. I'm not surprised when I see that our seats are front and center so that we find ourselves looking directly up at the emcee in a truly beguiling fashion. We're total prey for his sarcasm, I know. He's a smooth-looking black guy with clean, dreaded, long hair, a faint goatee, and cool demeanor, and I know from my interest in the NYC comedy scene that he is the omnipresent, seasoned veteran Lutsey Lampkin. As we order drinks, he's attempting to warm up the crowd with jokes about where people are from, along with crass jokes about sex. There's no doubt we're in for it.

Oh, so look who decided to join us," the comedian says immediately, interrupting his act to chastise Kate and I. "Where are you guys from?"

Kate is shy suddenly, but fortunately for her I'm an extreme extrovert and assume the role of spokesperson.

"Right here, man. Manhattan."

"You guys dating?" Before I can respond though, Kate blurts out no. And that's just perfect bait for any experienced comic like Lampkin.

"Ohhhhhh," he says, scratching his chin dramatically. "So ya'll is just fucking then!"

The crowd loves it and I find myself laughing a bit too, but Kate turns away blushing, which is the wrong way to be. If I viewed this as I date, I'd be down on her reaction, because if you ask me, taking a date to a comedy club is great way to find out about where someone stands in many ways, including--but not limited to--their sense of humor.

The emcee calls up the first act and she's awful. At one point in a moment of painful silence she says, "what do you want...we all know women aren't funny"--and that actually was funny. Not that I think it's entirely true; it's just funny to hear. I mean, I've come across many a funny girl, and Cassan is chief among them.

"O.K. everyone, ya'll ready for more show?" It's Lutsey Lampkin again, but his re-appearance is quick and funny like a fart, and it's disappointing to see him simply introduce the next act and hop back off stage. I hate when the most talented comedian is resigned to the emcee role for a show.

The pain continues with the next act. It's a white guy, overweight with bushy blond hair. He's wearing suspenders, which is a bad sign. Sight gags translate to bad comedians or bad writing at least, and he's no exception. But his act starts to improve after he finishes with the props.

"So I just got in from Kansas," he says, tugging on the right suspender." That shit is flat. Like Japanese women chest flat." Then he looks down at his prey (Kate) sitting front and center and he gestures towards her. "This woman has no idea what I'm talking about, do you honey?" He imitates Kate with a stereotypical bimbo voice: "Small titties? What are those? Don't cup sizes start at C+?"

Kate looks at me and rolls her eyes, and I laugh inwardly at her. She still hadn't gotten over the first attack by Lampkin and now she's apparently fuming. She clenches her little red purse tight and purses her lips even tighter. Me, I'm suddenly enjoying the guy a bit. It's a guilty pleasure at first, but then he begins to fall apart again and goes after me. Don't get me wrong--I can take it--but he's really sinking fast and he's resorted to forced jokes about the first guy in sight just to stay afloat. There's a whole science to standup comedy that I'd love to write a book about if only I had more stage experience and actual skill to go with my knowledge of the subject. For example, it's empowering to be able to go after people in the audience or anything else in the room for that matter if you can generate spontaneous humor. That's credibility and people always respect it. You should sprinkle it in or make it a big part of your act if you have some novel twist on it. Sort of like the comic Judith Freidlander. But when it's timed awkwardly or becomes a replacement for your act its obvious desperation, like now.

"Is that actually your shirt?" the comic asks me. I'm still in the black linen shirt, but luckily there are no traces of the espresso martini remaining.

"Yep." I look down for a quick examination and see that my left collar has flapped up a bit.

"What's up with your collar my man? You preparing for take-off?"

A spattering of laughs are audible, but nothing much. Hyperbole isn't funny unless there's the smallest ounce of quirky truth in it.

"I know your career isn't," I say. I sorta regret this rueful comment as much as I hated some of the things I said to Cassan back at the restaurant. The comic makes a quick comeback in the form of patronizing gestures and the show just moves on. But I can see that Kate's uncomfortable and not having a good time and I guess I'm not either anymore, so I whisper to her that we should go. We signal for our check and walk out as the comedian wraps up.

"It's great to get out of there," Kate says, applying lipstick. Those guys sucked!"

"I thought the emcee was good though."

"Hey, I know a fun place for a drink." Kate's eyes are beaming suddenly with life back on her terms. "There's this little gay piano bar around the corner you have to see. It's a trip." I can tell she's into me, which makes at least one woman tonight.

"Sure."

I dutifully follow, and we come upon a divvy tavern-looking place hidden in the middle of a residential cross street. Sure enough, the place is jam-packed and bursting with gay spirit from the moment we enter. Three men in cowboy gear are belting out "Come Sail Away" into the one mic stand beside the door, and it's so loud I have to read Kate's lips saying let's get a drink. The place smacks with fun for sure, though it's a touch too rowdy for my tastes at the moment with people hugging and yelling at strangers left and right. I consider an invention of special pants for such a bar where metal plates cover the ass and genitals, but I throw it back to the comedy universe like too small a fish.

Kate says something that I can't make out.

"What?"

She tries again, yelling, but I still can't hear her. She smiles though, so I just smile back since it's embarrassing to ask what she said again. But then she cups my ear and says, "you didn't hear a word I said did you?"

"No." I was had.

"All I said is I'm getting a whiskey. Want one?"

I do and she gets us a round.

"Like this place?" she lip-speaks.

"Giddy up!"

Another group begins singing "Dancing Queen" and we watch them go for a while. There's only a pianist to accompany the vocals though, and the crowd obviously loves that they are required to help things out. After a few songs it's apparent that a handful of the same adventurous audience singers keep taking turns as they go through "I Am What I Am" by Gloria Gaynor, "We Are Family" by Sister Sledge and "Freedom '90" by George Michael, and it never occurred to me until now how many gay essential songs there are.

Kate wants to dance and I'm lucky there's no room to do so. Instead we grab a table in the back room where it's quieter and sit for a while.

"So have you travelled anywhere interesting?" Kate says out of nowhere. She pokes at the ice in her drink with her stirrer and the whole thing feels like a Bond movie suddenly.

"You mean like what other countries I've been too?"

"Yeah."

"Well, I lived in Costa Rica for almost a year."

"Really. What for?"

"After college, I wanted to travel for a while and when I got to Costa Rica I got a bartending job at a surf camp and ended up staying there. Met this girl and all."

The girl, Sam, was the last I'd been with before Cassan, who I got together with right after I came back to the States.

"Wait, how old are you now?"

"27."

"Really?! I had you at 32. Do you get that a lot?"

"No, not really."

I resist asking her age, but she just blurts it out.

I'm 38."

"Really? I would never have guessed."

"I'm a cougar," she yells, laughing, and she clinks my glass. The whole comment doesn't sit well with me though, especially given that she also had mentioned wanting babies. There's just something a bit desperate about her, which is odd for her looks.

"What do you do?"

"You know: I'm in advertising."

"Oh yeah," she says, slurping her drink. "So what college did you go to?"

"Dartmouth."

"Cool. What was your major?"

Her line of questioning grows tedious again and she keeps staring too intensely at my eyes. Has she been out with a guy in the last 38 years? Maybe it's because of all this or maybe it's because I'm drunk suddenly, but I switch gears and tell her about the fight with Cassan. I tell her how I took my girlfriend to a nice restaurant, how things got heated and how she cursed me and threw her drink on me in front of everyone. She listens with gaping mouth and breathy laugh, perhaps taking some satisfaction in a vicarious dose of justice bestowed upon a member of the male gender.

"So wait, this happened tonight?"

"Yeah, just before I met you and Stacy."

"Holy shit! Are you OK?"

"Yeah, you know, I'm really not bad right now."

"What did you do man?"

"That's what I'm trying to figure out." I take an especially harsh gulp of my drink and feel the whisky sear my throat.

"So did you start it? Are you the bad guy?"

"No, honestly," I say, not appreciative of the accusation. "Cassandra--that's her name--has been increasingly different these last few months. I don't know how long. She has different friends and a more hip lifestyle and she's just not the same girl anymore. At first it was just stupid arguments that we never used to have and lately we haven't been on the same page and a lot of the excitement is gone.

"OK," Kate says, her jaw ajar. I have to admit, she's a good listener. "So you have no idea what went wrong?"

"I have some idea. It has to do with me not evolving into the hipster lifestyle she evolved into I think. But to be fair, there's stuff on my end too. She did say something and I get it. She said I didn't seem content with anything anymore.

"Is that true?"

I pause and take a drink while constructing the answer that I have been mulling over the last few weeks; the answer I know to be correct, but one I had never even acknowledged to myself officially."

"Yes. I mean, I guess we both got too busy for each other and interested in other things. We both only knew one job and one partner ever since college."

"What about the restaurant? What happened?"

"Well, I always asked her if everything was ok, and she always said yes and changed the topic. Then at the restaurant, I asked again, and she said things obviously weren't ok. Things had changed. *We* had changed. Then she said she's not even sure if this whole thing will still work."

"And then she threw a drink at you?"

"No, then I threw an ice cube at her chest."

Kate shakes her head like a penguin.

"What?"

"Yeah, I was shocked," I plead. And I realize I had forgotten all about that detail until now. "It was just a little piece of ice. It splattered like a big drop of water. It just happened out of sheer frustration but I tried to laugh it off like I was kidding. I think maybe it was frustration at myself as much as with her."

"And then?"

"And then she got all irate and told me I suck or whatever. And so I asked her why she's always talking to me in such vague ways about our problems and suggested that she's become too hip and prima donna and full of bullshit to even know herself. And then she friggin' threw her drink at me in the middle of the restaurant."

There's a moment of silence and bewilderment.

"I'm not a bad guy," I add. "Trust me. If you knew me, you'd think I was nice and sweet and upstanding and all that. All I'm guilty of is working a lot lately and being uncharacteristically out of touch with pop culture and maybe wondering if life is passing me by."

At this point, Kate pipes up with a bit of mundane advice that's worth a bit less than a pile of horseshit.

"Well, it doesn't sound like it's anyone's fault. People change and some-times they need different things."

"I'll remember that," I say, my tone indicating we're about done with this. I try to shoot her a friendly smile. On the one hand, I suppose I should be grateful to have this hot and presumably available woman so eager to play psy-chologist to a solo male stranger who she probably perceives to be an asshole. But then there are those maxims that women fall for assholes and that nice guys finish last, etc., etc., blah, blah, blah, Vinny Dam Diesel. On the other hand, my whiskey is nearly done. I slug the rest down, and we decide to get going.

✳✳✳

I light a cigarette outside the bar for the walk. But a walk to where?

"Well, if you don't want to go home, you're welcome to crash with me," Kate offers.

Ordinarily I would take this opportunity to run for the hills (if I was clearly single), but she's sort of right: I don't want to go home. I'm not ready for Cassan and I'd rather not be alone just now either.

"Yeah, is that cool?"

"Definitely."

One great thing I can say for myself proudly is that I've never cheated on a girlfriend of substance before and I'm certainly not starting now. I still love and respect Cassan far too much for that, and I even still lust for her sexually above anyone else. Still, I'm allowing for this immediate confidence-boost to take place. If I can so quickly roll into another situation with a woman in a matter of hours then what do I have to fear? If I were in another place in life--if Cassan never existed--I'd certainly give Kate a fair shake, if not for her personality that I find unmoving, then at least for her looks. And now I realize she probably does want to hook up. Of course she would, right? I'm vulnerable and she chose to come with me and we had fun and I accepted to crash at her place. I could tell her I'm not looking to hook up right now, but I decide to humor the situation; to clam up a bit, say little, and walk in offbeat strides. I secretly dwell on the concept of kissing. The idea that smacking lips says, "let's do this." Most of my past first kisses came from slipping into a casual rhythm with someone. The kiss just happened naturally. Success thereafter was merely predicated upon not having a horrific breath at the time.

"Why are you walking all far back?"

"Me? You're the one hauling ass. Did you know New Yorkers walk on average 10 percent faster than the rest of the country?"

"But you're a New Yorker too, aren't you?"

I don't know what to say to this, so I just smile and put out the cigarette. Then she stops.

"Are you O.K.?"

And of course I'm not O.K. and I realize how I can just say so and put any awkwardness of the Alan-Kate scene to bed--figuratively.

"I'm not sure." At this, Kate suddenly produces this sympathetic puppy look, her face accentuating her beauty so well that it must be the same rehearsed look she gives every young man on a stroll home. Her "closer" face.

We walk a few blocks and reach her place. It's an unassuming four-story brick walk-up on 80th Street that has this pointless little gate she has to unlock just to walk another foot to the building's front door. New York is loaded with pointless little gates. Aside from the gate though, the neighborhood is very different from mine. By day, the average Upper East Side citizen is a nanny or private school student and by night all you see are college kids skipping by in drunken stupors. Plus, the dogs seem smaller.

We hike up to the third floor and finally into Kate's one-bedroom apartment, which is a total mess. Her front door opens to a living room and the first thing I notice is a short couch with crackers seeping out into the cracks between the cushions. There's an ironing board just to my left and two pairs of underwear on the floor beside it. All of her decorations--strictly paintings of dogs--are crooked too.

"Want a drink?"

"Definitely. Any liquor will do."

I sit on the cracker-free cushion of the loveseat and look around wondering if I'll be living this way 10 years from now, when I hit my upper 30s. If I'll be single and living alone in a dirty, sullen walk-up, tilting my head ever so slightly to look at pictures of labradoodles on the wall.

"Why the dogs," I yell to her in the kitchen.

"I used to have some," she says. I shrug to myself, as if this was a complete answer. Kate walks back over to me.

"Here you go, rum and coke." As she hands me the drink, she looks at the cushions and sees the mess and cleans up quickly without apologies. She sits uncomfortably close, puts her drink down and looks at me suddenly. It's the fuck me look, and I recognize it despite not having seen it from Cassan in a month. And Kate's hot and I know definitively what I am going to do next and forgive me, please O my male brethren forgive me for...

"You know," I say, "You've been real cool tonight and I appreciate it. I know things are crazy, but I still technically have a girlfriend who I love and--"

"Hey, don't worry about it. I understand. You'll let me know if you are available again some day, right?" But I know she doesn't understand, because how could a hot, single, Manhattan bachelorette pushing 40 possibly? Surely she could hop in and out of relationships or be married with kids right now if she wanted. But what she really wants tonight is to prey on a cute, vulnerable young man and lure him back to her pad to score with him on a bed of crackers. I sip more rum and I vaguely know I'm being unjustifiably mean to her if only in my head, but goddammit, liquor and Cassan have potent effects.

As we talk, I wonder where things went wrong for Kate, or where they simply never went right. She starts telling me about how she was married once for two years and how she left him because they didn't get along. And how another engagement was broken off. There were never kids. She wants kids, she says, "but only if I find the perfect guy."

I go off on a sappy tangent, waxing poetic on the fragility of love. I ask Kate if, subconsciously, I could have fallen out of love with Cassan. Mostly, I'm just babbling to thwart the temptation of hooking up and I know I'm beginning to sound like an absolute bore, and so enough. We decide to go to sleep. But there's no way I'm sleeping on that garbage couch.

"Sleep with me if you like," she yawns. "Just don't hog the covers."

We walk to her bedroom and she lies down as I stumble into the bathroom in some surreal attempt to freshen up. I have to use her stuff and I find the process difficult. You'd think that after living with a girl for several years I'd be a pro, but there's so many niche toiletry products and brands and contraptions marketed to women that every female bathroom is its own unique entity. All I want is some toothpaste and a bar of soap, but I have to sort through loofahs, creams, scrubs, and hair implements, and inspect everything like a child. I finger-scrub my teeth with some vanilla-flavored toothpaste and climb into bed with Kate who is sound asleep. I check my voicemail and there are no messages. I turn off the lights and lie there for a moment. There's a good part of me that wants to start rubbing up and grinding on Kate. She is wearing these hot boy shorts and a t-shirt and how could I not? I resist the temptation though, and instead grab my cell phone type a quick text message to Cassan. It reads simply: Are you all right?

Chapter 3

I FEEL LIKE I'VE BEEN HIT BY A TRUCK. My head is spinning, I have to fumble around to find my sleeping left arm, and my mouth is so dry that I recall dreaming of water. Still dressed in last night's clothes, I crawl out of bed uncharacteristically early for a Sunday morning--Kate's alarm says 8 a.m.--and promise my body more sleep when I get home, when I return to civilization and far, far away from the dreariness that I've suddenly come to associate with the Upper East Side.

Beams of sunlight penetrate the bedroom through the blinds and I can see Kate's sleeping face, drooling beautifully amidst an enormous poof of pillow. I stand over her a minute, unsure how to leave things. Then I decide to give her a stupid little pat on her shoulder and whisper thanks. She just mumbles something incoherent back though, so I leave my business card on her dresser as a courtesy more than anything else, and then I tip-toe out of the room and make for the front door as though heaven awaited on the other side.

But I'm far from heaven, I know, stepping out into the blinding low-lying sun with my disheveled hair and attire. I flag a cab and give the driver my address and notice that his name displayed on the window partition is Khani Khani.

"What's your ethnicity?" I ask.

"Pakistani, my friend."

"Been driving a cab long?"

"I drive two years, then I go home."

"Do you like it?"

I watch him stroke his beard in the rearview mirror.

"I like, yes. How about you? What do you do?"

The thing about meeting people is, they always wanna know what you do. If you ask me, the question should be rephrased like, "What are you into?" I dunno, I guess I think people shouldn't be defined by their careers. Maybe I'm just turned off to my job lately. It's a great job for sure and it pays a small fortune, but the career has begun to own me. My free time is taxed heavily and there are boundaries and limits on creativity.

There is still no text reply from Cassan, so I get off a few blocks from home at this great bodega and gather all the tools necessary to get me through my hangover without having to leave my apartment for a while. I buy water, aspirin, green tea, and sit down to eat some sushi as I peruse the marketing and advertising news. I don't see anything about what I'm working on though, so I collect my stuff and head home.

Cassandra and I live in the West Village because we want to. That is, we have the means thanks in large part to the success I've had and in no part at all to the fashion design job she has. Not that she's unsuccessful. Rather she's very successful in a gig that--even after two promotions from entry level--only pays enough for her to help out with our utility bills and cover all her expenses and nightlife. So in a town where people often pick a general part of the city and then cross their fingers they find something to rent that approximates the size, locale, proximity to subway and price range they seek, we actually went shopping for our ideal apartment and I bought it with 30 percent down. We live in a nice one-bedroom brick townhouse on West 4th St., which takes a peculiar turn west of Avenue of the Americas and shoots northwest across every street in the neighborhood. Our place is between Charles and Perry streets, and our neighborhood is so charming that is seems to have no business being located in the city. The tree-lined cobblestone streets can be quieter than a country estate and the quaint restaurants and shops are more likened to those found in New England coastal towns than anywhere else in Manhattan. If you were transported right here, you'd have no clue that some of the hippest nightlife spots in the city are only a few blocks away.

I arrive at stone steps to our building and stop. I look up to our two windows on the second floor, jiggling my keys. What if Cassan is up there now demanding an Oscar-winning apologetic speech? What if she's got some intense ultimatum? What if she's--terror of all terrors--up there with someone else? Not having the mental fortitude to prepare for even one of these possibilities, I nevertheless I walk up for the door.

When I enter, I yell for her but she's not home. I check every room before dropping my bag of groceries on the kitchen table, and that's where I see a little note she left me. I pick it up and take a deep breath. It reads:

Alan, I hate what happened the last night. Terrible, awful, the worst. I regret everything even though you deserved much of what happened. Went back to Jen's and we're having another sleepover. I'll see you Monday night and we can talk then.

-Me

This is hard to interpret because it's not uncommon for Cassan to sleep at her sister's apartment on Sunday nights. Cassan usually picks up a bucket of cookie dough ice cream and they lay around in their pajamas catching up on the latest romance flicks they couldn't manage to drag their boyfriends to. Not that I don't like romance movies. One of my favorite movies of all time was Casablanca, and I think all the women I've ever dated will admit that I'm a romantic. My guy friends don't know that though--and I prefer to keep it that way.

I re-read her letter and by the fifth reading I feel a little better about things and about myself. The part about me deserving "much" of what happened is disconcerting though, and I do wish she signed it 'love, me' rather than the more casual 'sorry again,' version she went with. In any case, I decided to pass the afternoon watching comedians. Kate calls but I let it go to voicemail and she leaves a simple message: 'Hope all is well. I had fun last night. I'm here if you need me."

Next I fall into a little scenario that is completely foreign to me--something I believe people refer to as "boredom." Given my general apathy towards doing anything at the moment, I begin walking around my apartment just to move. I go in the bedroom and look at the new curtains Cassan bought; they're thick and maroon like those of a Broadway stage. I stare at them with arms akimbo, picturing an audience on the other side of the curtains, which are about to open to reveal...me! Then I go back to the TV and a movie is about to start. The screen flashes the warnings "V" and "AL" for violence and adult language.

"Violence and adult language? Where's my brief nudity," I plead aloud.

✳✳✳

Just then my phone rings. This time I pick it up and flip it open without looking and Elden Lewis, my college roommate of two years and my closest friend ever since, is on the other end talking to me as though I joined a conversation already in progress.

"So you see, my man, what we must do is gravitate towards one of New York's finer drinking establishments pronto."

"Elden? Where are you?!"

I ask because he tends to just show up unannounced in the city (taking the train from Boston), and I'm hoping that's the case now. He answers in his typical enigmatic fashion of course.

"Well, it's cloudy now. And warm and fresh like it's about to rain. If we're lucky we can find a window seat in a little pub where the garage door is up even as the water smashes down a foot away."

"Nice! You're in town!"

"I'm on vacation. Staying at your place and loitering in the village."

"Wait, where are you now?"

"Downstairs presently. Look out your window."

I don't bother. I just slip on a Yankees hat and run downstairs and out the door and sure enough there's Elden, standing there with his big blue eyes and his wiry light-brown hair as chaotic as 42nd St. He's dressed in army shorts and a badly ripped t-shirt that must be a decade old. He smiles like the Cheshire Cat and dances a giddy little jig before slapping my hand.

"Yeah, yeah my man! Let's go catch up!"

With Elden, you don't know what you're doing or why, and there's never any use in questioning any of it because there's never an answer that's logical to anyone but him--unless you listen long enough to see the genius in his perspective. He just does what he feels like doing most at any given moment in a real carpe diem sort of way, such as coming to New York to wander the streets, check out bands, hang with friends, and simply ingest life. His approach to living is therapeutic, and I've always felt that I could never really lose it in life having a friend so close and compassionate and so utterly fun and alive all at once.

We begin walking a few blocks west towards a place to sit and have a drink.

"So what are you doing here on a Sunday night?"

"School's out for summer! Just finished my last exam on Friday."

"Damn. That came up fast. How long can you stay?"

"I'm a big boy; I can stay as long as I like. But practically speaking, I should get back by Wednesday afternoon for some things."

Elden's working on a doctorate in philosophy up at Harvard and he dreams, he says, of one day sitting in his own little oaken study at a university and smoking a pipe while gazing out a bright bay window onto the campus's central lawn. He also makes money working as a part-time travel writer, and for this reason he puts up a fuss when we arrive at the bar I had in mind.

"What's this piece of shit? We need a more ideal drinking venue than this."

"Does it matter on a Sunday night?"

"We need something with a quality mix of décor, character and, ideally, antiquity. The crowd doesn't matter tonight though--I'll let that aspect slide."

So we backtrack a bit and I guide us to the White Horse Tavern, where Dylan Thomas drank an obscene amount of whiskey before dying of it all the next day, and this pleases Elden. We take in the dank aroma of stale beer passed down from generations before and the floorboards creek and moan as we approach the sodden bar that bears only trace remnants of its formerly elaborate carvings. Elden orders us two pints of Bass and two whiskey shots to honor the poet and we sit in the middle room at a table that must be at least 80 years old. And as we sit, we hear a crack of thunder outside and I can see the rain begin to pour down, just as Elden predicted.

"So your timing couldn't have been more perfect. Cassan's gone and I was actually losing my mind and bored as hell in that apartment."

"I thought you don't believe in boredom."

"Well, not boredom so much as apathy."

"Apathy? Apathy with what?" Then Elden looks around. "Excuse me," he says loudly to the few people in earshot, "I'm looking for Alan Jones."

"Seriously man. I'm like apathetic towards everything lately. Work. Having fun."

There's a conversation I'm holding off on of course and I'm just inching my way there. This won't be the cursory revelation I gave Kate. This is Elden, after all.

"I'm not sure what I am anymore," I continue.

Elden laughs a bit, trying to read me.

"You're a philosopher like me."

He grabs at his pint of Bass and takes a merry gulp.

I shuffle my head back and forth. I'm sure that not all of the sage perspectives of life have been recorded and there's no particular qualification we fail to meet.

"Maybe you're right. You know, I was reading about how the bible is littered with holes and problems."

Elden is already nodding as if he knew I would move things in this direction.

"For first," he says, cutting me off, "there's no reliable narrator. You have to have a reliable narrator. The bible has many narrators, such as the E, J, D and P according to Friedman. So what you have is your basic editorial nightmare."

This is beyond my knowledge, and while probably interesting, I can't hold off from the real subject matter on my mind anymore.

"Speaking of nightmares, I've got my own little one going on now."

"What's this?"

"Cassan and I. Things are bad."

"Ahhh, that it? Just fix it man."

"Well, it's not that easy."

"Sure it is. Why does everyone make relationships out to be so damn complicated? What's the core issue?"

"She says that I've changed for one thing."

Elden laughs and holds up his shot.

"Get it up my man."

It's in inopportune time for a shot, but I grab my whiskey and we throw them back. Elden lets out a long, satisfying "ah" and then continues: "So first of all, that's total bullshit. You're the same exact person from high school. She should be upset that you *haven't* changed at all."

"Well then there's the other side of the coin. She's says she's changed a lot too, and she has. Or she's trying to forcefully."

"Ohhh! I see. Now I get it. So she wants to dump you and try something new."

"Fuck man!"

"Alan, look. First off, you yourself told me you were worried about getting stuck with the same girl and the same job right out of college forever. You two are both just antsy in my eyes." Elden was there from the beginning when we all met in college, so he's extremely qualified on the subject of Cassan. "I still can't figure out why the hell you still like her so much."

"Love her."

"Love her, really like her, whatever. Either way, she's not that girl from our college days anymore. That girl was witty and funny as hell. I mean, she's still funny, but she's not really you anymore. In my opinion, this is a reality check that's been waiting to explode for a few years now."

Elden would strike anyone as emotionally detached and inexperienced in the ways of romance, but it's completely the opposite. In fact, I don't know of anyone who has been in more relationships or in love more than Elden. And it's not that he's bad at relationships or anything, because most are serious and passionate for him. But Elden just does what makes him the happiest at any given moment. If you ask, me I really don't understand any of it.

"I'm talking five years," I say, pleading with my hands. "And we live together. It's not like anyone else I've dated. This would be like parting with a family member."

"Whamo!" Elden yells. "Time for more shots then."

He's a big ball of energy as always, but even more so now. Obviously he's excited to have just arrived in town. But I know him. And I know he's also trying to cheer me up and play down the emotional significance that I should attach to the Cassan situation.

"Look," he says, "I say relationships aren't complicated because it comes down to one thing: are you happy together. If you still love each other then that will manifest itself and you will want to remind each other of it as much as possible."

"That's the thing. I'm not sure either of us is in love anymore."

"Wham! Well, I learned that when I was here last month."

"How did you know?"

"Because I'm an instinctive animal. It's how I maintain homeostasis."

"So that's why you predicted I'd break down and even cry this year?"

"Exactly. Three times on the crying in fact."

I nod my head in disbelief and disapproval for a moment. It just sounds ridiculous.

"Well you've got it wrong: I didn't cry."

"Yet."

"Fine. But if I finally do, that will be once, and then there will only be like 10 months left."

"I hate to say it, but that's not how it's gonna go. My prediction stands. I don't want to get into the specifics of how just now, but in the end, it's gonna be for the best man. You're great, but maybe you are not great to her lately, and she's not great to you; you're gonna run around meeting new people again and soon enough you'll find someone even better for you because you'll make each other happy, which is all you really need. And then--the best part--you'll get back your swagger and passion for life that's been down lately. Remember that?"

"But what if the next love doesn't stick?"

Elden closes his eyes and twirls his index finger around.

"Just keep it going man."

I know he's perfectly ready to delve into things for me on a much more complex and psychological level with all the patience of a vulture, but I actually feel a bit contented suddenly. Or at the least, I'm able to sufficiently shuffle it aside.

"You're right, damn it! More shots!"

With that, Elden jumps up and does a poor man's Riverdance.

I'm afraid to look at my watch on a "school night". All I know is I pumped about five dollars into the jukebox and heard all my songs plus twice as many we didn't pick. That's how long we stayed talking about my job, the semi-fiction philosophy book Elden's working on, his graduate schooling experience, my Kate experience, his last fling and just laughing at utter nonsense.

At one point later, Elden says, "People are so easily thrown by anything out of the norm. Watch this little experiment in psychology." With that, he moves to the center of the barroom and sits down alone Indian style on the sawdust-covered floor. I check my phone and watch him on and off for nearly five full minutes until a tipsy girl walking by stops and asks, "why the floor?"

"Must we sit in chairs?"

She agreed they mustn't, and asks to join him. So then I join in and her friends join in and we start singing off-key loud and horribly to the jukebox, even when songs repeat back-to-back.

When we finally leave, a wagon-style car packed with family pulls up at the corner outside. They're obviously lost and have no business being here. Not with kids at this hour on a Sunday. The father who is driving rolls down his window.

"Can you tell me how to get to 424 Houston Street?"

"That's easy," I yell back while walking away. "Just go to 422 Houston. It should be right next door."

Elden and I laugh ourselves back to my apartment and immediately prepare to crash.

"Don't wake me in the morning," Elden says, taking the couch in the living room. I say good night and head to my bedroom.

Then Elden yells to me through my bedroom door in the dark: "One good thing about this whole Cassandra thing...some peace and quiet in the morning."

I erupt into a big drunken laugh that's completely inaudible because my face is buried nose deep in the pillow. It's a sort of pathetic laugh though, because really I'm just laughing at the deadening irony--the tragedy really--that after my five-year relationship has come to a likely end, the only "good" thing I have to show for it is silence.

Chapter 4

SOMETHING FEELS DIFFERENT THIS MORNING when I step off the elevator at the 50th floor of my company's revamped Madison Avenue office building. The painfully cheerful receptionist in the lobby doesn't greet me with her customary blessings for a great day--greetings I have endured for all of my four years here--but rather snaps her head down to her monitor and begins typing feverishly. I don't bother to interrupt. Instead I walk past her and down through the glass doors that divide a veritable sanctuary from the madhouse that is the creative floor of HRGM advertising.

The main hallway of Creative is usually filled with designers and writers running in and out of offices cursing or jumping up in celebration to smack the pseudo-funky pear pendant lamps that dangle from the hardwood ceiling. It's no secret that everyone's job on 50 involves a constant flux of emotional highs and lows, but that's not the vibe at all now. Nobody is here. The hall is empty to a surreal degree, and I'm reminded of that scene in Vanilla Sky when Tom Cruise is alone in Times Square.

I have to walk all the way down the hall past the corporate modern art work lining the walls because I have this large corner office at the other end and to the left. I walk slowly, deftly, pivoting my head about like spy. Just as I approach the end of the hall where I need to turn, I hear some murmurings. Then I hear more. I can make out some words and then the sentence, "I think he's coming." I turn the corner.

"Congratulations!" a small group yells.

There, packed in the short distance between myself and my office door, the entire creative team stands holding balloons and drinking mimosas. They all burst into applause, whistling and hollering.

"What's this?" I ask.

"Baseball! They bought it!" It's the voice of my boss, Steve Beringer, who is the vice president overseeing all HRGM creative work. He pushes through the crowd and greets me with a huge grin and extends a hand for a high five. "You didn't hear!?"

Somehow I didn't hear. I come in later than Steve and usually he calls me or I gather all the latest news about my work through the internet before I even get on the subway, but this morning I'm still reeling a bit after the small drinking bout with Elden last night. When I awoke, I pounded coffee and water and stuffed toast in my mouth as I ran out the door, and the only thing I could deal with on my 25-minute commute was music.

"No. But I celebrated nonetheless."

"Yeah I can smell that," Steve says, slapping me on the back. "Well, we got the call about two hours ago. Major League Baseball loved everything! Not a single change. They want to roll out your soap opera campaign and they want to go big."

I'm not sure how to feel. Everyone's far too excited and it's really sort of annoying in a way. It's my show I guess, and I have the urge to make them all sit down on the floor and drink shots and sing songs like last night.

"Thanks everyone," I say, as someone hands me a mimosa. Then I add some hokey teamwork crap: "Well, if it was my idea, it was all your execution. It's not about me."

This is the proper thing to say of course, and it summons a bunch of touched faces and prompts Steve to start nodding like a madman. I can't let them down because a few years ago I was like them, all wide-eyed and full of hope and optimism. And what's more, most, if not all of them, will go on believing this is a dream, and their lives will consist of constant stress and entire weeks of daylight substituted by the artificial green-tinted glow that emits from pretentious and soulless ceramics. They'll no doubt acquire spouses if they haven't already, and the variety in their lives will be boiled down to talk of the highs and lows of their workdays and the different restaurants they relate these trivial tales in.

What's gotten into me? Where's that newfound passion that Elden promised me? I theorize that it's all allocated to hoping things with Cassan will improve and go back to how they were.

"Come with me," Steve says. He calls after a few others in the crowd and we walk two doors down to the conference room. I sink deep into the familiar leather swivel chair with a padded back that towers above my head--the very seat I've pitched hundreds of creative concepts in. Steve sits next to me and five others pull up to the table too, including the art director, the head of accounts, the marketing director and two copywriters that I manage. Steve clicks on the LCD projector and starts walking us through some slides. It's the same presentation we're all too familiar with, but he wants to hit on some high points from his conversation with the baseball people earlier in the morning.

"So they loved the whole operetta. Even the soap name and the new tagline," he says. He clicks on a remote and advances the slide. The blue screen features the logo of Major League Baseball and reads: MLB presents: "The Life of Game."

The big idea for the campaign came to me last summer when Cassan was between jobs and I took some much needed time off. We made a whole bunch of fun outdoor plans and then it rained--no exaggeration--for two weeks straight. It was like a biblical disaster. So all our plans got cancelled and she decided to go spend some time with her parents down in North Carolina. As for myself, I spent most of my unproductive time watching the Yankees on T.V. It dawned on me then that baseball is there for people for the entire 180 game season--sort of like a soap opera but real. That's when I realized that this is what baseball is all about. Your team is there for you all the time, everyday. It's much more than a game of balls and strikes; it's about being part of the players' lives.

So anyway, I pitched this concept to MLB, a campaign in the style of a soap opera called "The Life of Game," and they loved it. Then I proposed a second tagline to roll out with the campaign: "They're for you." It's a pun on "there," and they loved that too. And now I've just found out they are going with it, and it's nothing I didn't expect last night when I mentioned it to Kate and Stacy.

Steve advances a few slides while telling us that MLB loved all five commercials, especially No. 2. He stops on a storyboard for this second installment, a 30-second spot called "Rumors." The spot, like all the others, quickly juggles three story lines that build on the previous episode like a soap would. The first story deals with a female baseball reporter that a player broke up with, and she gets revenge by throwing him under the bus during a live TV interview. I giggled when writing questions such as, "do you think it was totally selfish of you take that extra base down by three runs in the ninth?" We see dramatic shots of both their faces over music. Cut to: San Diego Padres players haze a rookie by making him wear a blue baby bonnet when he's in the on-deck circle. He complains because he's superstitious and thinks that's what's causing his slump. Other stories are woven into other spots and, really, the stuff was a piece of cake to write.

I'm thinking this meeting is just about gloating as Steve begins to wrap up with more congrats, but then he finally gets at the real reason for it.

"So MLB is so excited that they are throwing an announcement party early tonight. They reserved the top floor bar of the Gansevoort Hotel and they are going to screen the whole operetta--the specs and storyboards. We need our whole team there. Arrival time is 6 p.m. and Kathy can set you up with a room there if you need one. Thanks everyone."

The small group stands and starts filing out but Steve stops me and asks me to meet him in his office. I walk ahead of him down the hall cursing inside. It's a terrible night for a work function, especially one I'll no doubt be an important part of. I need to speak with Cassan. I need to get out of it, but how? By the time I reach Steve's office, he's caught up with me and he closes the door behind us.

"Have a seat my man."

"Steve," I say, diving right into it. "I have a very important personal affair to attend to tonight with my girl. I can't go to this party. Maybe stop by later?"

"Ouch." He bites his lips and turns away a moment to think. "I know it's last second, but we need you to at least get up while Terry Giles is speaking. Nothing you can do?"

"This is crucial man."

Steve taps his pen on his desk and hums a bit.

"OK, tell you what. Just come later. The speeches don't start until around nine anyway and they will just be screening the campaign before you arrive. You can swoop in and out."

It's tough to let Steve down because he's actually a fairly cool guy most of the time, especially given the insanity of Creative and what he has to deal with everyday. He's pioneered the bar and poolroom on our floor and is always championing happy hours and raucous affairs. But today he's turned into a bit of a sap.

"Can you get there by nine and just speak for a minute. I mean, you can walk there in 10 minutes from your place buddy."

I take a deep breath. I could say, 'No, I can't come,' and why not? What's more important? Steve would never fire me and I'm not sure I'd care if he did anyway. But then I consider things the other way. Why should I sacrifice everything else in my life for a woman who may not love me? I mean, if she doesn't really care about me anymore then what's the point? To my knowledge, life doesn't work like the movies and sometimes there's just nothing you can do. You can't win someone back if they don't love you. But tonight, I can grab Elden and go to this hip party and have a fucking blast.

"OK, fine. I'll be there at nine."

Steve emits a palpable sigh of relief, kicks back and smiles.

"There's one more piece of business we need to discuss," he says, "and that's the matter of a raise."

"Another raise?"

"Well, yeah. We've got to keep our all-star happy."

I've come to react to these frequent raises with increased apathy. Every time I do something big I get one and my salary has already shot to a level I'd never thought possible. It's not that I'm complaining, but I declare that I enjoy them for purely unselfish reasons--namely, for Cassan's happiness. Her material interests were always fairly normal until she landed her job in fashion. Now she has one material weakness and that's for designer outfits from the hottest SOHO boutiques and trendy European shoes that seem to cost a hundred bucks just to look at. I recall how she said, "the only thing you'll ever love is you." That couldn't be further from the truth. I would agree with anyone who thought a great sense of humor and great nose for fashion in a woman an unlikely combo, but she has been pulling it off for the most part.

"I hope a 20 percent raise will keep you happy," Steve says. "How's that sound?"

That comes to a lot, especially for a 27-year-old. Far too much for what I do if you ask me. I mean, is it so fucking hard to think of a creative theme based on some research and then generate a few related ideas? What's your product? Is it soap? Then grab yourself some goofy characters and a catchy jingle or something funny. It's all bullshit anyway. For years McDonald's had the sing-song tagline, "We love to see you smile." Are you telling me the McDonald's

Corporation gives a shit whether you or not you're smiling as you're ten deep in line? I can't imagine two guys mopping the floor after a busy Saturday night having warm fuzzies thinking about customers. It'd be like:

"Man, thank God this shift is over...I'm shot."

"Yeah but it was worth it. I mean, did you see all those muthafuckas smiling?"

The raise is nice, but nothing monumental by comparison. Steve hopes the money will keep me focused, and I open my mouth to say I hope it will too, but I know for now nothing will. Instead I say thanks and "see you tonight," and I walk out.

✳✳✳

At 2 p.m. I give Cassan a call at work, but she doesn't pick up. No text or email or voicemail or social media messages. She usually gets out of work between three and four and I'm starting to fidget, so I decide to head home early. I leave my computer on and my jacket on my chair to suggest that I might just be down the hall or in a meeting and off I go.

It's cloudy outside but plenty warm for just my white dress shirt with oversized collar and my thin khakis. I head underground and the 1 train screeches up with perfect timing. I feel good. I can even go for a cigarette, and I buy a pack at a news-stand after coming up the steps and spilling out onto West 4th and Christopher streets. I light up and make the short walk home wondering where in the city Elden is and what sort of wacky spectacle he's probably a part of at this very minute. When I get home I check the mailbox but it's empty so I head up stairs, and when I open the door to my apartment I see Cassan sitting at the kitchen table.

"You're home early," she says.

"I, uh--so are you."

We're both quiet a moment as I drop my bag on a chair with suddenly shaky fingers. I walk past her to the fridge and crack a beer and take a powerful chug.

"Fun night with Elden last night?"

"Yeah. He just showed up announced like he does. How'd you know?"

"I saw him this morning," she says, pushing aside a copy of Elle Magazine that she was reading. "We passed each other on the stairs and he said to tell you he'll call later."

"Did you not go to work today?"

She sort of messes with this cute green blouse she's wearing and in the process she mutters, "no."

"How come?"

"I took a personal day and slept in at Jen's. I just needed to think a bit today."

"About what?"

"Yeah right," she says. She gives me this snide little smirk--the sort of smirk that can never be good.

"I mean about what, exactly? I mean, where are you at right now? Let's talk. Let's start now and talk through dinner and--"

"I don't think dinner would be a good idea Alan. Unless it's 130 degrees and I'm dying for someone to throw some ice at me."

"I'm sorry for that. Seriously. That wasn't me, you know that." I sit down beside her and grab for her hand, but she doesn't grab back so I'm really just resting my hand on hers. "I didn't mean to do that. I just--I just hated to hear you say what you said because I love you."

I feel terrible suddenly. I'm nervous and choking up a bit I think. I think it's the same for Cassan, but I can't tell. Her beautiful chestnut hair still flows in poignant streams down along her cheeks. All that's nestled between those cheeks now though is a stoic expression; the sort of empty stare people have while waiting alone in long lines. But then I can see that her eyes are a bit marooned and puffy around the lids.

"Let's just stay in and chat tonight," she says.

"Definitely. But I do have a work party to go to at nine. I'm being honored in part and I can't get out of it. And it would mean a lot to me if you would come."

"Seriously? What did you do now?"

I don't know what to say to this, so I say nothing.

"I mean--" and then she pauses. "I'm sure you were amazing with the base-ball campaign. And I'm sorry I threw a drink on you and I hated Saturday night."

"Your favorite drink--an espresso martini. That's what really made it hurt."

I manage to smile at her to ease the tension, but it doesn't work. We look at each other in an uncomfortable moment of silence before I break it by guzzling some beer.

"You've been drinking a lot lately I noticed."

"Fuck yeah. It's been a rough weekend, no?"

"I mean, like, the last few months." And this is annoying as hell to hear because our whole relationship was initially predicated on going out and drinking together and I don't recall that ever really ending. So I take another slug.

"I drink every day. Water, beer, orange juice. What of it? Don't make this about something it's not." And I sound like an idiot.

"What I mean is, I don't think you've been very happy either lately. You're not content with anything anymore. You don't laugh as much...you're not yourself."

"I see your angle here, and that's not going to work. Don't put this on me."

She reflects for a moment. Then she begins nodding her head.

"You're right. It's not really about anything specific on your end. I'm the same way. Let's be honest with ourselves. Things have changed a lot between us. We are passionate people who haven't been passionate lately. Maybe we owe it to ourselves to explore and experience the world more. I don't know Alan. I just don't know if it's right anymore."

"Exactly. You don't know. So maybe it still is. Or maybe it can be again. Maybe we can give it a try like a new couple."

"But we did give it a try Alan. And we're far from a new couple."

"Look Cassan, I love you. And I got another raise today and all I can think about is how it will benefit you." I gesture to my apartment. "All this...is for you."

"That's not the issue. It's not about money or your job or anything like that. I hope you know that."

"Well what the fuck is the issue?! All you want to do is run around with your new crew of friends lately and you never invite me along. What did I do?"

She braces her head on her hands and stares down at the table.

"I don't know Alan. Nothing." She looks back up at me with those dagger blue eyes and they slay me.

"Honey," I plead, taking a different tone. "What is it?"

Suddenly a tear streams from Cassandra's left eye and she bursts into a soft sob. Neither of us speaks. Her mascara smears her face like war paint. I reach over and dry her eye with the back of my wrist. I stroke her hair a moment, but then she brushes me off.

"I don't love you anymore Alan. I wish I did, but I don't, and I don't know why."

I feel my face cringe at that. Several emotions explode and scatter at once as though smashed from a piñata. They come on too fast to make any order or sense of them. Another minute passes.

"So what does this mean?" I know it's a desperate question. We know the answer. That's about the only thing I do know. She looks back down and wipes her cheek.

I stare a little longer in vain, then sit back deep into my chair. Across from me, and close--ever so close--is love and happiness and a life of laugher and the universe of all that matters; yet as the universe goes, all I can do is look and sense and anything but have, and as I stare at it all with passion and desire all that looks me back is a vast intangible expanse of emptiness. And I feel my eyes begin to water, but before I allow for any tears to stream I pick up my beer and walk out of the apartment.

Chapter 5

I DON'T KNOW WHERE I'M GOING as I wander from my apartment, but after walking a few blocks I come upon Washington Square Park and decide to sit and clear my head for a while. I think of Elden and what he would do post-mortem with a serious girlfriend and realize I can't cry and curse the world. Instead I simply grab a seat on a green wooden bench near the stone arch that ushers people into the heart of Greenwich Village and New York University. The problem though, is that the park is always so friggin' crowded, and at first I can't concentrate a lick because a group of skateboarders--kids in their mid-teens--are rolling by loudly on the sidewalk in front of me, jumping up and smashing down hard on the concrete with their boards. The bench is long and some of the kids sit a few spots down from me and light cigarettes and even a joint that they begin to covertly pass around. They're a real obnoxious lot--mainstays in the park--and they thrive on showing off in front of the doting teen girls that run up to kiss them after they pull off tricks. To be honest though, I can't see what's so impressive about these tricks. It boils down to a matter of limited options for teens to express themselves in cool ways. If you don't know how to show a girl a good time or you're not very interesting or you don't have any money, I guess you can wow them with a big Kickflip Indy. I tell you what though, you try holding onto Cassan's love. Now there's a neat trick.

"Yo, you wanna hit?" one of the kids asks me. He flashes a smoldering joint quickly in his palm. He's the only white kid in an ethnically mixed group and he's wearing a scully hat that's pressed tightly down over his long blond hair.

"I can't man. I'm a cop." I find myself once again so utterly aloof and apathetic that it's hard to care about any repercussions for anything I might do or say.

"Oh shit, for real?" His face loses color and that actually peps me up a bit in a cruel sort of way.

"Yeah, but don't sweat it. I'm off duty."

The kid offers me a "thanks" and spins to whisper to his friends, who in turn whisper to a few others. Within a few minutes the whole group drifts to a different bench.

✳✳✳

The winds have picked up and the temperature has chilled to the low-sixties, but I'm still fine in my work outfit that I didn't have a chance to change at home. I look up and watch the fast-moving clouds roll by and allow myself to slip into a reverie of sorts. I transport myself back in time to when I first met Cassan, when we were juniors at Dartmouth and still living in the dorms. Back then--and really for most of the time since--she was a blast; a sort of free-spirited hilarious girl who knew how to have fun. Our dorms were situated across from each other and separated by this quad where lots of cookouts and games were held and somehow our groups collided one day. I don't remember the details because we all spiked our drink containers with liquor, but eventually I got her alone and we hit it off right away. In this first conversation, she started telling me how she was exhausted because she kept waking up all night from a terrible nightmare she couldn't shake.

"What happened?" I asked.

"It was terrible. I kept getting cornered by all these guys who kept slapping my face with their dicks. All I remember were tons of dicks everywhere."

And of course that shit floored me. How could it not, coming from such an impossibly cute girl barely learning to stray from confines of innocence? Back then she dressed like an odd cross between a hippie and goth girl if you can imagine that. She always wore tattered jean skirts over sheer black leggings and let her then blondish hair freefall wildly. She rolled thick azure eye shadow out to her sideburns and slipped on rubbery bracelets from time to time. I'm not sure if her Jersey upbringing and some throwback '80s boardwalk fashion scene influenced her tastes. All I know is that she had an addicting look and feel that I surrendered to at once. Until then I wasn't attractive to non-mainstream fashion. I'm guilty of being overly picky and I didn't think she was my type physically either. She was more average than thin in build and a bit too fair-skinned. I told my friends I wanted a girl who had dark hair and was slender and named Mila Kunis.

Cassan was crazy popular too! Everyone always invited her to the most exclusive and happening parties and she was the sort of girl that all the other girls followed. She was hilarious and goofy but somehow cool at the same time. Even before I met her, I always noticed her ambling across the quad with her entourage close behind. I told her once that she reminded me of those New York dog-walkers you see walking 10 dogs at once, but she didn't like the analogy.

"So are the dicks really a nightmare or some Freudian representation of your desire to get gang-banged?"

"Shut it," she said, playfully pushing at me. "I can guess your sign I bet."

"You can't guess my sign."

"Let me see. Are you a cancer? You're a cancer aren't you?"

My smirk disappeared. I moved on without giving her credit for being right.

"Horoscopes are such crap anyway," I said. "It's like I don't know who I am when I read them."

"Dude, are you crazy? It's like free daily advice tailored to you."

"Yeah, well it never seems to apply to me. Or it's too vague. Don't tell me that I'm gonna put down all of my enemies. I wanna read something practical, like how I'm gonna sleep my ass off tomorrow."

Those days we never really cared what we talked about; all that mattered was how we talked. How we fired witty remarks back and forth like two giddy kids sensing a fresh and burgeoning romance on the horizon. The romance had to wait though. For reasons inexplicable to me then--reasons which are starting to make sense now--she kept dating this grad student who I thought was a total dud and had nothing in common with her. Some civil engineer or architectural guy named Dave who kept wooing her with grandiose visions of bridges he planned to build.

So I kept trucking on with my brief dating cycles, one after another, like I'd always been doing since high school. There was Megan and Jen in grades 10 and 12 respectively, both girls I thought I loved until I looked back in college and realized I just loved the idea of having a girlfriend in high school. They both left me, one for a football player, the other for a kid who sang real well but later came out gay and left her. But then so many more followed at Dartmouth, including three of my patented eight-month relationships. College works like dog years if you ask me, so hanging onto a girl for eight months equates to dating for at least three years in the real world. I had a slew of random dates and hookups as well, the sort of drunken flings that literally fall into your lap in college.

Finally, there was Sam, the tall, tough-talking girl from Alabama I met when I traveled to Costa Rica after graduation. My plan was to head south to backpack South America for a few months and learn Spanish and write a comedy routine along the way, but she sidetracked everything. I extended my trip a bit and she taught me how to surf and we shared a little shack at the surf camp in Montezuma we both worked at, though usually we hooked up on the beach at night before a regular audience of howler monkeys that we named as we fell asleep there alongside the edge of the sea.

Eventually I began itching to get my career started in New York. An English major and journalism minor, I thrived on writing and creativity and targeted advertising as my niche. New York was the capital of advertising and runner up capital to L.A. for stand-up comedy. I got settled into Manhattan and landed my current job and after dating for a while, the sweetest letter in the world arrived. A virtual novella from Cassan telling me, in effect, that she burned her bridges with Dave.

I can see I've been subconsciously gravitating towards this crazy conclusion--or maybe it's a perfectly rational one--that none of this breakup stuff is Cassan's fault. It's not her fault because she's not the person she used to be. She's right: she changed and I didn't. And so what you have is the old me taking issue with the new her, which is in essence the equivalent of me picking a fight with a stranger on the street. The old Cassan is gone perhaps, consumed by time, and maybe I should write all this off to fate and the "everything happens for a reason" crap that I'd hear if I bothered to share this with anyone besides Elden. But I haven't told anyone else because there's not too many friends left to tell anymore. Blame that on being consumed with work. And yes, I've been grumbling about my job and not having the time to really give stand-up comedy a real go, and I've been worried life is passing me by. Cassan said so in a way, and she's right: I'm not content with anything lately, and that doesn't make for a fun boyfriend. I guess I sorta sensed this the last few months. Shit, maybe I have changed.

Another thing: Looking back I can see how troublesome not having my own friends anymore was to both Cassan and our relationship. Elden came down frequently enough and there were always work functions, but Cassan used my social events to get in her own "me time," which revolved around her new fashion industry friends--tons of them. They came by the hundreds it seemed...men and women, hipsters, occult scientists, professional artists and the pseudo-homeless artists that frequented our couches. Cassan has made something of a name for herself through her job all those fashion parties she attends. It's just how things went for her in college, except her sense of humor and that innocent goofiness has been transplanted with a sleek and sophisticated wit and a general favoring of what was interesting over what was merely fun.

I tried to get along with her new crowd, and in my gregarious manner I quickly took to dominating the dinner tables and the pubs and clubs we hit whenever I tagged along. Despite this, I never clicked with any of them. They weren't my audience. They were a new audience for a new Cassan, comprised of fashionistas, hipsters, artist, occult scientists, and more.

This sense of detachment between Cassan and I applied to family as well. The first time she met my parents she picked me up at my Connecticut home on the way up to Dartmouth the spring of our senior year. She stayed for dinner and my parents and her volleyed questions with all the gusto of a Sunday morning political round table. My mother, an office administrator, and my father, a vice president of an electronics company, are extroverted and affable like me, and I barely even got in a word. She loved my mother and father she said, as we pulled away later that night.

We visited each other's families regularly. The last time on my side was a sleepover when my older sister and only sibling Amy came home to visit with her new husband Dale. Amy had gone to college in San Francisco and never came back, getting work as a graphic designer at an ad firm. I admit she turned me on to the advertising world initially. The four of us "kids" drank wine all night and got drunk after my parents went to bed. I had to pee and Cassan dared me to go in the bottle of chardonnay we had just drained. I did, and put the bottle aside and forgot about it. My mother found the bottle the next morning and, taking it for wine, put it in the fridge. To our horror the bottle was placed on the table before us the next night for dinner.

"What do we do," my girlfriend mouthed silently across the table, half-laughing at the situation. Amy looked at us both, mortified.

I had to act fast. I grabbed the bottle as my parents busied themselves around the kitchen, and in one smooth move I opened the kitchen slider door and heaved it out into the woods. Miraculously, we all sat down for dinner without a single inquiry about the bottle. And that's my last memory of Cassan with my family: Sitting down to dinner with a chilled bottle of piss on the table.

✳✳✳

Suddenly an odd young woman with very short blue hair and zebra stockings plops down violently on the bench next to me, snapping me from my daydream. She's attractive in a punkish way, petite, with a small nose and taut cheeks. She is wearing spikey bracelets and a lip ring and she's in the middle of an angry, curse-ridden conversation with what seems to be a boyfriend.

"Then get your fucking shit together Troy!"

She pauses. Our eyes meet for a second but she looks away, straining to hear against the wind.

"Well godammit, it sure fucking seemed that way." Then her call drops. She looks at the phone and yells, "Fuck."

I immediately feel guilty for even sitting next to her. It's a no-win situation. Talking to her might invite more rage. Sitting next to her in silence as if I didn't witness a thing would be awkward. I look over at her again and clear my throat.

"You OK?"

Silence. She doesn't even look at me, so I start to stand. Then she reaches out in my general direction.

"No. You don't have to get up. Sorry."

"Sorry for what?"

"I don't know. Being a bitch in front of you." At this, her phone explodes into a ringtone song I recognize from Cassan, "Anthems of a 17-Year-Old Girl" by Broken Social Scene. It carries on for about a verse then falls back to silence.

"Letting him go?"

She just sorta rubs her small head and cracks her neck a bit before speaking again.

"It's fuckin' done. Fuck it. It's over." She goes on muttering expletives while staring down at the pavement by her feet. Then she looks up at me, and waves her phone at me.

"That was our stupid song, but it's over. Do you know how to change it?"

"Sure."

I grab the phone and navigate to her music archive without any questions or words. There aren't any other songs on there, so I set the new ringtone to Melody 8. Then, in a quick, conniving, spy-like manner, I navigate to her contacts directory and add my number. For name, I enter the guy from Wash Sq Park and save it. It's a move I saw Elden pull once and I wanted to try it ever since. Then I hand the phone back.

"I just broke up with that fucker," she says. She flips off a pigeon that strolls by. "He's a motherfuckin'...pigeon."

I can't help but laugh at the disjointed metaphor.

"A pigeon? How so?"

"I don't know. He just is."

"Give me a dollar if I guess what he did," I say. I don't know why I'm proposing this or why I'm engaging this potential nut at all.

She looks at me curiously and extends her hand to shake on it. And I know I've got it nailed. This is a clear-cut case of cheating. It doesn't take a detective to sense that from the snippet of dialogue I heard. Nor does it take much to postulate that she's a bit of a mess. The odds, I figure, aren't too good that this is her first bout with drama in the 25 or so years of her existence. And then there's the hair. Blue hair by itself is funky and fun to me. Blue hair jumping into your life with such vehemence spells drama queen to me.

"You think he cheated on you."

She laughs, looks away a moment, then looks back.

"You win. But all I got is an ATM card."

"Forget it. Just give me the gist."

"Actually, I don't even care if he is cheating. Fuck it. I cheat. The bottom line is he's much younger, like four years, and I don't know what I was thinking. Too young for a guy."

There's this little habit of abruptly changing subjects that I developed from both good and bad sources. I like to think the good source flows from the creative juices in my mind. The bad source, perhaps, from too much alcohol.

"I love your button."

She looks down onto her army-green vest. There's a button that reads "Sucka bitches." It's nothing unusual per se. This is Greenwich Village, after all. But it's just the sort of thing Cassan would wear now and it makes me miss her--even the new her.

"Thanks. Now can I get back to my fuckin' story?" I laugh inwardly at her deadpan delivery. It would make for a good comedic style actually, and I sorta love her energy from the safe distance of being a stranger.

"I'm sorry. Out with it."

"Ah, he's just too young. How old are you?"

"Me? 27."

"See. Makes more fucking sense. You ever been spanked?"

"Huh?"

"Never mind."

She pulls out a cigarette and lights it. I do the same.

"Jade," she says and exhales.

"Jade? What's that?"

"That's my name, cutie. What's yours?"

"I'm just the guy from Washington Square Park."

She smirks and stands up, but I feel like my little sly tactic of entering my number in her phone gives me the upper-hand, even though I might regret it.

"What are you, afraid?"

"I think you're afraid," I say, unsure what we're even talking about. The whole thing is too friggin' strange. I'm not sure what to make of it or how much I like it, but it doesn't matter anyway. Jade doesn't say another word. She just walks off toward 3rd Street.

"That's right, go get my dollar," I yell after her. She turns back and smiles and exits the park under the arch.

✲✲✲

I laugh out loud in quick reflective summary of Jade's intrusion, at such a weird and pointless moment. If I were writing a book, I certainly wouldn't mention her except maybe to say that a "foul-mouthed female punk distracted me for a moment." But life is a book in my head, and it can use some spice lately. I know I've grown to be a bit of bore, relatively speaking. I know I've dedicated too much time to a job that's not for me. I have the skill of creativity, sure, but the career container is inadequate. Copywriting was never a dream. It's worn me down slowly like the burning of incense, and nobody's looking hard enough to see the process until one day you wake up and see your friends are nearly gone and the woman you love is telling you she doesn't love you anymore.

Still, I feel good. I feel better, anyway. Credit Jade in part. I suddenly love hearing about other relationship issues, having them myself. Beats the hell out of any professional therapy you can find.

I realize I'm even up for this work party tonight, which will help me re-engage. My watch guesses that it's 4:45 p.m., but it's a strange and stupid watch with a rubber band that I bought at the surf camp in Costa Rica for two bucks. There's a teeny yellow warped surfboard that serves as the hour hand. The hand for the seconds is a little peeled banana that bends into the northwest quadrant of the face, accurate no better than plus or minus 10 minutes. A banana is a horrible choice for a second hand on a watch. Bananas are only good for two things, one of which I saw in a porno. All I know about the time for sure is that I should call Elden and move on.

Chapter 6

THE PHONE RINGS THREE TIMES before Elden answers with a question.

"So what's the plan Chakazulu?"

"We're going to a party tonight for my baseball ad campaign. You're my date."

"I love it. Can't you see how this whole Cassandra debacle is already working out? It's like Hanover revisted." He's referring to Dartmouth, where we shared a room that became the dorm hangout.

"Yeah, maybe."

It turns out Elden's only a few blocks away at a divvy little underground pub off MacDougal Street. I begin the short 10-minute walk along West 4th St. under the early evening sunlight and I can feel the near-summer energy that pervades the streets. People scurry about everywhere, hopping in and out of tenements with bicycles or leashed dogs, casually patronizing shops and easing into outdoor seating at restaurants for dinner. I take slow, purposeful strides against this grain of action at first, but pick up the pace as I recall my promise to myself in the park. Re-engage. There will be no more thoughts of Cassan. Not tonight anyway. And I know I have the temporary power to make it so like in video games when you jump up and grab a star of invincibility and try to enjoy it while it lasts.

I reach the spectacle of MacDougal with all of its tattoo shops and sidewalk artisans and dynamic characters and find the pub and walk down a flight of stairs to enter. The place is dark and empty except for my boy Elden and three older men he's throwing darts with, and the first thing I notice is that one of the men is dressed in a crimson and gold monk's garb.

"That's one bullseye for me if you would good sirs," Elden says. He retrieves his darts and sees me.

"Alan Jones! There he is! Gentleman, the man I've been telling you about, the top ad man in New York, and a real hoot."

I stare perhaps a little too long at the ornate old man, so Elden continues.

"Alan, this here is Topek. He's a Buddhist monk and owns a little Tibetan artifact shop next door. And these Caucasian gentlemen were born in America, blah blah blah."

The monk offers me a bow and I join them all for darts. After that, Elden and I grab a sub-par sushi dinner down the street and he excuses himself to cavort in front of a group of female NYU students. I watch him twist and turn his way through an animated story à la the comedian Dane Cook, and after about two minutes of that he sits back down at our table and mutters, "too young."

"So are you ready for tonight?" I ask.

"I should be asking you that. You have a speech?"

"No, I'm just gonna wing it. I'm really not in the mood for more awards crap to be honest. Not to sound conceded, but you know what I mean." I pause thoughtfully, realizing I'm about to immediately break my pact of not discussing Cassan.

"I talked to Cassan. She told me she doesn't love me anymore."

"Didn't she already tell you that?" Elden takes a drink after asking this, but keeps a pensive glare fixed on me.

"No. Before she said she wasn't sure. But before I came here, back at the apartment, she said flat out, 'I don't love you anymore.'"

Elden taps the table and looks down for a moment. Then he looks back at me.

"I think you don't love her anymore If you did it wouldn't have come to this."

"What?"

"I started to tell you this last night, but I didn't know how to get at it without you blowing up. But honestly man, the last few months you were talking about her differently. And love's a two-way street.

I consider this, which I owe Elden given his impeccable track record of accurate analyses and advice ever since we became friends. Still, he's not beyond reverse psychology to help me move on.

"I didn't cry by the way," I tell him. "My eyes started to water, but I didn't shed a tear."

"Look man, you know I'm not rooting for any situation that would cause you to shed a tear. But why do you think I even made that prediction in the first place?"

I realize that I never stopped to consider that question before.

"Yeah, why did you?"

"That will dawn on you in time."

"I think you've been hanging around Topek too much talking like this."

I look at my watch and change the subject by relaying details about the party, but Elden's looking around the room and scratching his head in wonder. Then he cuts me off.

"There's two types of intelligence in the world: Intelligence and *perceived* intelligence. Memory plays a big part in the latter.

"OK. Why bring this up?"

"Topek and I were talking about intelligence and this was the point I tried to make with him. I was trying to explain that some people are flat out smart and others only *appear* to be smart because they have such good memories and know a lot and they can bring in good contextual examples, but they can't make connections and understand things quickly like truly smart people can."

"So what am I?"

"You're intelligent. Except when it comes to women of course. And speaking of which--Cassandra--she leans towards perceived intelligence. She's has that unearthly memory so she can test well and pull out facts on the fly that blow people away. But you're highly creative and you destroyed your S.A.T.s and seem to excel at any discipline."

"OK..." I'm wondering where this is going, but it's going nowhere. Just a pick-me-up speech I guess. Elden goes back to scratching his head and watching girls come and go, but I can see he wants me to inquire more.

"So what are you then?"

"Me? I'm intelligent too I guess. And maybe perceived intelligent as well because I have a lot of random knowledge. Comes from over-schooling."

I start laughing just to fuck with him.

"Oh, no, no, no. You're a whole different and additional category of intelligence. You're idiot savant."

"How so?"

"Well you don't know about anything except philosophy."

"Which is everything," he says, toasting my chopsticks. And then it's time to go.

✳✳✳

Hotel Gansevoort stands the tallest building in the Meatpacking District in the far west teens. By day, the area still maintains some semblance of it's old self. Butchers in blood-stained aprons scurry along broken cobble-stoned streets attending to animal carcasses that dangle before turn-of-century warehouses. At the same time, the district has become one of New York's trendiest, and all of this now juxtaposes with haute couture, frequent star-sightings, hip restaurants and some of the city's most expensive private clubs. It's the trendiness, though, that rules completely when the sun goes down, and that's the case now as we arrive. We press the button for the hotel penthouse and the elevator doors open to reveal a jazz band and waitresses serving hours' devours to a well-dressed crowd on a panoramic outdoor patio. We grab drinks from the open bar and walk past a swimming pool to the west side of the wrap-around balcony. From there we can see about a mile stretch of the Hudson River, which looks tranquil and sullen save for harbor lights shimmying off its surface.

"Nice view eh?"

Elden and I turn to the speaker and it's my boss, Steve, munching on a kabob.

"Yeah, not bad."

"So Cassandra looks a lot different from the last time I saw her," he says, addressing Elden.

"I gained some weight, did some things with my hair," Elden says. I introduce them and explain quickly that Cassan wasn't up for a party last minute tonight.

"Well, glad you made it anyhow. It looks like they're going to get started. We'll just call you up briefly Alan. Excuse me."

Steve departs and suddenly I spy someone who looks very familiar--a smooth-looking black guy with short dreads wearing sunglasses and a white sports jacket. Then it hits me.

"Hey man," I tell Elden, "That's Lutsey Lampkin, the comedian at the comedy club I went to on Saturday."

"Any good?"

"Yeah, he's always pretty solid. I want to meet him."

Elden and I walk over and the timing is right--a woman he was talking to has just walked away and left him alone.

"Lutsey Lampkin," I say, as if we are old friends. "Caught you hosting at the Comic Strip on Saturday. Good set." While I know a lot about comedy lingo, I'm unsure if you can refer to hosting as a "set."

"Hey, all right! Thanks man."

"I'm Alan, this is Elden."

"Lutsey."

We shake and his firm grip pinches some skin on my index finger under a silver ring I bought in the East Village.

"All right, all right. Don't get too excited," I tell him, wincing a bit.

"Sorry man, I'm just not used to such puny hands," Lutsey counters. "Nah, let me stop. So are you guys with baseball or the ad firm?"

"The ad firm. I created the campaign and he's a friend. What are you doing here?"

"I'm gonna get things started in about two minutes."

"Really? Like doing some comedy?"

"Nah, I'm gonna juggle for a bit. Yeah man, what else would I do?" He holds a straight face for a moment and then laughs.

"I'm just playing. So yeah, my agent called today and said they're looking for someone to set a fun tone and introduce the players. It's crazy man; I get so many calls for corporate shit all the time." Then he pauses. "Wait--you said you are Alan. Are you Alan Jones?"

"Yeah!"

"Oh, all right. Nice. I'm supposed to mention you too. Got your name on this note card."

It's not ideal, but cool nonetheless. Cool that it's Lutsey that is. Sadly, this is about as glamorous as things get in my professional world. Ideally, a comedian would introduce me as a comic about to take the stage as opposed to some advertising employee.

"Yeah man, I dig the campaign. Respect," he adds, and bumps his fist to mine.

"Yeah, well I wish I had your gig. I've always wanted to make a living in standup." I'm a bit nervous like I always get talking to comics who are like gods to me because they're living this dream of mine, even though a great majority of them are jaded and melancholy and typically complain about it more than anything else. That doesn't seem to be the case with Lutsey.

"You ever get up on stage," Lutsey asks.

"Yeah. I was a regular headline at an amateur night at the New York Comedy Club.

"What happened?"

"You know. Girlfriend. Work. Life."

"Hey, someday baby. Never too late."

"Yeah someday."

"Seems like you got it set up good now though, no?"

"Not really, man. I just sorta lost the passion for it, you know? I don't even know what I'm going to say tonight. I haven't prepared anything."

"I hear you man. That happens in comedy for me too."

Elden has been swiveling his head side to side while following our volley of conversation as though he was watching a tennis match, and finally he chimes in.

"Alan my boy, I know what you should say to crowd. Get up there and just give 'em the old *Three Words Routine.*"

"What's that," Lutsey asks.

"When you get on stage, you just say, 'Three words,' and maybe even hold up three fingers. Then follow that with something ridiculous. Something like, 'Elephants for all.'"

Lutsey laughs, instantly appreciating Elden's relative insanity. Then he contributes.

"Or you could say, 'Three words: Let me home.'"

We all crack up at that one, and I'm seriously pondering each suggestion.

"I like it," I say, agreeing it has to make no sense. "It's like the *no soap radio* bit.

"What's this?" Lutsey's smile could light the rooftop, and I think for the first time that he might be high.

"Basically," I say, "Elden and I tell someone a joke that makes no sense and we get a bunch of other people to all laugh at the so-called punch-line. Every time, without fail, the person not in on it laughs simply out of peer pressure because he doesn't want to be the guy who doesn't get it."

"I like it," Lutsey says. "Tell me one."

"OK, so there are two elephants sitting in a bathtub together."

"Two *Swedish* elephants," Elden says, as if there is some significance to this.

"Right. Swedish elephants. And one elephant is scrubbing his ass." I do this unnecessary little scrubbing motion as I talk. "And he says to other elephant, 'hey elephant, pass me the soap.' And the other elephant looks back at him and says, 'no soap...radio!'"

At this, Elden bursts into laughter and we slap hands for added effect. Lutsey starts rolling too.

"And people laugh at that shit?"

"Every time!"

"All right, all right. Now we need three words for your opening man," Lutsey says.

"Exactly," Elden says. "So what then?" He stares at me wide-eyed.

"I don't know. Maybe something like, 'Three words: Call me Ishmael.'"

We all burst into laughter again and Lutsey pushes his hand towards my face.

"Yo, hold up man, hold up." He laughs some more. "What the fuck does that mean?"

"From 'Moby Dick'," Elden clarifies. "That's perfect because a lot of people will know it and they will try to read into it. Hawthorne right?"

"No, not Hawthorne." I scratch my head. "Damn. That's gonna bother me. Who wrote that?"

"I thought you were an English major!"

Just then we hear a loud chime.

"Oh yo, I gotta go introduce everyone now," Lutsey says. "See you guys after. Alan, man, make it happen!" And then he scampers off to the neighboring large room where the crowd is gathered before a stage set up. Elden and I follow. Lutsey puts his drink down on the stool and jumps up on the stage and takes the mic.

"OK everyone. Please gather round. Tell those people in the other room to get their asses in here." But it's still too loud and stragglers are still networking or clamoring by the patio bar.

"Close the bar for a minute or something goddammit," Lutsey continues. "Children! Children!"

He laughs, attempting to balance discipline with a light-hearted atmosphere.

"Greetings everyone, and thanks for coming out tonight to celebrate Major League Baseball's new ad campaign by HRGM!"

Applause follows and I spot the HRGM contingent--the group from this morning's meeting and their significant others--clapping across the way.

"I'm Lutsey Lampkin, your host tonight." Now I'm just a lowly comic here in the city, so when I got the call to emcee this event tonight, I got all excited because I thought there would be some ball players here. But you cheap bastards didn't get one. I know the Yankees are pricey, but couldn't ya'll have brought in a few Mets? Maybe toss them $20 per hour? But, once I learned about the campaign we're here to launch tonight, I saw the connection. I watched all five TV spots today and read the print and other media vehicles displayed on the patio and I gotta say, they're hilarious! They're smart and fresh and made me want to watch baseball again. Even the Mets."

A cell phone goes off, and Lutsey stops talking and stares the executive down.

"Do you need to take that sir?" And then to everyone: "People, please turn down your cell phones--unless ya'll got some shit cell service. Seriously now. This campaign is gonna hit hard: TV, radio, print, internet, outdoor, indoor, El Salvadore. And I swear it's the best campaign I've ever seen."

Lutsey winks at the MLB execs in jest and then carries on about the purpose of the event, which is to preview the campaign (which I missed by arriving late) and to introduce and thank the key people involved. Elden and I look on and drink silently as the baseball commissioner speaks followed by an MLB executive. After that, Steve takes the podium.

"Major League Baseball is at the core of Americana," Steve begins. He continues on for five minutes, ultimately drawing the connection between baseball and a soap opera before segueing over to me. "In great part this decision was made possible by the creative and intellectual genius of one individual that I am both honored and humbled to work with. You are all familiar with many of his ingenious creatives. Ladies and gentleman, please allow me to get out of the way and bring you the all-star behind the new homerun approach to communicating what is truly great about baseball, Mr. Alan Jones!"

If everyone gets 15 minutes of fame, I hope these don't count for me. I approach the podium aloof and bored with the proceedings despite a solid applause. All 100 or so attendees are on their feet clapping.

I walk to the small stage, realizing I still have an empty martini glass in my one hand. I feel the liquor traversing my veins as I set the drink down on a table near the stage and climb up.

"Go Alan!" Elden yells. "Give'em passion!"

As I prepare to speak I look around at the well-dressed audience. Then I spy Elden again who's wearing the same old jeans, a t-shirt and a look so comical I nearly laugh into the microphone. I look to my left at Lutsey who gives me a ceremonious nod and to my right I can see Steve proudly whispering to someone. And I've reached the pinnacle of fame in this career and it's hard to imagine things any better in this career and for the very first time I can see quite clearly that I want out.

"Thanks everyone," I say, pausing to let the applause subside. But that's all I have rehearsed. And that's fine, because my words couldn't possible represent my beliefs about anything now. Not about what sort of career is best for me, or what sort of woman is right for me, or about anything related to what I want or need from life for that matter. And the reason is simple: I don't know.

And in a life as confusing and cloudy as this, the only thought that manages to push into my mind at this exact moment is that Herman Melville wrote Moby Dick. And pulling only that thought, I go on.

"Three words," I say, holding up three fingers emphatically, puckering my lips and nodding intensely at the crowd.

"Call me Ishmael."

The resulting silence could fill the Grand Canyon. Silencio. But off to my left I hear a snicker, and I look to see Lutsey covering his mouth. And then there's a whistle and a single source of clapping from the crowd, and it's Elden. I drop my hand and say "thank you," and bow. And with that, others in the crowd begin clapping--the early adopters, misguided and fooled as they are. I wonder for a second if maybe these words do equate to some brilliant inanity that I missed. Maybe *I'm* the idiot savant. In belated unison, the entire audience erupts into applause. I turn and shake an executive's hand and wink at Steve, whose face is crinkled with bewilderment.

Lutsey and I have to walk past each other for me to exit the stage and for him to take the mic and keep the show rolling. As we approach each other, he's shaking his head in approval.

"Great job," he says to me below the applause. He takes my place at the podium and continues to babble on to the crowd as Elden and I head to the patio to take full advantage of the open bar. Within seconds, Lutsey rejoins us.

"Now this is what I'm talking about!" he says, toasting us.

✳✳✳

We stick out the party for another hour, which is plenty of time for Elden in his embolden and unsolicited advances to attract a cute corporate woman in her late twenties. Her hair is pulled back so tightly it's painful to look at, and she's dressed in a pin-striped suit which--for this gathering--implies to me that she's with MLB's marketing department. Meanwhile, Lutsey and I hit it off famously, talking the entire time about his comedy career in New York and his wife of six months and about my own comedy aspirations that have been festering since childhood. I scare him with my knowledge of the field, speaking intelligently as I rattle off performers, acts, venues and dates as though I were talking about rock stars and concerts.

I catch myself suddenly. I'm a fucking total bore to him! Talking about comedians that Lutsey has probably met and even shared the stage or friend-ships with. But he listens on, fascinated, and I'm finally convinced of his authenticity when he dovetails into a sincere speech on passion and motivation and how hard comedy can be without good friends around to constantly push and inspire him.

"Comedy can be the world's loneliest profession," Lutsey says. Then he adds, "There's a real party I'm supposed to hit up tonight and lots of comics will be there. You wanna come with?"

I check my crooked banana/surfboard watch and it's between 11:40 and midnight. My buzz is kicking in and feel good.

"Yeah, for sure."

"What the hell's that thing?" Lutsey asks pointing at my watch. "What do you got, a little fruit dish strapped to your wrist?"

"Someone's gotta wear it."

We're ready to go, but Elden's not. We finally find him making out with the executive blonde on lawn chairs beside the swimming pool. My interruption is purposely shameless for the fun of it.

"Hey man, are you ready? We've gotta get going. Do you want to join?"

"Where?"

I look at Lutsey, curious myself.

"Party in the East Village," he says. "Good times. Big space."

"Nice. Be sure to take lots of pictures." And with that Elden smiles and turns back to the woman for another kiss.

I don't protest, knowing full well that despite his frequent advances and spontaneous courtships, any woman Elden meets has a chance of yanking him off the shelves of the singles market. Elden is not a player in the traditional sense; he's neither overly confident nor insecure. He's not concerned with gathering notches on his belt and he's never concerned with awkwardness or inadequacies. Beneath his quirky shell lies a sincere romantic who genuinely listens to people and their stories and strives for connections. He has no fears of commitment or love but speculates thoroughly to find it.

"You two look like a perfect match," I say to them as we leave. We laugh because Elden looks like something out of the Dukes of Hazzard with his frayed jean pants wrapped around the woman's pinstriped suit. Without looking, Elden flashes us the middle finger in one hand behind the woman's back. Lutsey and I get on the elevator. Just before the doors close, I catch one last glimpse of Elden looking every bit like the happiest man in the world (as usual) with his head nodding vehemently and his limbs flailing about against the backdrop of the Hudson River and the shadowy yet twinkling buildings of New Jersey just beyond.

Chapter 7

WE TAKE A CAB EAST across town to the offbeat streets of the East Village, the capital of Cassan's new crowd and location of her home away from home--her sister's apartment. If I were alone, I'd squat down a bit, lest she see me and take me for a stalker or the sort of weak-minded sap that can't pull himself together. But I'm with Lutsey, and hanging with him has only helped fuel my newfound detachment. He's one of New York's premier new comedians and this fact absorbs my mind as I begin transferring the credentials of my new friend to my own status and slip into a daydream while Lutsey fields a call on his phone. Suddenly, in my mind, we're New York's hottest new talent. When we step out of the cab there's sure to be paparazzi from at least the local publications like Time Out and Page Six of the Daily News. A few cameras will flash and the headline tomorrow will read, "Jones Stands Up," which I imagine refers to the successful conversion from ad copywriting to standup comedy and my indifference to the unwitting success I've just turned my back on. The sub-headline will say, "Splits with Fashion Beau and Moves Forward."

When we arrive, I tell Lutsey I've got the cab fare. He replies, "damn straight," and we step out onto Avenue C. The scene contrasts drastically with that of the Meat Packing district and my reveries of fame. The streets here are dirty and empty at this later hour and I'm wondering how good of a call I made in coming along. No pool bars or paparazzi anywhere. Rather, we have to dodge all these gigantic piles of black garbage bags awaiting early morning pickups as we work our way to the red steel door of an otherwise unassuming three-story loft building.

"Say again, whose place this is?"

"Hey man, I came with you," Lutsey says with a wink.

"You don't know?"

"It's cool. I've got friends here."

The buzzer is broken and we can make out music and voices inside. Lutsey wraps on the door with his fists for a while, but apparently no one can hear it.

"Shit, man," he says.

Just then, the door flings open and Lutsey grabs it. A loud burst of dance music blows two cute Latino girls out onto the sidewalk. They stumble drunkenly in their jean skirts, laughing and holding onto each other for support, and they don't notice us until they reach the street and turn back around.

"Yo! I know you!" one yells, pointing at Lutsey. Her friend slaps her arm.

"No you don't stupid!" her friend says.

"You guys wanna smoke with us?"

"Maybe later chicas," Lutsey says. "We just got here." And with that, we walk inside.

Hip-hop and dance-oriented parties usually aren't my thing, but I'm ready for it. I'm ready for anything. We walk into a dimly lit room that's jam-packed with people grinding to a loud, pulsating beat. Immediately I feel Lutsey tug my shirt and I turn to see him point to a staircase and mouth "follow me" over the noise. The stairs begin roughly ten feet across from where we came in and as we begin to ascend I'm struck with a bit of giddiness. I feel great. Nothing beats that early stage of drunkenness where you literally feel the liquor gently coursing through your veins yet still have all your wits about you; where you accept all the quirks of life with unbridled enthusiasm. And what a perfect place for the perfect buzz! It's hard to comprehend the sight as we make our way up the uneven homemade steps, except to say that the apartment resembles a funhouse more than anything else. To my left, a maroon wall supports bizarre paintings and distorted mirrors that are unyielding in terms of any practical reflections. There's no wall on the right though, so I can see up and ahead that the second floor is better lit, but with red filters or bulbs on the scattered lamps that illuminate a different crowd--a room nearly as full as the first floor, but without the dancing. We hop off the stairs onto the second floor like you might jump off a slow-moving tram at an amusement park and everyone is squared off and close-talking or working their way toward a long wooden bar where two guys pour drinks in a frenzy.

"Keep going up," Lutsey says, and there's a spiral staircase we transfer to. I follow close behind, realizing that all three floors of the brownstone are part of one big apartment.

"So you do know who lives here?"

"Yeah. My manager Ian," Lutsey says. "He's also co-owner of Liberal Arts."

"No way!" Liberal Arts, I know, is one of the best and hottest comedy clubs in the city, except it is not exclusively a comedy club every night. They have music and poetry nights and such as well.

"Yeah, and it's his birthday and he wanted to throw down on a Monday since comedians all work weekend nights."

The top floor has a much different feel. A smaller group of about 15 people mingle and talk easily over the relative quiet; the first floor music is reduced to a muted thud and drowned out by some soft playing trip-hop--Morcheeba, I think. Tacky red velvet lines the walls and seats everywhere and I love it. It's the sort of place you only seem to come upon under the influence and embeds itself in fragments in later dreams; the kind of place you know you'll never make your way back to and end up wondering years later if in fact it even existed at all.

I figure Lutsey has spent a lot of time hanging out here. We walk over to a small and inviting tiki bar in the corner and he taps the back of an older, 50-ish man in a hip sports coat and a yellow cardboard party hat strapped onto his large head. The man turns around screams when he sees Lutsey.

"There he is!"

"Happy birthday Ian!" Lutsey says.

It makes perfect sense that the name Ian belongs to such a pale, blonde, Scandanavian-looking face. Before they involve me though, I give Lutsey a little hand motion that indicates I need to hit the bathroom and he gestures to a very narrow hallway behind me. There's a small line of just two people. The problem is that they're women though, which equates to waiting for four men, even if the women do go in pairs. I plan to introduce myself but they're engrossed in some sort of chat that I quickly realize is about Lutsey.

"Him? Really?"

"He was on Comedy Central like a year ago."

"What's his last name?"

"I don't know. Just Lutsey is all I know."

When I rejoin the group, Lutsey is breaking away from a conversation, as he always seems to be doing. I grab a bottle of beer from an ice bucket and go up to him.

"Yo, I just overheard someone say you were on Comedy Central?"

Lutsey balks and sips at some sort of mixed drink he just got.

"Yeah, you didn't know that shit? I thought you knew everything about the comedy scene." He says the last few words in a goofy voice and frames it with hand quotes.

It's true, I know a great deal and pay close attention, but between work and Cassan, many things slipped through the cracks.

"It was probably a one-shot thing goddammit."

"What do you mean? That's just the first step."

"Yeah well..." Lutsey is more preoccupied with scouting out the room.

"Come on man, let me introduce you to everyone."

A few feet away, five people are slouched back on a red velvet couch that curves around a graffiti-tagged door serving as a makeshift table. All of them are engrossed in a story, but Lutsey makes a shameless interruption.

"Ok ya'll, listen up." All five heads stop and pivot up at us. "This is my boy Alan, and I expect that you'll extend to him every courtesy you might extend to each other."

"Does that mean I have to fuck him?" yells a woman with caramel skin and long, smooth black hair. Everyone explodes into laughter, including Lutsey. He pulls me in close for a second and gives me a sorta bear hug.

"Alan, this here is my wife Candice. Don't fuck her."

The idea of Lutsey being married still shocks me. He mentioned it back at the Gansavoort and it was hard to process then, but they do make immediate sense to me as a couple upon seeing them together.

"Oh, why you always have to be so controlling Lutz?" Her words are slurred and she's visibly tipsy and I like her right off.

Lutsey continues with introductions, left to right, his arms still around my head. "This dude right here is Ian. There's not much to say about Ian though," he says, while scanning the group. "Nah, I'm just playing. Ian lives here and it's his birthday. Next you got Vivian, then there goes Candice again, and then Phillip, and then my man Greg."

"Check it out Phil, another white boy to keep you company," Greg says to Phillip, despite the fact that Ian is white too. Phillip is a chubby, awkward sort who quietly nods and I can't imagine how he fits in here. He's not even drinking. I ask him where his drink is, just because I feel like I should say something.

"I don't drink alcohol anymore--it's a depressant."

"You know what's depressing," I say, "a party without alcohol."

The man next to him laughs at this and smacks Phillip on the back.

"Served bitch!"

It's Greg, who I recognized right off though. He's a hyper comedian I caught several times at the Comedy Cellar on McDougal. He's wearing a white Addidas jumpsuit and a white hat with a black brim, which I know conceals a shaved head. He must be in his late-30s because he's been a comic for so long, but he has this fun, nice, young-looking face that perfectly matches his energy.

"Yeah, yeah," Lutsey chimes in. "Like a host telling people, 'Thanks for coming. There's plenty of milk and shit in the kitchen.'"

Greg cracks up and mumbles something incoherent about cookies and milk, and everyone laughs.

"Alan here is a comedy aficionado and aspiring comic," Lutsey tells Greg. "My man just got an award tonight for creating Major League Baseball's ad campaign."

"For real? Congrats man."

"Thanks," I say. He couldn't know that I revere him with far more potency.

As Lutsey talks, I sit down on a chair with rollers opposite the couch facing everyone. I smile when I catch Ian with a comic expression just beneath his birthday hat. I'm guessing he's high or on ecstasy.

"So you're a comic, Alan?" The question comes from Phillip, who tries to look sincere despite his ridiculously grooved aqua shirt replete with huge butterfly collar and enormous purple polka dots. I'm guessing he's like a manager or something for one of the comics.

"No, Lutsey's just messing around. I did some open mics a few years back is all." Something Jerry Seinfeld once said in an interview comes to mind and I share it with this crew. The interviewer asked when Seinfeld first knew he was very funny, and Jerry said, "Everybody was funny back in high school. The only difference was that at some point they all just got jobs." The group loves it, and

I feel completely as ease as I always do with strangers for some reason, with the exception of my past attempts at standup.

"But really," I say, "Besides being a regular at a shitty amateur club a few years ago, it was always more of dream than anything else."

"Yeah, well you wouldn't be dreaming about my pay check," Greg says. "I paid down all my bills and had just a five dollar budget to go out with last week."

"What'd you buy with your five?" the other woman Vivian says. Before he can respond, I cut in and answer for him.

"Buy? Fuck that. He invested it," I say. "Gotta be smart." I tap my head with my index finger simultaneously.

Greg loves it and expands on my comments.

"That's what I've been saying man. Figure with a 10 percent return, in ten years I could have six dollars."

I bring up and begin impersonating Louis C.K.'s classic bit about money and how he only had five bucks in the bank, which he couldn't take out because there's no fives in the machines. I go on in flawless execution about how the bank charged him $10 for not having enough in his account so that he was left with negative five: "I wish I had nothing. But I didn't have that much. I had *not five*. I can't afford to buy something that costs nothing."

Lutsey and Greg go off on being broke some more and it's like a free show with all new material to boot. I sip my drink and recline deep into my chair, enjoying the old familiar feeling of hanging out with good funny friends again, before most of mine moved far away and were replaced by Cassan's too-serious gang. I feel right at home. I feel like Alan Jones again.

"Lemme hear some of your material Alan," Vivian says. I'm caught off guard by this, and I wonder if this is the norm when comedians get together, if they challenge each other like rappers might battle. I don't even know a thing about this Vivian woman.

"I'm sorry, who are you?" I cast this in a jestingly insulting tone for the sheer reason that I feel so inexplicably comfortable with everyone.

"Oh shit! I like this guy!" Greg says. He slaps my hand. "You tell her Alan!"

"Who am I? I'm the fuckin'...I'm the Michelin Man, motherfucka! Where'd you find this guy Lutsey?"

"Easy Viv," Lutsey says. "Alan's cool." He covers his mouth as if to speak privately to me, but remains loud on purpose. "Vivian is a comic too. And a mean son-of-a-bitch."

"You know I'm kidding," I say.

"I know sweets. And I'm not mean," she playfully punches at Lutsey. She's a tall, thin, Latina, and a fairly ugly girl. I imagine her looks have helped engineer her harsh demeanor over the years. "So let's hear your jokes."

Everyone looks at me. Suddenly, I recall one of the reasons I gave up on comedy to begin with, which is that I didn't care about telling jokes. I've always been more about writing them. And of course, I can't think of any now.

"I'm telling you guys, I'm not a comedian," I protest.

"According to Lutsey you are," Candice says. A look of intrigue overcomes her cute, freckly, face.

"He's never seen me on stage. And that was just some open-mic years ago."

"Oh, spare me the mothafuckin' excuses," Vivian says with a smile.

"Yeah, give us a laugh then," Ian chimes in.

"I, uh...retired my material."

"Get the hell out of here! Coward!"

"I really don't remember much and I'm not in performance mode." They all continue to look at me in a uniform silent deadpan as if they rehearsed this tactic, so I can see I need to say something. Finally I recall at least something.

"I had a bit about people taking forever at ATM machines. I say how this guy in front of me is rolling over his 401K, he's taking out a second mortgage on his house."

"You're gay," Greg says, playfully heckling me.

"Everyone's gay now," I fire back. "I feel all embarrassed being straight and shit."

And this gets everyone laughing.

I feel looser for some reason, so I try to slip into stand-up mode for a bit.

"I talked about Chinese restaurants," I say. "Like I always think they're messing with me. They're all smiling and treating me like royalty over some strange mythological dish. I'll have the Unicorn. The waiter nods emphatically with a big smile. 'Yes Sir!' He walks away laughing. For all I know I ordered a loaf of dog shit. And what's up with the duck sauce? The waiter explains: 'We take many ducks, then we *squeeeeeeze* the ducky sauce out of them.'"

For reasons I can't fathom, it's on. This isn't the way I expected the party to go, with me sort of auditioning as a comic suddenly. I even get the sense that Lutsey is a bit nervous for me.

"I wish could remember more and I have tons at home. I have this habit of writing down anything I find funny like some working comic, constantly digging for new material. I have notebooks full of bits and even routines, but I was never satisfied with any of it."

"Word?" Lutsey says. His face and tone are so serious for some reason that I stop to laugh, which makes the others laugh.

"Yeah. Word."

"Let's hear another one," Ian says. He's sitting so far to the end of the table that I forgot he was there. Ian, the manager of Lutsey. Ian, the manager of the renowned Liberal Arts comedy room!

"No, no. I'm done."

"It's my birthday, and I want to hear more." He dons a smile and sits back with full expectations of entertainment.

As comfortable and outgoing as I've gotten with this all-star group, I again plead that I don't have material ready to go like a working comic. My every day sense of humor is more about reacting to others and telling stories now.

"So let's tell stories then," Ian says.

I start to think, but Greg saves me. He suddenly goes off about some heckler situation he was in recently and then Vivian and Lutsey go in turn. Lutsey talks about how he got pulled over swerving all over the road while his girlfriend was going down on him. "I pleaded head," he says.

This reminds me of the time Elden and I both got pulled over in New Hampshire, so I jump in.

"My friend Elden and I were driving in separate cars in New Hampshire once and a cop pulled us both over. We were sort of taking turns cutting each other off on the way to his house. We were only going 30 and it was on this wide main street and nobody was on the road, but it was stupid of course."

"Were you guys wasted?"

"Luckily no. So it wasn't a DWI, but we got assigned 150 hours of community service for reckless driving."

"Damn. 150 hours," Candice says, with lovely brown eyes that seem to pop off of her cute face as though they are on springs.

"Isn't reckless driving a good thing? You didn't get into a wreck. That shit's wreck-less" We all look at Greg, owner of this comment, and I give him a resounding payback "boo." He laughs heartily and throws an empty cup at me.

"So anyway," I continue, "we looked around and found this great option to work at an aquarium. It was ridiculous. I mean--get this--Elden was assigned to feed the sharks! He loved it! He'd get all high in parking lot and then just go in there and feed sharks-- just because he was driving terribly! College students studying marine biology would kill for this, but we got it because we were driving like idiots.

"The gig wasn't as great for me though at first. They assigned me to the touch tank, which was bullshit. I had to pull all these sea creatures out of a tank and show them to the kids and come up with educational facts."

"You know about sea creatures?" The way Greg asks this cracks me up, and I feel a sense of giddiness that rivals his hyper mode.

"Not a thing! I couldn't believe they gave me that job, so I just made shit up. There would be like 20 kids gathered around me pointing at a crab they wanted see, and I had to pick it out of the water. It would be all snapping at me and I'd drop it because I didn't know how to hold them. And I had to make up some sort of educational speech. If it was bluish, I'd be like, 'this is North American blue crab.'

"But I listened to the real employees and learned my stuff eventually. Then they had me feeding dolphins and seals later. We became like professionals. I'd walk to get lunch and pass Elden with a headset on standing in water teaching 50 people about stingrays. It was ridiculous!"

"So you just kept working there," Ian asks.

"No. Like half-way through our service hours they called us both up to the office. This douchebag manager said, 'Um...we just learned you two are *not* marine biologists! Is that true?' So we were like, 'We never said we were.' The truth was, we were just some schmucks who got pulled over for reckless driving and they fired us on the spot."

And then I announce I'm off the hot seat.

"I like it," Ian says. "You should get on stage."

"What?"

"Yeah, why not? Hang out, practice your craft. It could be the perfect breeding ground for you."

"Damn Ian, you Norwegian prick. You're always working," Greg says.

Ian rubs his fingers implying money. As I watch everyone interact, I feel like I'm in high school or college or even how I did the first few years of dating, when I used to go out all the time. Back when I was the ringleader. And I suddenly realize how easy it is to get that all back. Just like tonight. There's a lot to be said for being with fun people and having a crew. I've felt so isolated with Cassan the last few years and when your good friends are gone, New York can feel like the loneliest place in the world.

Things get quiet for a second and then Candice finally pipes up.

"So Alan, you like advertising?"

"Baby, what'd I say about messing with Mr. Jones?" Lutsey yells.

"I'm not messing with him! Settle down."

"I'm over it," I say, trying to include her. There's a palpable sort of tension between the couple and I can't figure out if it is entirely playful. Lutsey asks if I want a drink to which I gesture "of course," and he walks off. The rest of the close-knit group launches into boisterous, cross-table chat, so Candice comes around to take Lutsey's chair next to me.

"You known my husband long?"

"Maybe four hours."

"Really?" She seems taken aback.

"Yeah, why?"

"Just seemed like you guys were pretty tight."

"You would have heard of me though, no?"

Candice sighs and in doing so I can see she's tipsy.

"Not necessarily. I mean, not when you're married to a comedian."

"He's crazy fun though."

"Well, I love him of course. But it's no secret that we haven't seen each other much lately."

I'm listening carefully. I'm buzzed, but attentive and engaged.

"I mean, he's trying to rediscover himself," she says. "With his comic persona and style I mean."

I nod empathetically. I faced the same challenge in my brief run, failing and bailing.

"But for some comedians like Lutsey, I guess it's hard for him to separate the stage personality from his own personality sometimes. So he's been off lately and I'm trying to stay out of his way."

"Not like I'm not interested, but why would you tell me this?" I have to ask, and Candice sighs. I want to add something like, "*I mean, damn, we just met,*" but that comment stays in my head. She twirls her tightly braided hair and adjusts her black skirt, which contrasts nicely against her light caramel skin.

"Because I'm stoned." She laughs. "Nah. I guess because I was hoping to get a fresh perspective on him, you know? I mean, I know these people pretty well and I don't want to bring it up in front of Ian of course--even if he is aware of it and all."

I don't know what else to offer up at the moment and I feel like a bit of a traitor. It's not like she's cutting Lutsey down, but it's awkward nevertheless, and I have to keep looking over my shoulder to see when he's coming back. And then I see him coming, saying quick hellos on the way.

I told you not to fuck her," Lutsey laughs, handing me a beer. He kisses Candice and the three of us form our own little side circle, which gets interrupted only by the occasional plucking or knee slapping by Greg.

"So everyone here is a comic except for Candice?"

"Everyone in our little circle here at least," Lutsey says.

"Even that quiet guy Phillip?"

Lutsey and Candice both laugh at this.

"Yeah, he was on Last Comic Standing, Candice says. But I'm with you. I don't know how.

"Cause he's funny baby. I tell keep telling you." Then Lutsey addresses me: "Made it to the quarterfinals with this slow, dry style and observational humor."

And they ask about my love life and I tell them like an idiot, like I've told everyone already. But I tell the story about Cassan with precision now, omitting the zillion little thoughts that had consumed me until nearly the moment I'd met Lutsey. And then I have another beer. And then I have another. And soon enough the warped surfboard on my watch tells me it's past 3 a.m. and I know I'm not making work tomorrow. Not on time anyway.

"You guys live around here?"

"Queens, and we're gonna get going. It's late and the party is dying down."

"I don't think I can stand up," I say. I consider the trek back to my apartment in my drunkenness and I think how sad it will be to return to a bed devoid of Cassan. What if I lost it and took a cab to her sister's place and yelled at her from the street like in someone painful movie scene you might cringe at watching? I don't know this new, single me very well, and I'm liable to say or do terrible things. My recent introspections have taught me that I've grown occasionally ruthless, if always apologetic--spurts that are the rest of my waking hours thickly veiled by my more familiar sincerity and sweetness. Perhaps they are symbiotic, the sarcastic me and the sweet me. So I decide that I'll eat the couch. I ask Ian if this is cool and he is happy to oblige. Lutsey looks like an Escher drawing in my stupor as I try to slap his hand good bye. They leave and I fade out.

Chapter 8

SOME MORNINGS--MANY MORNINGS--I awake groggy and clouded and I tense with negative recollections of the previous evening. These are the events that infallibly transpire once I surpass a drunken threshold. Secrets blown, drunken dials, flirtations regretted. And often there is the attendant pounding of the pillow in frustration. When I began dating Cassan, those mornings faded away and have only resurfaced recently. I suppose that's one of the primary functions of relationships in general--to appease the stupidity, to keep people in check. As I awake fully clothed in a mummified position on my normal right side of the bed, I begin thinking back on the previous evening. I recall putting myself out there in front of Lutsey and his comedy crew and hope I didn't embarrass myself. I vaguely remember bumping into a drowsy Ian outside the bathroom around 6 a.m., and him mumbling how I needed to come by his club soon. And then there was the cab home before crashing again in my own bed.

Suddenly I sense that something is wrong here. There's the hangover, sure, but there's something more--some essential element that is off. After sitting up a moment, I realize that my eyes are taking especially long to adjust to the daylight. And that's when it hits me: the curtains are gone! Those thick red stage curtains that I'd come to love. The curtains I imagined myself emerging from as a performer so many times. In their absence, two large windows reveal a grayish dull sky and what appears to be rain pattering down on the trees and the brownstones across the street. And there's more. Much more. A quick scan around the bedroom reveals that all-things-Cassandra have disappeared. Gone is her massive shoe rack and shrine of belts and her speaker towers and framed photos and her tablet and the little cedar desk it sat upon. Her entire vanity has disappeared, along with all her clothes that occupied a quarter of the apartment. I stumble out of bed and walk into the bathroom aching, and I see that all of her toiletries are gone too. Finally I work my way into the kitchen and on the counter I see another note penned in black from my recent ex. There's really no need to read it, I know. The trail of emptiness she left me on the way to the note foretold the blow. But I do read it:

Alan,

I hate to do this in writing, but I am moving in with Jen and you ran out before I had the chance to tell you. This probably isn't much of a surprise to you, but for the record, please consider us officially broken up. I hate to write this, and I would like to talk to you if you want to call me or maybe meet me, but please know that I've made my mind up and I need to move on. I think we both do. I will always care for you and I hope we can be friends, even if that takes some time. Who knows about the future? I wish all the best for you always,
Love (but, well, you know),
-Cassan

My body trembles and I fight it. I open the fridge and some lonely chicken pad thai stares back at me. I take it out and just sorta look at it for a moment and then I put it back in the fridge. I can't eat now. I debate taking a shower, but relent to the thought of the effort involved. I pick up my cell phone from the kitchen table and see that the battery is dead. It died somewhere in the wee hours of last night. I plug in the charger and turn it on and see five voice messages. I sit down and listen.

Message #1: Yo, Lutsz here. Good hanging out with you man. This fuckin' cab ride to Queens always sucks, doesn't it babe? Not you Alan, that's my wife. You're not my babe. Anyway, it's late man. We were talking about you and we wanted to say good hanging. Peace.

Message#2: Hey Sundip. It's Elden. I think I'm in love. Not in the Alan sorta way though. More like a happy way.

Message #3: Hi Alan, it's mom. I haven't heard from you in a while. Please give me a call when you can. I love you. Call me. Love you. Bye-bye.

Message #4: Alan, buddy, it's Steve. It's 10 a.m. man. I take it you partied pretty hard after that ceremony. No worries, but give me a call. I want to make sure you're ok and that you'll be in to work at some point today. We have some important baseball stuff to go over.

Message #5: Alan, it's Mike. Steve asked me to call. We haven't heard from you and Steve wanted me to check in to make sure everything is all right. OK, thanks.

I look up at the clock above the table and see that it's 1 p.m. I know without consulting myself that I'm not going to work. I do consider calling back Steve about the baseball stuff, but I'm too weak and weary and apathetic to even begin the process just now. Fuck it. What child's play really, when I think about it. So basically, baseball is like a soap opera because during the season it's with you every day. Got it? Good. I'm really pacing in circles now, and thinking in circles too. So we've got baseball, which happens every day. Then we've got myself, a copywriter who realizes that people follow baseball everyday just like people might follow a soap everyday. Great. So that's it. That simple connection is why I'm a great success? That little thought is the professional culmination of 27 years of life experience and of schooling and of tens of thousands of dollars spent on college? The reality is, once a connection is both appreciated and approved for a campaign, any kid with an imagination can fill in the blanks for the commercials to follow. So what do I get out of it? Money. Money and the loss of the woman I love. It's a negative gain. I'm in the red.

I stop pacing. I need to go somewhere. I go to my dresser and open the middle drawer with a bit of force, knocking over some photos of old friends and one of my photos of Cassan and I in Vegas. Some other things topple too, including random items I accumulated from past ad campaigns I worked on such as autographed golf balls, model racecars and a creative copywriting trophy in the shape of a large pen. In the drawer, I spot my favorite blue hoodie sweatshirt frayed from years of wear lying strategically on top just the way I like it. The sweatshirt was a gift from my parents when I left for college, and I use to live in the thing at Dartmouth. I have this bizarre habit of always keeping it stacked on top of my other shirts, maybe because it's the oldest item of clothing that I own. Some things just have history I guess. I throw the sweatshirt aside though, and dig up a pristine long-sleeve white t-shirt and sling it on. I'm going out, I just don't know where.

I grab one of the few remaining items in my fridge--a beer--and wrap it in a paper-bag and walk downstairs. I head west, and fish for my phone without any luck. It's rare to leave my phone behind, but I press on. As I walk, I mull over inanities and simple concepts without thinking, as though my mind is broken. Things like "baseball=soap opera." Big fucking deal! I own the field of copywriting. Everyone seems to say so, except Cassan (who was all that mattered). Then I realize my mind is working just fine. It just didn't know how to apply itself. For a moment I consider that I should just launch full-force into stand-up comedy, if for no other reason than laughter being healthy for the soul.

"Na," I say to myself out loud. A young female runner in a windbreaker hears me say this as I pass her, and smiles at me. I barely glance back, focused suddenly in this drizzle. Comedy is a pipe dream. What else could I excel at? I recall what Elden said about how I could excel at anything, and with that thought I take a very pleasing gulp of beer and cross over onto Greenwich Avenue. I'm right by the White Horse Tavern, where Elden and I went when he rolled into town the other night and I think to call him, but damn--no phone. I carry on west past the tavern, across Greenwich and Washington streets, and even across the West Side Highway, which is especially dull and empty on this dreary Sunday morning. Finally, I come to a stop. I have no choice. It's the end of the road. The light rain continues to tickle my head as I take a seat on a park bench at the edge of the Hudson River.

And man, time goes! Where does it go? I sip some beer in consideration. Time is measured well through déjà vu, when you find yourself holding or looking at the same thing you held or looked at before, or through a feeling you recapture. Only then do you consider the metaphorical bookshelf ends--the then and the now--and all the events that transpired in between and all the time that elapsed and how much you accomplished or fell short of achieving. I last sat on this bench in the early fall about six months ago. I had just finished a jog along the highway and came to rest. It's strange how details of a forgotten, trivial event can come back so vividly later. The sun sat low in the early evening. Autumn had settled in. I looked across the river at the leaves taking color, brilliant and cavorting for one last explosion of delight before withering into nothingness. I remember that it was a Wednesday and I had just found out I would be moving to the HRGM team assigned to sports and the Major League Baseball account. And I recall how Cassan said she would be out that night with the girls and how I agreed to meet them later for a last dance at a nearby club. I felt a vague sense of happiness then, but not for the state of our relationship. My thoughts were entirely on the new assignment at work. And I can see now that even then she unhappy with things between us.

"So she wants to dump you and try something new." I can still hear Elden's words ringing in my head. OK, sure. But the thing is, why can't *I* try something new? Try everything new.

I finish off my beer while looking at the ringlets of rainwater on the choppy river. I've made a decision, I know. I've made it on a subconscious level in various degrees over the last few days. Hell, maybe the last few months. An enormous decision I've been trying to ignore, pushing and squeezing it down into much too small a box and now that box has burst open. All I really need is a phone, which I may have subconsciously left behind in one last vain stab at resistance.

The decision is to quit my job. At this point, I don't see how I can't quit. It's not an ideal job, not something I love. An accomplishment? Sure. In terms of advertising copywriting, I've arrived. I'm an *IT* player. There's buzz and heat around me and I can go to just about any agency on the planet. There's room for creativity and cathedral ceilings for pay. And yet, just as I've hit the pinnacle of success in a career I sort of fell into, I've also reached the lowest of lows personally. Cassan was right. I've become less interesting and passionate as a result of my job. And now my work has led to my loss of Cassan. It's a paradox and I think I finally get it. But what do I need? I need something much more appealing, not only to myself, but to others. Not the dream job per se, but maybe the dream job in the eyes of both myself *and* the woman I will be with next.

I can see now that my success at HRGM was one bullet point on a long career resume. It boils down to direction, which I never possessed. I never thought about specific fields like real estate law or hedge funds or zoo keeping.

All I knew was I wanted to do something creative and fun. And the same with Cassan: She was just another accomplishment. Through her I have solid relationship experience under my belt. It's better to have loved and lost than to never have loved like Bogart says, and I get that now.

So that's who I was--a free-spirited, care-free, creative guy, always laughing and having fun. The sort of perfect bio you'd read in a dating ad. It reminds me of lesser Hedberg joke that goes something like, "I had a stick of Carefree gum, but it didn't work. I felt good blowing that bubble, but when the gum lost its flavor, I was back to pondering my mortality." That's how I felt about who I was, chewing that Carefree gum. That's what I lost, and that's what I'm going to reclaim. All I really need is that phone to complete the square of mental freedom. The phone, Elden, and who knows then? Maybe Lutsey, and a career in standup comedy. Or maybe something entirely different? Everything entirely different!

One of the most unheralded benefits of close friends is the sounding board they provide, even when they are not around. Especially when they are not around, when their biases and knee-jerk reactions are combed out and all you are left with is the meat of their viewpoints echoing in your head. To this end, I wonder how I might explain all of this to Elden, even though my primary goal is to explain it all to myself. How I might knead it over and sprinkle it with romanticism, idealism, humanism and optimism--all the good isms really. The isms central to who I *used* to be. The person Elden knows. And I'm not going to let jobs and break-ups destroy me. Not on my watch, and not on Elden's.

The gig is up, I realize. It's time to start anew. And suddenly I have all the answers, I know all the mysteries. I can tell you about cosmology, cosmogony, infinity, totality. A grid emerges, and I can envision it as clearly as white latticework on the porch of a country home. There's an x-axis and y-axis running horizontally and vertically respectively. On the x-axis one plots careers. On the y-axis, relationships. Anyone's life, I see now, can be plotted on this grid, and I need to begin the search of this grid in efforts to plot my own life. I can see, for example, my recent position 20 notches up on x and negative five clicks on the y. And at the intersection of these two lines I was a superstar advertising copywriter dating Cassandra, a fun and funny girl who was nevertheless shallow or whimsical and aloof to my finer qualities. I can see clearly now how small of a sample size my own life experience has been. A palpable wave of carpe diem sweeps through me, and I need more. More plots. One plot isn't enough! It's the desert island-stuck-with-one-book routine. How would one know that the plot was perfect? Ideal? No, no! I need to branch out, to make little marks on as many points on the grid as I can. It's all so plain and obvious now. I need to date as many women as I possibly can, sample as many careers as I can. Only then can I narrow the possibility of regret. Only then can I make informed decisions on how to plot my own life. And of course there are too many combinations for any lifetime. But should anyone sample just one? Instead I'll shift from (20, -5) to (12, 4) and become a carpenter whose dating an actress. Just for a week. Then I'll make a perpendicular adjustment so I'm flirting with a hippy. On plot $x = -3$, $y = 0$, I might be a single real estate mogul. And even the negative values will be positive experiences! My arm explodes with goose bumps as I stand and down the remainder of beer, and this energizes me all the more.

✳✳✳

I jog home and hop in the shower and formulate a mental to-do list while massaging my hair under hot water. Ah, life! You crazy son of a bitch!

I step out back out of the shower dripping with water and anticipation as I sling a towel around my waste and grab my phone. Steve picks up after one ring.

"Steve Dresmer."

"Steve, it's Alan.

"Alan!"

"Some bad news I'm afraid."

"Are you OK?"

"Never better."

"Okaaaay. You sound pretty hyper."

"The bad news is I have to give notice on my job."

The other end is silent. After a beat, Steve asks if I'm high.

"In a sense you could say."

"Are you fucking with me?"

"No sir."

Then a semi-pleading tone.

"Alan?"

"It's not the company, Steve, it's the career."

"The career?"

The conversation would be much more difficult without my newfound zeal, but I decide to ease the blow anyway with a promise of hope for Steve.

"I just need some time," I say.

"Why? Time for what?"

"Well, for one thing, Cassan just left me," I say, trying to throw some sense into the equation for him.

"What? When?"

"A few days ago."

I can almost here a sense of relief on the other end, as though Steve figures that I'm simply exhibiting the rash actions of any love-sick young man. And I'm happy to let him do so for now.

"I'm sorry to hear it Alan. I didn't see it coming. Still, you need to let it breath. You can't tie it in with your whole career."

"But it's more than that. I need some time. I'm not sure how much. And I can't promise I'll return to advertising at all."

"What are you talking about?"

We are both silent for a moment. Finally he continues.

"Listen, Alan, I'm not going to go into a big speech about how people over-react to breakups. Instead I'm going to give you two weeks paid but not officially accept any of this talk about you quitting for now."

"Sound fair?"

"Yes," I fire back.

"The campaign is well outlined, so we can proceed without you for now. But let's get together over a beer in a few days to discuss this."

"Sure. Next week."

"And Alan, if this is about you courting other agencies, you'd tell me, right?"

"It's not about that Steve. I give you my word on that. If advertising is for me, HRGM is for me."

With these understandings firm, I hear Steve breathe again on the other end. He parts with a final, "All right Alan. Take care of yourself for now and call me if you need anything. I will be following up and checking in on you."

"Thanks Steve," I say, while creating a mental checklist of new-world activities and possibilities and plotlines in my mind. And I consider that he is really a great guy and tell him so before hanging up.

Immediately after hitting the end button on Steve, I call Elden.

Elden picks up in three rings.

"There he is! I figured you forgot I was in town one last night."

"Where are you," I ask.

"I'm shacked at Caroline's place from last night. She's at work."

"So Cassan moved out," I say, anxious to get to it.

"I love it!" he yells. His response and tone is unexpected yet somehow appreciated. He can take any news, whether bad or tepid, and instantly flip it upside down and present it back with a joyful shine.

"Oh, hey, and I quit my job!"

"Wham! Seriously?"

"Seriously."

"My goodness. Alan Jones re-shuffling the deck. Let's go celebrate!"

Chapter 9

'm plotted on my newly minted grid as a single and unemployed male, point 0,0 perhaps, which I figure is not altogether too removed from being widowed and retired. That's not me though. I'm a ball of energy and passion, and I know this plot point won't last long.

The drab, gray afternoon has given way to a big, proud 6 p.m. sun, and I feel comfortable walking down Bleecker Street in light jeans and a purple t-shirt. June is here. Summer is here. Elden is here. He had left for Newport to do a freelance travel piece now that he is on break from school. Just days later, he grabbed another train back down to Manhattan to see both his new baseball executive girl and I. We made plans to meet up for dinner at a solid Mexican restaurant in my neighborhood, Diablo Royale, and when I arrive, he is sitting on a rickety bench outside wearing sunglasses and a nice white shirt that contrasts with his patent torn cargo shorts. The shirt is the same from the Hotel Gansavoort party a few weeks ago--his special occasion shirt--and Diablo Royale is always a great event for Elden, like most everything he experiences in life. The first thing that strikes me is that he is puffing away on a cigarette.

"What the hell man! You don't smoke." I say this in lieu of hello as I approach to him.

"Caroline does," he says. I'm just honoring her." He grabs at his hair, which is a golden, rustic hue under the sun, and he pushes it away from his forehead.

"Is she meeting us?" I ask.

"No, we said our goodbyes. She plans to come visit me up in Cambridge next week."

Inside, our hostess walks us through the saloon-like dining room with its "Hell is Empty, All The Devil's Are Here" quote by Shakespeare etched into the walls. She seats us at a wooden table beside the cantina-style glass doors swung wide open for us to gaze out onto the charming corner of West 10th street. Elden is giddy for one of their Margaritas, and he tells the waitress without consulting with me two bring out a pitcher along with their nachos with picadillo beef and cinnamon sugar pita chips.

"Detailed as ever," I say.

"Aw c'mon now. Ordering is an art you see."

I just look at him anxiously.

"So what's the plan kid," Elden asks.

"I need to start over," I say.

"Agreed."

"I still get paid for a few weeks from HRGM. Steve took it pretty well."

I could care less about the money though and might not accept it. I've saved enough to be fine for a while, maybe a year comfortably. All I care about is the latticework: the new grid of infinite possibilities and the renewal on life. I take a slug of sake and launch excitedly into my whole theory of the relationship-career grid and Elden nods along furiously, taking great delight it in all.

"And what's the goal," he asks.

"To find the ideal woman and the ideal career." We share a mutual laugh for a moment at the ostensive ridiculous of it all, but I do mean it. "What do you think?"

"I suppose it's a sage theory, though I'm not sure how practical really. I mean, all you are really saying is that you are open to meeting anyone or trying any career. Am I right?"

I consider the simplistic light he casts on this for a moment and I'm suddenly unsure.

"I dunno. I guess I need some rules. I have to. Otherwise I might as well just turn to the first woman I see in this restaurant and ask her out. That can get tiresome."

"Maybe you can appropriate your plots into quadrants like say, entertainment for careers, rather than spraying it all over?"

"No, no," I say, shaking my head. "That defeats this open mindset. Whatever, whoever comes my way that might interest me has a shot," I say. "So long as the basic criteria is met."

"Oh! So the basic criteria is still in effect."

Elden knows from our previous chats and theories that the relationship criteria for me are three-fold. For me, a woman must be funny, smart/witty, and somewhat creative, or at least someone who can appreciate creativity or the arts. As for careers, my criteria are more undefined than ever.

"What if a standard bell curve apex comes your way?" He is referring to the theory we have about how really cute (but not super hot) women tend to have the best personalities. This is due to more social development without the conceit. More specifically here, Elden wants to know if I would waive some of my criteria, like say a good sense of humor if a girl I liked came my way.

"I'm holding my ground," I say. "Plus I need to narrow the field somehow. I know I value these three characteristics the most in a woman, so I'm opening myself up to anyone in this field."

Elden scratches at a chin stubbly enough to be considered a goatee, although his lighter hair makes it hard to see.

"Interesting though," he says. "We never considered the 3-Quality-Model contradicting the Personality-Attraction Bell Curve. Are we losing it?"

Suddenly we both burst into laughter at the complexity of how it all sounds, of how we like to make it all out. We regroup quickly but before I can answer, Elden hits me with a tough question.

"Suppose you meet this so-called ideal woman or find the ideal career on the first shot? How do you recognize it as ideal? What is ideal?"

I'm prepared for this though. I had continued working out my master plan the last few days.

"The answer is five things."

"You sure it's not three words," Elden laughs, referring to the Moby Dick gag.

"Nope. Five plot points, or at least five relationships and five careers at some point, even if they are not all paired up."

Elden drains his first glass of Margarita and pours another. He has a habit of wanting a fresh drink when he anticipates some engaging dialogue coming his way.

"You know," I add, smiling, "My uncle's a dirty bastard. He says there's actually only two things that are important in life: tits."

Before he can react, the waitress suddenly appears to take our order. Chile Relleno for Elden and fajitas for myself.

"OK," I say, capturing Elden's full attention. "The x-factor to this is that I've decided not only to pursue new plots on the grid, but I need to do it five times. That's five different girlfriends and five different careers."

"Why five?"

"No particular reason. Five is a nice smooth number and a reachable goal. But more importantly, this gives me a roadmap."

Elden scratches at his itching chin again while considering this.

"So in a month from now, let's say you are a professional comic dating a Victoria Secret model. You wouldn't just call it quits?"

"Nope. Because how do I know that even that is perfection? Plus, wouldn't she be too far to the right on our attraction-personality curve?"

"But you can't tell me that four more lesser experiences--or like you say, plot points on your grid--are going to inform you much differently."

"Maybe not," I say, "but I have to go deeper. If I don't throw myself around the world a bit, I might never feel satisfied. I've known just one girl-friend and one career since college. That's unheard of today, even for recent college grads."

Elden still balks at this.

"I need to digest this," he says. "I just caution you not to taint your experi-ences with your concepts of idealism. You can run around dating as many women as you like, but if you keep looking for the same thing, you really aren't experiencing anew."

And of course Elden has a good point. He wouldn't be Elden if he didn't. But I feel great about my plan and I know there's nothing wrong with having some criteria to start with. It's not like I was born yesterday. I have a head start. I know of many qualities in women I definitely do not seek, and I have a pretty good idea what moves me."

"I'll try to keep as open a mind as I can," I say.

"Zippadoo," he says, wagging his finger happily at me.

We polish off our second round of drinks while having fun considering potential plot points.

"Maybe you can be a beekeep," Elden says. "Or an inventor or a turkey baster. Maybe you can hit up some career fairs to start, and then on the same day try some speed dating. Sign up for some online dating sites too since you are so big on criteria up front. You can customize right there. Or you can really aim high. You can become a prince of an exotic country with five wives for efficiency in your plan or become a poet and then a nomadic artist who only communicates through degrees of smiles and date isolated women who have never heard of television."

And on and on Elden goes in the way that Elden goes. As all men of passion go I suppose, with constant streams of energy and ideas and intoxicating perspectives.

✳✳✳

After a scotch dessert, Elden and I walk the neighborhood to see if I can immediately score a job. The early evening is cool and dry and even now at 8 p.m. the near-solstice sun remains well above the horizon. We pass several restaurants posting help wanted for wait staff, and cabinet shops seeking craftsmen and various retails shops in need of cashiers. We walk into a SEE eyewear shop in Sheridan Square and Elden asks if in fact glasses can reflect the transient nature of mankind, "for *his* sake," he adds, pointing at me. The baffled clerk responds simply, "can I help you?" as if Elden hadn't already engaged him in dialogue. We laugh our way out of there at that.

Next we begin stopping at pubs we pass that advertise for bartending help in order to "scout it out" as Elden puts it. We need to go undercover as mere barroom patrons to sus out the atmosphere, potential colleagues and general working conditions. Our rule becomes one beer per pub. I don't want to take a bar job though for the sole reason that I have already experienced working as a bartender at Dartmouth during part of my senior year.

"Come on Alan, you need to stop being such a finicky bastard," Elden finally says when we resume walking.

"I'm not being finicky," I protest. "I can't just grab a bartending job tonight because you want free drinks when you visit. I know your angle."

"Do you think I'm *that* shallow? This is your career we're talking about man, or at least the first of many to come. And by the way, you don't have to stop precisely at five you know. You could, in theory--which is all this whole grid *thang* is anyway--plow right past five careers en route to 20 before you find the perfect one. Especially when you can fall back on advertising or give comedy a real go at any given moment."

Elden is right of course, and I'm just about to concede as much, but a chubby old man in front of little wine shop suddenly interrupts us.

"Don't you think this looks a lot better?" the man asks us.

He is simply watering down the sidewalk in front of the shop that he apparently owns and a timid young protégé of some sort looks at us in frustration.

"Why, yes," Elden says. "Your store façade is now quite refreshing to behold."

"See kid, that's what draws them in," the old man says to the scruffy-looking young man. And then, to Elden: "I try to tell the kid, you hose down the macadam and the store looks much more appealing." The younger man could care less, and being in his early 20s he seems annoyed with being referred to as a kid. Elden eats this older character up though, the goofy logic registering succinctly in his mind.

"What you may consider too, is perhaps some sand and a boat and a little waterfall."

I look up at the sign above the storefront that reads "Elmer's Fine Wines and Spirits," and just below that, "Help wanted."

Elden has beaten me to the punch though.

"Would your fine shop make room for an over-qualified gentleman seeking temporary employment sir?" Elden indicates myself and the old man glosses me over.

"Sure. We can always use some talent in here. Do you know your wines?"

"Somewhat," I say, admitting that I'm no connoisseur.

"Well, go on in and meet Kevin the manager. Tell him I sent you."

"I'm sorry. Who are you?" I feel rude asking, but this strange guy brought it on.

"I'm Don," he says. "I own the place."

"Is there an Elmer?"

"That was my father, but he passed."

Elden hangs back with Don and the kid while I go in to meet Kevin. The store is a tiny little affair, maybe 600 square feet with nothing but wine bottles on display in wooden crates stacked wall-to-wall. There's also an island of these wine crates right in the middle of the room, so I walk around the stack to reach the old, oaken counter. Behind it, a smooth-looking man of about 35 with blond hair and a boyish face is at attention. In front of him is a bottle of open wine and a few Dixie cups and a metal bucket.

"Welcome," the man behind the counter says. "Try some wine? Just got in the new vintage of our house wine. Bouchet." He offers me a sip, which I take before announcing my raison d'être.

I inform the man that Don sent me about a job, and the man introduces himself as the manager. Kevin.

"Don is not your ordinary guy," he says.

"I already learned as much. Is watering down the front sidewalk your primary marketing vehicle?"

Kevin laughs and begins to explain several other quirks of Don's, such as the booby traps he has set up in the back room to thwart criminals and his extreme take on customer service that ensures the store will never make money.

"Don's doing it just because he loves the customers and to keep his father's legacy alive," Kevin says. "He doesn't need the money. Anything he makes just pays for the wine and salaries. He has an enormous heart, I'll say that."

I explain my background, which both impresses Kevin and takes him off guard.

"So you want to go from that world to a wine clerk?"

"If you offer me a job I'll explain it over the course of the first week," I say.

And with that, I'm hired. Career No. 1 is underway: a clerk for a fine wine shop. Assistant manager in fact. Kevin confides that he's happy to have someone who can fill his shoes when he takes vacation next month, including bookkeeping, inventory, pricing, and scheduling the younger part-time staff, or "the kids" as Don calls them. Am I kid now? The tough part will be getting up to speed on my fine wines, which I find rather appealing. We shake hands and I'm asked to start in two days.

When I head back outside into the twilight, I see Elden engaged in some sort of intense conversation with Don. He has his arms the old man's shoulders even.

"And that's all you have to remember Don," Elden says. "Point of contact. Tender eyes." They both break off from the intensity and look at me.

"Hey kid," Don says. "Did you get the job?"

"Start in two days," I say, suddenly unsure who is boss. All I know is that now I'm a kid.

"Great. And you're a comedian?" I look at Elden who shrugs with apathetic guilt for revealing my side passion. The owner's large button-down dress shirt accentuates his bulbous stomach as he steps towards me. He smiles and reaches to shake my hand, but stops just short.

"You don't have any germs do you?" His pitch is high, his cadence slow.

"None that I know of."

"Wonderful. What's your name?"

"Alan."

"Great, kid."

✳✳✳

Elden and I head back in the direction of my apartment where he left his travelling bag. Sadly, he needs to catch a train back to Boston.

"What the hell was that all about?" I ask.

"Your new employer is gold. He loves his shop and the regular customers and he cares deeply about selling great wine to people. A real passionate Zen master."

"You think?"

"I was just telling him to stay true and how the world needs more people like that nice round man."

He wants to know quirky particulars like whether I thought the clerk reminded me a bit of Matthew Broderick and if I might feel a bit stuffy in such a little shop.

"You think you'll be happy?" he asks.

"I don't know. But it's work," I say in jest. "Who knows? Maybe this could be perfect. Maybe this is my gateway to owning a vineyard out west or some dreamy gig I never saw coming.

"Wham!" Elden yells. "That's the spirit!"

"Pun on spirit," I say. "Maybe I buy this shop one day and spin it into a little money-maker. Like this thing." And I point to my ass.

When we reach my apartment, I give Elden the keys to run up and get his stuff while I light up a cigarette on the sidewalk. I use the brief time alone to consider what I've just gotten into--the pros, the cons, the possibilities. I shrug it off with the notion that I won't stay there long anyway with four more careers looming. When Elden comes back down we make tentative plans for me to come visit him in Boston.

"You're a manager now. Just schedule yourself off anytime and come on up."

I can tell he enjoys my dedication to this offbeat movement and to this casual acceptance of a much lower manifestation of my education. We giggle about the whole thing like idiots for the first time since I was "hired" while he hails a cab. Then we share a hardy guy hug and he hops in the cab and yells "Penn Station my good man!" and he speeds off in a blur of yellow.

I remain standing on the street, smoking and considering my new world. Five careers and five women. I don't have a black book and I'm not ready for speed dating or online dating and so I prefer to start organically on the girl front. I need to get out there and meet people in the natural environment, if you can call Manhattan that. And there's a text message on my phone that Kate sent earlier in the night that reads, come out and play, and I smile at the perfect symmetry of it all.

Chapter 10

Three months later.

I'M LYING IN BED NAKED WITH KATE around noon on the Friday of Labor Day weekend, wondering how she managed to hang onto me since June. I don't know why I'm dating her really. The conversation has been an exhausting, typically one-sided discourse by her on the pros and cons of her career, friends and family. Normal things, and perfectly fine topics of course, but she drones on like a cicada bug in an incessant hum that lulls me to sleep.

I am antsy now, and I start poking her in random spots, making different, goofy loud noises with each poke. I even imitate the sound of a buzzing fly and move my finger about like a fly that periodically lands on different parts of Kate's face.

"Quit it Alan," she says. "That's so annoying!"

What I have learned by dating Kate is that she is a mess. And I don't just mean her apartment. There's some hollowed out chunk of passion inside her that makes it terribly hard to connect with her well on anything. She began taking painkillers daily after her career in television commercial acting fell apart and she was forced back into secretarial temp jobs. She maintains a network of shady ex-boyfriends who keep her supplied with Vicodin, and with whom she still sleeps with as she continues her quest for the perfect guy. I feel bad that I'm not this perfect guy for her sake. The truth is, the sex is great, but it's the only thing holding us together.

And so, as I lie in bed, I consider my new plot on the grid, which is wine shop manager dating a depressed, neurotic mid-life crisis type about 10 years my senior. Her listening skills are a big part of the problem too, and I've secretly taken it upon myself to serve as her relationship counselor, skillfully hinting at areas of improvement to help her land her next man. I want to tell her to hang in there, that I, too, am searching for the perfect relationship, but it's not the sort of thing you tell a girl that you are seeing.

"What time do you have to be at work," she asks.

"Soon."

"Do you miss your old job being the hot-shot ad exec at all?"

"I was really just a copywriter, but yeah, it's a refreshing change of pace."

We lay in silence a moment, and suddenly I feel like I need to defend my new job. I begin to tell her about my growing fascination with wine that has resulted from my mandatory studies at Elmer's.

"Bordeaux," I say, "is still king. Have you ever sipped a $600 bottle of Bordeaux?"

"No."

"It tastes like smooth grape juice. Doesn't burn at all, but you still get the most happy, tingly feeling."

I go on to explain how a tour of Elmer's--which Don proudly offers to the big-pocketed wine connoisseurs that frequent his shop--reveals the store to be deceptively large. How a single, narrow walkway seeps back behind the counter and branches off into countless tributaries of thin, winding aisles of wine crates containing varietals from all the world's appellations as far back as the '40s.

Kate yawns, and I decide to stop talking.

"I thought this was only a temp job for you," she says.

"It is. Maybe another month." And I mean this. It's time to move on--not just in terms of a career, but from Kate as well. Things have grown stale and she has to feel the same way. It's the way any two people will eventually feel when they are not highly compatible. And I think to just break it off right now, but I don't have the heart or the energy, so instead I make a loud, steamroller sound effect and topple back on top of her.

When I arrive at Elmer's at 2 p.m. the place is already bustling. Holiday specials line the store. The wind chimes on the front door produce a steady stream of annoying music as people come and go. The tiny shopping floor is packed with customers, most of whom are regulars. In sharp juxtaposition to the elite wine clientele are the drinkers that burst in from the street demanding malt liquor in paper bags and nips of Jack Daniel's and six-pack cans of beer. Yet for these patrons, Don's intrigue remains every bit as lofty.

"Hey buddy," says a sweaty man in an electric company uniform who approaches me at the counter. "You got any Rolling Rock back there?"

"Sure we do," Don says, sizing the man up. "How's business? Electric?"

As they talk, I fetch the beer from the walk-in cooler with its bizarre custom pulley system that opens and closes the slider. This is just one of the many ancient contraptions that help produce the character of the store. In the backroom there is a single thick string that struggles to hold up a massive metal junk structure in place some 50 feet above the ground, and the store manager Kevin and I laugh as we stare at this in utter disbelief during cigarette breaks in the backroom. For that matter, there are all too many things to laugh about when considering Don's habits and eccentric practices that we have to contend with. My favorite is the Manager's Manual. This hearty, 40-page document instructs on everything from how to teach seasonal gift-wrapper employees to fluff a ribbon with scissors to how we should line the office windows where we eat with newspapers so that customers can't observe us chowing down. Page 32 deals exclusively with the steps for closing up, including how to place a wooden board across the spiral staircase leading up the office with the rationale that burglars would bang their necks on the board in the dark and tumble down the stairs and thus their mischievous plans would be thwarted. On and on the manual goes with products of Don's strange mind--a mind Elden fully appreciates.

About an hour into my workday, one of the regulars works her way up to the counter. She is a woman of about my age with an average build, dressed as usual in a suit and holding her customary bottle of Chardonnay. Her slightly disheveled brown hair and baggy eyes likely point to work-related stress although the rest of her features are delicate and cute enough. I've seen her come in every Friday and occasionally on a weeknight as well, always ordering the same single bottle. Part of the fun of the job for me is making witty little remarks about everything to the customers and getting conversations going with everyone near the counter. This woman never joined the dialogue though, instead opting every time to smile politely and silently until she received her change and left. For this reason, I say nothing now, but suddenly she initiates the conversation.

"You know," she says in a soft, higher-pitched voice that contrasts sharply with her power outfit, "I'm just going to cozy up with a movie and a bottle of wine tonight. Do you have any good movie recommendations for me?"

"What genre," I fire back, ready for the challenge. I do admit to a haughty opinion of myself when it comes to judging movies.

"Well, I don't know if it's your thing, but maybe like a romantic comedy."

"That's half of all Hollywood films ever made," I say. "Lucky for you I'm in touch with my romantic side. Does it matter how recent it is?"

"No. I'm just starting to become a movie junkie, so I've missed out on a lot."

At this point, Kevin--who I have come to befriend--comes to the counter early from a break to help others in line. He's trying to do me a favor buy freeing me up to continue talking to the woman. I suggest the movie *Casablanca* to her first and foremost of course, but she balks at the black and white format. Then I suggest *Breakfast at Tiffany's* even though the color in that one is reflective of its age--early '60s I think--and I rather wish it was just black and white. She considers this and then I give her a few more.

"*Forgetting Sarah Marshall, Love Actually, Romancing the Stone, Groundhog Day, Jerry Maguire, When Harry Met Sally.*"

It annoys me somehow when she says she has only seen *Love Actually* and *Jerry Maguire* but it is refreshing to hear that she wants a romantic comedy that is heavier on the humor side, so I recommend *Groundhog Day*.

"Thanks. What's your name?"

"I'm Alan."

"Thanks Alan. I'm Diane. I'll let you know what I think next time I see you." And with, that she's gone.

✳✳✳

I get off work at 9 p.m. and the plan is to go see Lutsey who is headlining at Liberal Arts tonight. Despite our frequent text messaging, I haven't seen him in person since the party at Ian's three months ago. The only reason for that I guess is that I have endured something of a dark age since Cassan left me. Even now I still miss her. Or more accurately, I miss who she was and what we were before those last few months. Furthermore, I had called Steve from HGRM and told him that my advertising career would remain on indefinite leave. The real price of this move was that I missed the daily company of my old colleagues. Aside from the various rebound distractions with Kate, I became relatively isolated. I drifted into a lazy rhythm of sleeping late, reading the Onion, fiction, entertainment and sports news, and Timeout New York over lunch in a circular patronage of neighborhood bistros.

Eventually I cheered up. After a few weeks of working at Elmer's, I began writing down a whirlwind of humorous thoughts. This became my one saving grace during this period of detox and transition from my old life and the emotional roller coasters I endured. I attended live afternoon readings from visiting poets and authors in homage to my literary schooling, slipped into comedy shows alone at night, and took an improvisational comedy class for a month. I figured any reputable psychiatrist would have prescribed humor. As my arsenal of comedy material began to build, so did my general vigor. And so, after all this time, I'm finally up for making my way to midtown east and Liberal Arts.

The comedy club is jammed when I arrive but the hostess finds a single seat for me at a long table of mixed groups off to the side against the back wall. Suddenly the emcee introduces Lutsey as the headline act for the night. Music erupts from house speakers overhead and Lutsey runs up to the stage in his trademark boisterous wobble that is purposely uncoordinated with long, exaggerated strides. And right away I see he braided his hair since I last saw him. He leaps onto the slightly elevated stage, which is practically on top of the audience in the fairly small, intimate room. He places a glass of water down on a table in front of the brick wall behind him. The music fades out behind the applause as he grabs the microphone and begins pacing frantically to the chagrin of the spotlight.

"Wow. No take backs now," he says. "Ya'll clapped and cheered and shit and I haven't done anything yet." The crowd laughs, taking in his fun demeanor while his big eyes gleam back at them. "What if I start talking about how I love terrorism and shit? Ya'll have to go home saying, "Why did I clap for the motherfucker?""

As Lutsey carries on, I notice that his act is not entirely as blue, or dirty, as he made it out to be. Generally speaking, when you can be very funny without talking about extremely dirty things all the time you become more marketable. This is just common sense. You leave the doors open to network television roles and specials like he landed on Comedy Central in the past.

"I found a new apartment for a great price," he says. "I was like, 'what's the catch? What, it's got roaches? A 10 story walk-up?' And the landlord was like, 'no, it's got ghosts.'"

Lutsey scrunches up his face in disdain.

"A ghost? Shit. If that means you're knocking a $1,000 off the rent, sign my ass up. If the ghost appears, I'll just start masturbating. Ghosts don't want hang around while some dude is masturbating. Or I'll lock myself in the bathroom and take a shit. That ghost will disappear in a second."

Again the crowd erupts, as do I. It's thoroughly entertaining stuff, and much of it is new to me because I'm used to seeing him in the emcee role where he picks on the crowd rather than doing bits. The set lasts for 30 minutes, after which Lutsey steps off and heads my way, slapping hands with the audience on the way.

"There he is!" Lutsey says, when he reaches my table. I shake his sweaty hand as the people at my table all stare, and Lutsey suggests that we head over to the bar so we can talk. I'm glad we haven't missed a beat since we last saw each other, and as I follow him I think how weird it is that the last time I watched him perform we were strangers to each other. That's part of the charm of living in Manhattan; the connections, the ease of networking and sharing drinks with people who are industry leaders in any field you can imagine.

We grab a seat at the bar and Lutsey orders us two drinks that he claims are on Ian.

"How you been, bitchy?"

"I'm good." And the truth is, I'm great now that Lutsey is here. I feel like I've been shot with adrenaline. I'm ready to climb a mountain or run out and party or get up on stage and do a set of comedy. "Great set man!"

"It's all right," he says. "Nothing all that new. I need some solid new material. You've been writing?"

"Actually, yeah. A lot has been coming to me in the reprieve. But nothing polished by any means. Not anything that works for you sadly."

"Eh." Lutsey waves my comment off and sighs. "Truth is man, I'm think I'm losing steam."

"Get out of here. You just killed them. Pick a good analogy pretend I said it."

Lutsey smiles and thanks me again.

"Maybe. But things have been rocky with Candice to be honest too."

"Really? Sorry man." I had hoped things might have improved between them after Candice confided in me at Ian's party.

"Yeah, but that's not for now. What about you? What's this you've been texting me about trying to find the perfect job, the perfect girl, the perfect... everything? Leaving advertising and shit? What the fuck?"

"As advertised. I just felt like I wasn't moved by my job anymore. I want to get out there and make things all great again, you know?"

Lutsey takes a sip while staring me down for a moment. Then he toasts me.

"I do know." And we laugh at the melodrama in his response. "Nah, but seriously. I'm impressed. I don't know why, but I am. So are you thinking of trying comedy finally?"

And at this, I launch into an explanation of my five-step-plan. His eyes pop when I tell him how I will try dating five different women and work in five different careers, hopefully within a year.

"Like in the movies," he says.

"What do you mean?"

"You know what I mean. Like when a guy has to date a bunch of women. What's that movie with Meg Ryan?"

"When Harry Met Sally?" I say, thinking of Diane at Elmer's.

"Yeah."

"But that wasn't a list of women he had to date."

"Whatever man. What about a Christmas Carol?"

I laugh at this comparison, especially coming from him.

"Really? A Christmas Carol?"

"Hell yeah. He has to meet all those ghosts and shit."

"So yeah, something like that then," I say, conceding his point.

"That's crazy man." Lutsey scratches his chin in thought, much like an Elden surrogate.

"So what about standup comedy? Will you make it one of your five?"

"Good question. I'm thinking yes." And I tell him again how I've been writing and even sheepishly admit to the comedy class I took, and we both decide that this is all part and parcel of a standup comedy career. That is, I am already involved in the comedy career by virtue of working on an act, which is even more than half the battle. So this is the second job of five then I tell him.

"Oh, you mean you count that wine shop job?" Lutsey knows about this through our text messages.

"Yeah."

"So you *were* serious? How do you go from a top copywriter to retail?" The question is valid. I often can't believe it myself, but I'm happy with the decision.

"Kate just asked me the same thing."

"Oh, yeah. How's that going?"

"I'm ending it soon. I have to, right? Even if I did like her."

Lutsey looks at me for a moment and smiles.

"One down, four to go?"

"Yeah." I fight back my own smile, knowing how ridiculous my plan sounds.

"But with the wine thing, what the hell do you know about wine?"

"Everything…now," I say. I burst into laughter. Maybe it's because of Diane, but I'm reminded of that scene in *Groundhog Day* when Bill Murray says, "I don't worry about anything anymore," and I share this with Lutsey who luckily knows the scene and we both start dying.

"OK," he says when we collect ourselves. So you manage a wine shop now."

"Yeah. It's kind of cool. Something laid back and interesting while I figure out what to do next, ya know?" I stop talking, but Lutsey continues to look at me in wonderment. Then he snaps out of it with a shake of his head and fires back his drink.

"Man, it's just odd is all. I mean, I don't know you that well really, but it still strikes me as odd."

"I'm reinventing. What can I say?"

"Whatever works man. But here's how it's gonna go down. Pick three more jobs and get them over with so you can do what you know you want to do. You told me the night I met you that standup comedy has been your real passion. So that's it. You're a comic now too. And I'm gonna help you get there."

"You? You just told me you are losing steam yourself."

Lutsey is about to explain, but suddenly the towering proprietor Ian interrupts us.

"Alan Jones!" he says, drawing out the words with that Norwegian accent. "So when are you taking the stage here?"

"Hey Ian! New talent must be hard to find these days. Don't you have a million seasoned comics out there you'd rather recruit?" And I mean it. I've bumped into many aspiring comics in the city the last few years, most of whom get their start through open mic nights that require them to bring friends to defray the costs of such a spectacle. These are called "bringer shows" as you have to bring someone to get stage time.

"Of course I do," he says. "But this is what I do. I cultivate talent." I took a similar approach with Greg and Jimmy, and now I have to tap-dance to book them here. Lutsey thinks you have promise too. We all like you and you are in our circle now and so forth."

And I'm flattered. Sincerely. To have someone in the industry tell me I have potential is good to hear, but that's based on one drunken night hanging out and he's never seen me on stage.

"OK, OK," Ian says. He gets up and pats my back. "I know you came to see Lutsey and I have to go handle some things. But I have to say, it's not often a comedy manager slash house owner tries to woo a guy with absolutely no experience." He scratches his head in jest while walking away. "I don't think it's ever been done actually."

Lutsey turns back to me as if his manager never intruded.

"So when are you gonna get on stage?"

"Soon," I say. This just spills out of my mouth without any thought and for the first time I realize that I will definitely give it a go again--an unencumbered, serious attempt this time, with the advantage of industry people on my side.

"I'm lovin' it!"

"What are you doing, a McDonald's commercial," I ask, referencing the McDonald's tagline. Lutsey laughs after I share with him the thought I had about an unenthusiastic McDonald's staff behind closed doors."

"There you go. That's a bit right there," he says.

We carry on for a while discussing comedy bits, pausing occasionally to watch comics on the bar monitor performing live in the room just beyond. We can't see them from our angle, but we can hear the intermittent explosions of laughter from the crowd perfectly clear. After one of the comics leaves the stage, I address Lutsey on a different topic.

"So what's the talk before about you losing steam?"

Lutsey shakes his head and a few of his braids flop about.

"I don't know if I'm gonna make it man."

"What do you mean," I ask. "At what?"

"Comedy."

This catches me a bit off guard. I instantly recall how Candice said something about Lutsey trying to rediscover himself as a comic, but I hadn't really bought into it at the time, or at least I was too drunk to remember until now.

"What the hell are you talking about? You just headlined and had a great set. You're on stage somewhere in the city like every night. And you had a comedy central showcase."

"That was a long time ago. I've lost my heat. I only headline at Liberal Arts these days, and that's because my manager owns the place." He rattles off NYC comedy clubs he hasn't played in a while except to host. "The thing is, I'm sort of typecast now as an emcee. And I get my own sets in showcases a lot but I'm seldom the main act, even after eight years of this shit."

I dwell on this, still unfamiliar with the inner-workings of the industry. I'm fairly confident that Lutsey is the best and most experienced host in the city. But I see his point. He hasn't turned the corner. It's like aspiring to be a movie star and landing in commercials for the rest of your life.

"You're still pretty young. Many comics don't make it big until way later on."

Lutsey considers this.

"I mean, I hear you," he says. "But the thing is, all my contemporaries in the industry are headlining all over the country, getting movie parts and what not. I'm 32, and I worked my ass off and I'm getting pretty burned out doing the same shit."

It's hard for me to pep him up without full disclosure on his part, so we sit quietly for a moment.

"Is this why you say things are rocky with Candice, or are you down on comedy right now because of her?"

"I don't know man. Maybe being down on my success has me being a bit moody at home. It's my fault. And she's a great girl and she gets my frustrations so she's giving me space."

"So it's not too rocky? Not like a break up thing?"

"Man, I hope not. But I feel like I kind of break up with her every week."

"No you don't. You just end up re-confirming your commitment each week," I say. This was more of an educational guess as I'm unfamiliar with the intricacies of their relationship. Lutsey smiles warmly though.

"Yeah, maybe. I mean, I love her, but I have to figure shit out. Maybe I should try five different careers."

"No way. You are a comedian. We all know you belong on stage."

By way of thanks, Lutsey orders more drinks for us. A final round he says, and when they arrive he proposes a toast.

"To new friends!"

We clink glasses and settle back into a fun rhythm.

Chapter 11

FEW THINGS IN THE NATURAL WORLD EXCITE ME MORE than the feeling of a beautiful fall day in the northeast. There's a surreal element to the crisp, promising air as the wind jostles the leaves and swirls the brilliant hues of greens, yellows, oranges, and reds like a painter tackling his palette. I step out into the brisk October afternoon with the high noon sun meandering through puffy clouds in the otherwise cartoon blue sky. I have the day off and have no plans whatsoever, so I dress in jeans and a white long-sleeve t-shirt and a thin black jacket and decide to hit a different part of town to maybe sit and write some comedy material. I hail a cab and I don't know my destination until the driver asks me.

"Battery Park," I say. Visions of writing over a beer at the Battery Gardens restaurant with its view of the New York Harbor and the Statue of Liberty bounce in my head. As I walk through the park toward the water, I get a call from Kate.

"What's up," I say.

"Hey Alan. I was wondering if we could get together tonight."

"Can't tonight," I say, which is utterly untrue.

"Maybe just for a drink? I want to talk about us."

"Is this break up sort of talk," I ask playfully. Kate doesn't know how to respond and she fumbles over a series of beginnings.

"It's just--I mean, what I want to discuss--what I think we should—"Wow! So it *is* break-up talk," I say, helping her out.

She is silent for a moment. When she resumes talking, I can hear the relief in her voice.

"Kind of. Is that so wrong?"

"No, I think I'm holding you back."

"Actually, I kind of met someone while out with the girls and I sort of got his number. I might have called it too."

"That's great," I say. "Seriously."

"Really?"

"No harm, no foul." Maybe we'll get along better as friends.

"I'd like that."

I feel wonderful when we hang up. If there was one true dark cloud on my day it was the knowledge that I needed to break things off with Kate before they moved any further. And there it is. Done: The most benign, simple break-up in history. The God of Comedy, Louis C.K., had a great relevant bit when I caught him at Caroline's recently. He talked about how he got married, which meant he couldn't leave now. "And then I had kids," he said. "And I thought, 'man, I could have left!'"

I hardly dwell on the Kate breakup another minute. I'd been egging it on for a while really, and so much the better for both of us.

✳✳✳

I sit at a patio table at the restaurant and nurse a cold beer as I watch the Staten Island Ferry shuttle back and forth from Ellis Island, its passengers all wide-eyed and excited on the way out and tired and let-down on the return trip. I pull out my computer and jot down a few funny thoughts that come to mind about commercial jingles and sex and online dating despite my lack of experience in the latter. And after another beer, I decide to embark on the long walk home on such a great day, armed with a pleasant buzz and the thought that I need some exercise.

I head up Broadway and cross Wall Street and note how quickly the women have begun their retreat into the cover of bundled clothing. Cassan once told me that fall begins the season for stowing away unwanted calories behind a fortress of wool and cashmere. It was during this time of each year that we devoured Pepperidge Farm cookies--Bordeaux in particular--and drank lots of thick stouts while ignoring her occasional utterances to the effect of joining a new sports club come February.

When I reach TriBeca, I take a break. I order vodka and soda and sit at a sidewalk table and flirt with my waitress. I begin to write down some more thoughts. I've never been the type to spout off pick-up lines, and at bars I typically cling to friends. But the pick-up spiel can't be avoided in clubs. The music's loud and all you can do is dance over to someone or yell something stupid to a girl while waiting in line for the bathroom. For this reason, if the world were broken down in terms of pub guys and club guys, I'd be a pub guy. Let the records show that every possible word you can say to a woman is a pickup line. You can't avoid it. If you so much as say "hi" to a woman, she perceives this as a pickup line, and I can't bear the judgmental scrutiny. Still, I have my moments.

I resume my walk, feeling the pleasure of the daylight three-drink buzz, and I feel like I'm on top my game. On the fringes of SoHo I pick up a merging sidekick, a very cute and slender blonde-haired woman about my age, wearing business casual attire beneath an unzipped trench coat. We exchange looks and keep on walking at exactly the same pace for another few blocks. Along the way, I uncharacteristically grin at girls I pass and received blushing smiles in return.

So at Spring Street I bang a left, expecting to lose my sidekick femme fatale, but she too makes the turn, and despite the fact that I have the post, we somehow resume our perfectly parallel stroll. Then, without provocation and without thought, I turn to her and actually execute a pick-up line of sorts. I simply say: "We might as well be talking."

That was it. A simple line that she doesn't even react to for a moment, and I wonder if she even heard me. But then I notice her smiling.

"Yeah, may as well," she finally says.

"Might as well," I said, correcting her for no reason.

"May as well," isn't it?

"I dunno. Might be."

We walk another four blocks on cobblestone streets past art galleries and chic fashion outlets. It's an indirect, highly impractical route home for me, but I don't let on. We stop a block short of a school just letting out and the streets ahead are crowded with loud kids, and suddenly the woman catches me totally off guard.

"How are you at phone sex?"

I'm floored by this, but I roll with it.

"District champion." Sure I've never done it. But how many people have with strangers? How many people are actually experienced experts? Worst case I suck and she hangs up on me.

"Ok," she says. "What's your number?"

"TRY-MULE," I say, and then add the area code for her.

"No it isn't," she says. But it's a widely known fact amongst my family and friends that this is accurate information. So I stare her down."

"Dial it and I'll pick up. Promise."

She distorts her pale face with a cute, wry smile, her wide, green eyes fixated on me all the while as she backs away.

"I'm calling you in 10." My asinine route makes this impossible though.

"I'll be home in 15," I say.

"I'm calling TRY MULE in 15."

I flag a cab to get home even faster. I close the curtains on the early twilight sky and change into pajamas and a t-shirt and hop in bed. Not knowing what to expect, I conjure up the most blissful experience in my mind. This, combined with this cute girl's image in my head, has me fully entranced by the prospects of phone sex. I adjust my pillow so that I can lay in bed comfortably upright. Just then my phone rings--five minutes early--and it cautiously displays "restricted number." I pick it up.

"Hey hot stuff," I say, which is horribly cliché and so un-me. But I'm ready to roll with this.

"Hot stuff?" The voice on the other end sounds thrown.

"What, too personal?"

"Do you know who this is?"

"Well, I never did get your name."

"Yes you did. It's Jade. Remember?"

"Jade?" I wonder if this is some sort of quirky role-play.

"No worries. I couldn't expect you to remember. It was a quick chat a few months ago."

"A few months?" I say.

"Yeah. I knew you didn't know who this was. I met you in Washington Square Park over the summer. You were a sneaky bastard and programmed your name into my phone. Took me awhile to find it and solve the mystery."

I lay quiet a moment, retracing the steps of my life. Then it dawns on me. That girl from the park, back when I was about to go to the HRGM party!

"Oh! Yeah, I remember you. Blue hair. Sexy. Right?"

"That a boy!"

"Well, shit! Why would you call me now?"

"I'm bored and newly single."

"So you called me?"

"I'm in the mood for a date tonight with someone new."

I let the line go quiet for a moment, struggling to make sense of it all. I draw blanks. Then my phone lets me know I have another incoming call--a New York number.

"Hold on. I was expecting a call, and it's coming in now. Can you hang on a moment?"

"Fine," she sighs.

I switch over.

"Hello?"

"I want to suck your cock like the naughty bitch I am."

"Hello?" I say weakly in response. I don't know what else to say, and I'm suddenly trembling a bit. It's the phone sex girl, and I know instantly I'm not up for this anymore, Jade having ruined it, although in an acceptable manner.

"Then I'm going to--"

"Hi," I say, interjecting nervously. "Sounds nice and all. Can you hold up a moment? I got this call on the other line that I took because I thought it was you."

"Whatever."

"Are you going to hold?"

"Do you want me to?"

"Not so much," I say.

She hangs up and that's the end of that. I shrug and click back over to the other line.

"Jade?"

"Still here hot stuff. But even more bored than when I called you."

"Sorry. It's just that phone sex is kind of new to me."

"Phone sex? Who said I was looking for phone sex?"

I cringe at my mix-up and try to quickly fumble through it.

"I mean, not phone sex. I mean--what kind of date?"

I can hear Jade exhale a cigarette on the other end.

"I wanna bowl. Wanna go to Bowlmore with me tonight?"

Distorted images of the abrasive, blue-haired punk with her "Sucka bitches" button repopulate my mind.

"Yeah sure."

"Cool. I have a session at 9 and then we can get our bowl on."

"A session?"

"Yeah. Didn't I tell you what I do," she asks.

"Uh-uh."

There's a pause on the other end, and I brace myself for something crazy.

"I'm a pro-domme."

"What's that?"

"Do you know what a dominatrix is?"

"Yeah."

"That."

I recline deeper into my bed considering this bizarre occupation. And I find it fascinating that I will be going bowling with a woman fresh from whipping or beating some poor guy or whatever else it is that a dominatrix does. I can't imagine a dull conversation with her later.

"You can come watch if you like," she says.

"Watch? Me? How?"

"I have a session with a voyeur client later. He likes to be watched as I dominate him."

"No, no," I say. "If it were a woman, maybe. What is the place like?"

"It's a dungeon. How about you come pick me up at 9:15. The place will be empty and I'll show you around before we bowl." I agree to this and we hang up.

As I shower again, a painful thought pierces my mind. I hoped for more from myself, and more from Kate and from my first new career as a wine shop manager. And I have a queasy feeling deep down that I shouldn't be getting involved with Jade and her dominatrix lifestyle. It's not me. But as I lather my hair, which has grown ever so long and shaggy these last few unkempt months of mine, I remind myself that there are so many plots on the grid of life and to refuse one on the basis of someone's work would be hypocritical. Plus Jade might end up meeting the *Three Criterion* of being smart, funny and creative. I know she's cute, which is bonus criteria. And then, without any warning, I slap the shower wall in a burst of anger. Anger directed at myself I know, for losing Cassan and perhaps for allowing myself to become a martyr for perfection--for the perfect relationship, the perfect career, the perfect everything. I feel like there is some angelic, put-together version of myself observing me and judging this foolish effort and I hate that it all smacks of an asylum resident liable to snap at any second. I quickly recollect myself and think of comedy bits and laugh about my lot in life and the stories I will have for Elden. All is normal, all is well. And I'm still so young at 27. What's there to stress about?

I walk over to the Jade's dungeon on East 8th St., just around the corner from University Place and Bowlmore Lanes. I ring the buzzer and a female voice on the intercom tells me to come up to 3A. I walked up the dark, rickety stairs, and knock on the unassuming black door and a gorgeous Asian woman welcomes me. Before she can introduce herself, Jade comes around the corner.

"Hey cutie," she says. "Alan this is Sue. She's the receptionist. Sue, Alan."

We all nod and smile at each other and I'm not sure what to say. I begin to wonder how big the place is, how many employees, how many "sessions" are going on right now behind the many doors off of the long corridor I see ahead.

"Come on," Jade says. "Let me show you a room."

I follow Jade down the dark hall while admiring her petite body, which is clad in a rubber skirt and t-shirt. She is wearing fishnet pantyhose and black high heels that make a sinister clack on the hardwood floor. When we reach the forth door on the left, she opens it and turns on a light and summons me with her fingers. I step in to a deceptively large room that has large mirrors on all four walls and oversized drawers and cabinets and a vanity and a creepy looking medical chair that you might be made to recline in at a doctors office, although this chair has straps around the head, arms and legs, and it rather conjures thoughts of Frankenstein. There's also a small door that is opened to reveal a bathroom.

"What do you think?"

"I'm not sure. So what were you doing in here with your last client?"

"Nothing too extreme. His was new and he basically wanted me to spank him and talk dirty to him and tease him and we did some bondage."

"Bondage," I say, blankly.

"Yeah, you know, tying him up." She opens one of cabinets to reveals all sorts of ropes of varying colors and sizes. "Like, with rope. Haven't you ever been tied up?"

"Nope. I never seem to run into kinky girls for better or worse."

"Wanna try?"

I shrug. I figure when else will I get the opportunity, and from a professional no less. Jade tells me to strip down to my boxers in a matter-of-fact tone--which is kind of sexy--and she has me sit down on the carpeted floor. Then she grabs a white rope of medium thickness and begins to tie me up. The material is curious and fairly soft to the touch.

"It's a synthetic rope," she says, grabbing another. "This is called the Shibari style, which is a Japanese method of bonding in sensual positions. I'm just doing quick, half-assed knots so you get the idea."

I say nothing as she rubs up against me and eases the rope up and down and all around my body. She pushes my legs open and my arms back, and soon enough she is done. Then she pushes me and, without control of my bound limbs, I easily topple over onto my face with my ass stuck up high in the air. She gets behind me and massages my rope-strewn back. The massage would be nice if not for the discomfort of the rope.

"So what do you think?"

"I'm not a fan."

Jade laughs and undoes a few of the knots so that my hands at least are freed, and then my cell phone rings, a call from Lutsey.

"This will be quick," I say. She shrugs and keeps working the knots as I take the call.

"What's up man," Lutsey yells on the other end. There is loud noise in his background.

"Not much."

"Wanna come hang at club?"

"Uh--I'm kinda tied up right now."

Jade laughs out loud as I say this, and Lutsey hears her voice.

"Oh, I got you man. OK, well listen quick. You listening?"

"Yeah, I'm listening."

"OK. So Ian just booked you for Sunday night. You're gonna do six minutes on stage at Liberal Arts."

"What! What are you, high?"

"Shit, I wish I was. All I'm doing is helping you get your plan in motion."

"That's only four days away," I protest. "I can't do that."

"Sure you can. And I'll help you. Call me tomorrow and we'll sort out your material and practice."

Jade finishes untying me and sits on the freaky table and watches me on the phone. I look at her for a moment while thinking, and she pumps her fist in a go-for-it sort of cheer, despite having no idea what I'm talking about or to whom. I almost feel sick suddenly--nervous already about going up on stage for the first time in years and I feel my heart racing."

"Well, I hope Ian isn't expecting anything good."

"Don't worry about it. He knows you're green. Sunday nights are pretty dead and he had a lot of comics that had to cancel. If you don't go up, he'll probably book a puppet show."

"Fine," I say. And I can't believe it.

"Atta boy! And Alan."

"Yeah?"

"That girl you're with...is that some *new*?" By this he means to ask if Jade is a new girl for me.

"Yeah."

"Pimpin'. Call me tomorrow."

We hang up and I exhale deeply.

"Is everything OK," Jade asks.

"I'm not sure. I just got booked to do some standup comedy at a club in the city Sunday."

"You're a comic?"

"I'm not sure. Aspiring, mostly."

"Can I come? I'll sit in the front row and laugh my ass off at everything. Promise." We look at each other through new eyes. Hers the eyes of surprised interest, mine the eyes of terror.

"I hope you're the only one who comes. Let's go bowl."

Chapter 12

"**I**T'S EASY TO BLOW PEOPLE OFF WITH TECHNOLOGY," I say to nobody in particular. I'm rehearsing with Lutsey at Liberal Arts and before I can go any further he stops me.

"Wait, wait. Did we do this one?"

"I forget," I say. It's definitely huge to have him policing my material, but the writing isn't my biggest concern. Performing the material is what worries me.

It's 1 p.m. on a dreary Saturday, and this is the third straight day Ian has let us come in to practice before the place opens. I've been working on my comedy set from 10 a.m. until 2 p.m. each day before heading off to Elmer's at night. I shared some of my material with Kevin at work, and even ran some of it by Jade in bed the last few nights when I got home. Lutsey and I have mined all of the jokes I have written--both old and new--and we came up with four and half minutes for my set. Now we're testing other bits to get me to six minutes.

"Well *excuuuse* me. I'll let the master get back to work," Lutsey says. He sits down in the front row of the small, empty theater as I pull the mic off the stand again to resume my act, and I pace on the small stage that is only several feet away from him.

"OK. So...It's easy to blow people off with text messages. You just type <u>be right back</u> or <u>I'm in the bathroom</u>. I wish you could blow people off in person like that. They come up to you and start talking and you say, "I'm sorry. I'm in the bathroom"".

Lutsey smiles and looks at his stopwatch. He flashes a finger to tell me I have one minute left, and I press on.

I hear Ian laugh from the back of the theater and wonder how long he has been prying.

"Time," Lutsey says. "Not bad. What did you think?"

"Like a self-evaluation? I guess it's OK. It was a funnier bit in my head."

"The best material usual is," he says. "But it works the other way too. Some stuff isn't funny on paper until you use your voice and gestures to make it gold on stage."

I listen like a soldier being addressed by general and nod. There certainly are many successful comics with bad material. They just have a great personality and stage presence that people relate to and enjoy so they do well. And they have people writing for them.

We work on the technology material for a while, adding more depth to it. Then we run through the whole short set several more times. Lutsey occasionally heckles me and I try to handle it, but if I get heckled I'm a dead man.

✳✳✳

I awake around noon fully dressed again, and I realize I passed out while rehearsing late into the night. As the comedian Steven Wright would say, it was the next night. The big show starts at 8 p.m. today and I can't recall ever being so nervous in any of my previous standup experiences, or for any HRGM presentations for that matter. I guess it's because so much more is at stake. Now comedy is a possible career. Now there are people coming to see me. I don't want to let Lutsey or Ian down, and I don't want to botch a fast-track opportunity in what could be the ideal job.

Elden calls me around noon, confirming that he can't come down from Boston, despite already making this abundantly clear last night.

"I feel terrible I can't be there," he says. "The universe and such." And his reasons are more than valid.

"Don't worry about it. I'd rather you come once I get more comfortable anyway." This is complete lie. There could be no face more comforting to see in an audience than Elden's, no matter what I might be doing on stage. What throws me though, is that Jade calls around 2 p.m. to say that she can't make it either. This comes after I carried on about the whole thing with her every single night since we started hanging out.

"Sorry sexy. My main client has to see me tonight and I can't turn down a thousand dollars."

"Whoa! I guess not."

One positive is that tonight's show is not a "bringer show." I don't have to bring friends in order to be *allowed* on stage where I proceed to perform for free like in my earlier days. Liberal Arts is a major comedy club and I will have a real, paying audience of some sort. Plus I receive confirmation that Kevin and another guy from Elmer's are coming, as well as a few pseudo friends from HRGM.

I call for sushi delivery and shower and try on a hundred outfits, ultimately deciding on a blue linen shirt and jeans--the ones Cassan had spilled her espresso martini all over in the spring. I add a necklace of thick silver beads that shows slightly beneath the shirt and a black belt with a large silver buckle that complements my black shoes.

"Showtime," I say to myself in the mirror, and I head out.

I arrive an hour before my impending doom on stage and meet Lutsey for a drink at the bar.

"Relax," he says. "You'll be fine. Plus, you're a good-looking guy. If you bomb, just smile at the ladies."

Ian comes over all leggy and wide-eyed and partially lit I think.

"Here's my new champ, yeah?"

"I can't promise much my first time out."

"Don't you know Alan? Just the fact that you are getting up there and filling a hole is great thing. I don't care if you tell knock-knock jokes. You are doing me a favor."

I feel like he's right, but I shouldn't--Ian is the one providing the favor. And it's a huge favor. I could have only dreamed of such an inroad back when I used to perform at open mics in the backrooms of offbeat and out-of-the-way pubs and burger joints.

We talk and drink as the audience begins to file in. The good news is that it's a Sunday night crowd, which tends to be a more sober, less obnoxious lot. I notice most are couples of all ages and in good spirits, most likely after a hearty meal. Their giddy procession takes them quickly past us and into the theater where they begin taking their seats. The bad news (for me) is that this is indeed a crowd. Larger than any I've been in front of before.

"What happened to Sunday nights being dead," I ask Lutsey.

"Must be the bad weather all weekend. Everyone needs to get out and do something. Let's get backstage. This thing is about to get going."

My heart begins racing as I follow Lutsey through a curtain, and then through a narrow, dirty hall to a green room. There are two coffee tables and a monitor so we can follow the show and there is also a refrigerator stocked with beer and water. Three other comics are seated at one of the tables sharing an engaging conversation about terrible audiences they have encountered before.

"Easy on the alcohol until you finish your set," Lutsey cautions. "You don't want to start slurring up there. You want to be sharp. Let them do the drinking until you're done."

"Anything else?"

"You're on second. Just be funnier than the first comic. Oh--and three words baby! If you can get up and say that shit in front of all those executives, this should be nothing."

Suddenly the house lights dim, and music pumps through speakers. The voice of an unseen man welcomes the audience to the show and the emcee is introduced. He's a Latino guy of about 40 who I met earlier and he begins to warm up the crowd. After five minutes, a female comic that I have never seen emerges on stage and launches into her routine.

"Where the hell did she come from?"

"There's another room like this on the other side of the stage."

"Damn I'm nervous."

"I always get nervous before going on too," Lutsey says. "Once you start talking up there, it becomes much easier than you think. All those nerves just die away. I guess it's because we get preoccupied with the act."

We don't talk to the other comics in the green room. I have a hunch Lutsey asked them to leave me alone. Occasionally one of them leans over to ask him something or to share a quick inside joke, and I can see they all revere him. Lutsey is the man here. He's also the fifth and final act.

"Who's on after me anyway," I ask.

Lutsey is starring up at the monitor and without looking at me he says, "Stephen Reese."

And I feel like I've been kicked in the gut.

"Stephen Reese? From Saturday Night Live?"

"Yeah, you know him?"

"You asshole!"

"What?"

"Why didn't you tell me that?"

"Does it matter?"

"He's going to shred my act. Shouldn't he go on right before you?"

"It's all good. Relax man. Stephen is still a novice at stand-up. He's an actor."

We both continue watching the show quietly, but now my heart is racing doubly. I suppose they want the better comics to follow the lesser acts to highlight them more. I keep telling myself I can't lose here, but it doesn't help. My hands start shaking a bit. My heart thumps harder. I struggle suddenly to remember my first line.

"What's my first line?"

"A lot of tourists here tonight? Then go into Priceline."

"Right, right."

My hands tremble more as I pull out my note card and review my jokes. There is a rousing applause and the emcee takes the stage again. Just then, Ian emerges and tells me I'm up. I can't believe it. I don't know what I'm doing here. I—

"Hey Alan," Lutsey says. "After we're done, let's go celebrate. You up to party tonight?"

Lutsey is trying every sort of psychological tactic he can think of to calm me down. This nonchalant approach seems to have the best effect.

"Sure. If Candice is cool with it."

He waves his hand at me.

"Bah. It's cool. Just go do your six little minutes and we'll talk right after."

I follow Ian around the corner and suddenly I'm on the side of the stage watching the emcee.

"You may have seen this next comic at the bar while you were walking in." All the way from the West Village, please give it up for Alan Jones."

The crowd applauds and my world takes on a dream-state quality as I walk out toward the microphone. As I remove the mic from the stand with sweaty palms, I realize that everyone is a shadow. The spotlight smashes my face and blinds me like a high noon sun on a cloudless day. This helps somehow, not being able to see faces well. I begin talking, almost as if on autopilot. *Lutsey was right*, I realize. As I begin talking, the nerves calm instantly and I'm focused.

"So is anyone from out of town?"

"Miami!" a table of younger women yell collectively.

"Really? Did you girls book your flight with Priceline?"

"No."

And I know I should be looser and off the cuff with them, but not tonight. Not on my first real show. I stick to my lines.

"Good for you. It sounds like a great deal Priceline, doesn't it? Name your price. C'mon. Really? You know you're getting fucked somehow. You type in $50, and they're probably like, 'Fine. He can pay his lousy $50. But as soon as he takes his seat, we piss on his face.'"

There are a few chuckles, but this doesn't come off nearly as well as I rehearsed it. Still I push on.

"I was on a flight once and this kid on the aisle in my row asked me to switch with him so he could have the window seat. And I was like, no!

"'Why not,' he asked me.

"'Because it's cool! I'm not giving up my window seat. What are you, high?'"

I'm actually doing this! I fend through the spotlight and see smiles and hear laughter. My resolve stiffens as I delve into more familiar material.

"So I live in New York and when you live in New York long enough, lots of little things get to you. I was in line at the ATM and this one guy in front of me was on the machine for 10 full minutes. I'm like, what the hell is he doing!? What is there to do besides type in a number and collect your cash? But this guy is up there rolling over his 401K. He's making out a will. He's taking out a second mortgage on his house."

This gets some laughs. Then I launch into the true story of the station wagon family that asked Elden and I how to get to a specific address.

"'How do I get to 420 Houston?'"

"'That's easy,' I told him. 'Just go to 422 Houston and it should be right next door.'" Then I add: "Like I know all about every address in New York. 'Oh--424 Houston? You mean the Smiths? Actually they're in Jersey at a wedding tonight.'"

I segue into another thing that annoys me about New York--the customers in bodegas that treat the place like a casino, buying alcohol and cigarettes and a million lottery tickets and Powerball numbers as they hold up the line.

"Nobody wins in Powerball," I say. They should just call that Blueball. You know why?"

I pause unintentionally, forgetting why myself. Finally a man up front yells, "why?"

"Because your balls never come sir." I do a mock drum roll and a stupid little dance that is all funnier than the actual joke. It's horrible, but I needed some filler. Just a few more minutes, I tell myself. And I press on.

"I bought a bottle of soda and walked out of the store, and when I untwisted the cap, the flip side read, 'sorry, you lose.'

"I was like, 'fuck you, I wasn't even playing!'"

This works well with the audience and I even hear one of the Miami girls say to her friends, "Oh my God, I hate that too!" I offer the audience a thoughtful pause, just as I rehearsed. Then I add a premeditated afterthought.

"I just want to call their VP of marketing and be like, 'you're the one who lost bitch. You lost a customer.'"

From there I move into my bits about technology and then heaven and I close to a fair applause. I thank the crowd and walk off stage and Lutsey and Ian are there to give me high fives and bear hugs.

"How was it?"

"You did great," Lutsey says.

"Just what I hoped for," Ian adds.

After Lutsey finishes his thunderous, superior set, the two of us head over the bar. We see the emcee wrap up the show on the monitor and the crowd slowly files out all excited and a bit loopy after completing their two-drink minimum purchase requirement throughout the show. The people have to walk by the bar to exit and many stop to offer a "great job" or a "very funny" comment to Lutsey, and few compliment me as well. We shake some hands, and Lutsey even signs an autograph. A few of the people decide to stop and have a drink at the bar, including the four younger women who said they were from Miami during my set. They couldn't be more than 22 or 23.

"Hi Alan," the cutest of the group says. She's a tall, thin thing, and her long bleached-blond hair practically melts into a bronze tan. "We liked your show."

"I appreciate it," I say.

"I hate when bottle caps tell me that I lost!"

We laugh together while the other girls try to order drinks. Lutsey has turned away to talk to another comic.

"So you said you are from Miami right," I ask.

"Yeah. I've been living here since I graduated college and my friends just came up to visit before I move back down south."

"Back to Miami?"

"No. Key West." And she yells a loud "woo" that her friends join in on as they pass her some kind of fruity drink.

"I'm Amber."

"Of course you are," I say. The name just makes a world of sense for her, and I tell her so.

She goes on to tell me how she graduated from college and how she has a good job lined up through a family friend at The Citizen news in Key West.

As her lush lips move, I debate if she might be hot enough to fall on the waning side of the personality curve I crafted with Elden. There are exceptions to that curve, I remind myself. And I can't imagine how this hot, impossibly Floridian girl managed to get through four years of college in New York, so far from the warm weather and white sand and booming sun that Amber must have been cast from at birth.

"How do you keep that tan going," I ask her, pointing at her arm with fingers that no longer tremble from stage fright.

"I spent the summer at home. I came back to New York to hang out with friends and to start moving stuff before my lease ends. I move in less than two weeks."

"Well we better get together soon."

"Yeah, better," she says, holding a stare on me. And I feel like a rock star on the smallest possible level. I get on stage and tell sub-par jokes for six minutes and then sit down to await my female prizes? For the first time I understand how the public can dredge conceit from even the most humble of men.

Lutsey comes over and hands me a drink and introduces himself to the girls who all giggle and ask questions about his act. They want to know what was true and, facetiously, if he really masturbated in front of a ghost.

After a while, the girls say they are going to Karaoke at Iggy's in the Upper East Side and they invite Lutsey and I to come. We all hop in cab and keep the party rolling. Lutsey and I perform a shameless pseudo-duet of "Roadhouse

Blues" by The Doors, and I watch in drunken awe as Amber and the girls sing "What's Up?" by 4 Non Blondes, and I practically fall in love with her. Somewhere on the stage, Amber and I make out and then make dinner plans for later in the week and eventually the lights blink for last call.

Chapter 13

REPTILES AND HAMSTERS SURROUND ME in Jade's Alphabet City apartment as she opens a bottle of merlot. This is my first time visiting her large pad despite spending five nights together this week.

"I thought I told you," she says, handing me my glass of wine.

"You said you loved animals, but I didn't know you were an animal lover."

Jade has just finished telling me what an animal rights activist she is. She spearheads the New York PETA office, and our plans tonight were delayed because she had to hand out leaflets protesting the inhuman treatment of a bird.

"I love animals," I tell her. "They're delicious!"

"Not funny at all."

"A little bit, no?" She stares back at me. "You know I'm kidding."

I'm as against animal cruelty as the next guy, but I can see this information hints at a lifetime of debate over what I can eat and wear and enjoy in the movies. That's not what really bothers me though. It's everything else. She's moody and all attitude, which I confused at first with repartee. I should have known better when I first met her at the park, but I just didn't care at the time.

Both of us are wearing nothing but underwear, and a tremendous sense of guilt overcomes me. I shouldn't have been fooling around with Jade. This can't last, but I can't just run out on her now; not after she so proudly showed me her recent paintings of animals in urban landscapes, and not after spending some lovely time in the 69 position with her.

We're in the kitchen, and she is busy working on her "specialty" which is sautéed veggies over whole-wheat pasta. As I fetch her a pot, she decides to resume an earlier lesson she gave me in politics.

"Don't you think that someone should murder Sarah Palin."

"I don't know."

"Seriously? Don't tell me you're are a moderate."

I gulp, imagining what she would do if I were a republican.

"I'm a registered independent," I say, which is true. "I don't allow my attitudes to be influenced by a party affiliation." I add that I studied journalism in college where I was instructed not to choose sides so we could be objective reporters. I didn't pursue a reporter's job after college though. I told my professor at the time that journalism is too passive and how I didn't want to spend my life writing about what other people are doing. Plus, I knew I couldn't get by on an entry-level reporter's salary when I moved to New York.

"Ha. No such thing. There are no true independents in the media. Someone always influences them. By higher ups or by corporate affiliations or whatever."

"Blah, blah."

"What?"

"Nothing," I say.

I admit I enjoyed her company the first few nights, but I was stressed as hell about the comedy and it felt good to bounce my jokes off a willing ear at night--not to mention having a professional from the world of erotica to help me fall asleep. But each night, new pieces of Jade's life clicked into place and the puzzle of our incompatibility is now complete. Sure, Jade's creative, but what else is there for me under the essential *Three Criterion*? Her intelligence is of the bookish sort Elden talked about, and I suspect that she picks topics and studies them and then rattles off arcane facts and anecdotes to sound like an authority. And when she's not blowing me off for her masochistic clients, she's attacking me from her extremist soap dish. I had considered her profound sense of entitlement and loftiness as a sense of humor, but I can see I am wrong here, too.

"Are you getting snippy Mr. Jones?" Jade crinkles her mouth and spanks the air. Then she passes me the lettuce and tells me to start working on the salad, and something in me just snaps.

"I'm sorry...I can't do this," I say suddenly.

"Do what?"

"I need to leave."

"After all of this?"

"After all of what? You know what, I don't think I even know your real name, do I?" I'm grasping at a random straw here, I know.

"Of course you do. It's Jade asshole."

"Fine!" I yell back, defeated, yet brazen.

"Where are you going?"

"I don't know. I need to move on."

"Are you serious?" She processes the situation quickly as I'm heading out the door and yells after me, "People pay thousands just to be with me for a night you cocksucker!"

I keep my head down as I walk out the door. It's a total disaster; a train wreck I certainly didn't plan for, but there's no turning back. I needed to rip the band-aid off. This is awful of me, I know. What's gotten into me? Is it Amber? Latent frustration or stress over the radical changes in my life? My heart stings when I reach the bottom of the stairs. What Jade saw in me was perhaps that elusive normal, decent guy in her life--or at least a sketch of one--and now that guy is walking out on her. Yet it's the best thing for both of us.

As I leave her apartment building I consider how close I am to Ian's block. The area feels vaguely familiar from the party Lutsey took me to. I pull a cigarette out of my pocket, light it, and look up at the cloudy, dark sky. Here I am, in all my glory, on gridpoint 2,2: a wine shop co-manager who just broke it off with a professional dominatrix. To be fair, people didn't pay Jade for sex as she assured me--they paid for fantasy fulfillment, role-playing, or a fetish. And that's what I feel like I'm doing now. I'm role-playing every aspect of my life.

I start walking west away from Alphabet City. Who I should call? What I should do? I call Elden and get his voicemail. Then I try to come up with some comedy material about bad breakups, and the little lines that come to mind are more scathing and threatening than funny. Elden texts me back. It reads: <u>I'm running a powwow. Call you later.</u>

I keep walking, turning the break-up concept over and over in my head, but nothing funny really clicks. So I think about Jade's apartment and then I decide to work the animal comedy angle. By the time I reach the East Village, I have a few semi-humorous thoughts in my head. I ruminate on how passionate and obsessed animal owners--especially single ones--can become. Perhaps you never know how much a pet is part of your family until a veterinarian asks for your pet's last name.

"Um, Jones," I would have to say. But it would be much better to give a pet a last name that is different from your own.

"What's your pet's name?"

"Skipper," I might say.

"So it's Skipper Jones, then?"

"No, Skipper Wellington."

"Your last name is Wellington? We have you down as Jones."

"My last name *is* Jones. But his name is Skipper Wellington."

When I reach 2nd Ave. at 4th St., I come upon a comedy club I never heard of called the Eastville Comedy Club. I decide to pop in for a drink and to do some research by watching other comics go at it. I grab a glass of Glenlivet at the bar and there's a sign touting tonight, Monday, as Open Mic Night. This dampens my mood on watching comedy here because I want to see some seasoned comics on stage. But then it hits me. Why don't I just go on myself? What better practice than just getting up on stage without any plans to do so. Plus, I'm sure I can learn by watching the mistakes and shortcomings of others at my experience level. Lutsey and Ian would applaud the initiative.

I get signed up, but I'm like 10th in line. I look around the small crowd, which is composed of tourists, a few couples, and all the other comics waiting to go up, as well as friends they have dragged to see them. Most of these aspiring comics look pale and jittery as they wait, rehearsing their routines in their heads rather than paying attention to anybody on stage. I down two glasses of scotch as I use my phone to type up a routine. We can have 5-10 minutes. But as the liquor sears my throat and warms me up, I find myself dwelling on Jade again. I feel awful that I walked out on her the way I did. I quietly pound the table with my fist. A sudden sense of isolation overcomes me, and my mind wanders to worst-case scenarios in life. What if I never find happiness in a career? What if I never find another woman like Cassan? What if I never find myself in general? I had always lived a life of optimism that was reinforced in college and through my success and my relationship out of college. Yet here I am in this suddenly sullen new realm of despair that finds me sitting alone drinking scotch and writing bad comedy for an audience of indifferent amateur comics. Even the few real audience members have grown tired of the sopho- moric and unrefined acts and have either left or engaged in conversations at their tables. And this is my world now, just as a busboy (serving double duty as the show's host) calls for me to take the stage.

I grab my scotch and walk up slowly up to the tiny stage, feeling a bit tipsy. I take the microphone off the stand and look out the room of 20 or so people, maybe half of which are paying me any attention.

"Anyone dating here?" I ask.

Nobody responds.

"I hear you. Fuck it, right?"

"I'm single again, but I don't want to date online because I'm afraid of the profile name I'll end up with. Maybe some woman writes me and tells her friend.

'He seems so charming and romantic.'

'What's his name?'

'PixieStick27.'"

This opening bit is one I used on stage before, back during my first bout with standup a few years ago. A man seated solo a few rows back chuckles at this, perhaps to be polite. This gesture is offset however by two couples seated together at a table to my right. Two women and two larger, muscular guys about 25-30 dressed in soccer shirts. They are all drunk and the guys are talking loudly in strong English accents, with no regard for me onstage at all. I try to ignore them.

"It's the same when you try to get an email screen name. I tried to get one on Gmail without any numbers in it, so I went for all these variations on Alan Jones and everything was taken. So I got all frustrated and just typed in <u>eatmon- keytastemonkey</u>. And Gmail says, 'sorry, it appears that name has been taken.'"

A few more heads turn to listen. At least I sound more seasoned than the other comics in this lousy show.

"So Gmail offers me similar names," I continue, "like <u>eatmonkeytastemon- key54</u>, which is funny to me because that means there are 53 other <u>eatmonkey- tastemonkey</u> people out there. Then I had to apply for a job. So now my resume has <u>eatmonkeytastemonkey54</u> in the upper right. Interviewers are probably still having a good laugh over it. And that sucks, doesn't it? Wondering what the interviewers are saying when you leave? I always imagine the worst. Like they're going, 'was that guy seriously applying for a position? What a piece of shit.'"

Most of the few remaining people laugh. I stand for a moment in silence looking back at them, wondering if I should test the new bit on animal names. And then I push into it, immediately missing key set-up points, and I completely lose confidence in what I'm saying. Finally, I stop.

"This is a lesson in death," I say. A blast of discomfort fills the room, and I know from having seen many bad acts before just how terrible this makes even the audience members feel. The loud English guys even turn around to size me up. And just like that, things have begun spiraling out of control for me.

I stumble over my words a bit and nervousness engulfs me. With a great hesitance, I push into another joke.

"You know the expression *all things considered?* Like when people say, 'All things considered, I had a pretty good time.'"

"No, never heard that expression mate," one of the Englishmen says. I try to ignore this and continue with the bit.

"Shouldn't we take for granted that people say things taking into consideration as much as possible? You never hear someone say, 'you know, taking absolutely *nothing* into consideration, everything is great. That's not considering that I lost my job and my girlfriend and I just shit my pants.'" The joke was supposed to go differently, but I forget how.

"Did you shit your pants then?" says the other half of my heckling duo. They both laugh, and the women at the table shake their heads and try to shush their men. There are so few other people in the room that I can't ignore them any longer.

"No," I say, turning and looking down at the men. "Just an amateur night joke. Settle down."

"So you lost your girl and your job mate?"

"Yes," I say. "Yes I did." And now this whole thing is shot to high heaven. I want to just get off the stage now that his has become a public therapy session.

"Well don't try to be a comic," one of men says again. I can't believe his annoying persistence. The last thing I need here and now is a heckler. I feel like my whole existence is on trial. I plan to just exit the stage, but something holds me there a moment. Uncontrollably, I fire back at the man.

"Are you guys a couple?" I ask, indicating the man and the woman next to him.

"You betcha."

"I knew it! Look at that everyone. A couple of douchebags. Sitting right in the front row of all things."

I try to walk off on that sour note, but the man storms over. He hops up onto the stage and with muscular arms he manhandles me, pushing me up against the brick back wall.

"I'll fucking wreck you," he yells in my face. The two women from his table and even his heckler friend yell for him to stop. Then the friend runs up and starts to grab the man off of me. Suddenly the largest man in the whole club--the bouncer--is on top of us all. He grabs both the men and shoves them aside and tells them to leave the club immediately. To my surprise, they comply without words. The women apologize to me as their party heads out.

"Shows over anyway," the bouncer announces to anyone remaining. I was the last comic standing--standing alone on stage, rattled and red-faced. I go to the bar and ask for a shot of whiskey and my check. The bartender gives me an additional shot on the house to apologize for what went down, and I throw that one back as well and head out.

I call Elden again from the street corner and light a cigarette with shaky hands. I could scream or tear up I think, but I'm calling Elden so I steel myself against it. The phone keeps ringing and he finally picks up, talking loudly over a noisy background.

"What's up Rumpshaker? Are you outside my dwelling?"

"Are you drunk," I ask, for no particular reason.

"Does a cow tip?"

"It's Monday, right? What's going on over there?"

"A party. We just finished exams. Soon you'll have to call me doctor."

I'm quiet for a moment so Elden asks if I'm OK.

"Yeah, I'm fine. Just nearly got into a bar fight."

"Wham! How did that go down?"

"Ah, tell ya later," I say, rubbing my eyes.

"Are you OK?" He sounds concerned suddenly.

"Yeah, I'm fine. Go back to your party," I say, regretting that I called. "I'm really buzzed and tired and I'm gonna go crash. Call you tomorrow."

Elden wishes me well, and as we hang up, I have a sudden desire to call Amber. I figure you always start with some free chips when faced with a new woman. And she's probably partying with her friends from Miami, maybe at some dreaded Karaoke bar right now. I could join them and I could even handle a baritone solo if I have to--maybe *Walk the Line*, by Johnny Cash. The idea sounds appealing, but I know it's a bad one. I can't let this negative adrenaline get to me, and the best bet is to get home and hide and just meet Amber for dinner with a clear mind as planned.

Chapter 14

AMBER DEVEROUX IS THE NAME, and a lovely one at that for this green-eyed Floridian girl. I can't keep my eyes off her as we scan the menu of pit barbeque dishes at Blue Smoke on 26ᵗʰ Street. The restaurant--Amber's favorite--is especially busy for a weeknight, and we had to wait at the bar for 45 minutes to sit down.

"I'm starving," she says, despite her petite frame.

"Are you French?" I ask.

"You mean because of my last name?" Her accent is succulent and flavored with a hint of the south. "I'm like a quarter French. My grandfather is from Quebec, but my mother is from Fort Lauderdale. How about you?"

"I'm a mut, but my parents are both from Connecticut."

When the waiter comes, we order sampler platters of ribs and salads and corn bread and light beers. When he leaves, I tell Amber all about my background and how I came to be in New York, and even how I came to be single and essentially out of a career right now. I talk a little about the career side of my five-step plan. This has the slightly intended effect of making me sound adventurous and laid back, which Amber claims to be herself.

"I roll with things, you know?" she says. "Going out and having fun. I love SEC Football, which ya'll can't understand being from the north."

I nod, admitting my distaste for college football as opposed to the NFL. But this is one of the few things we disagree on. She continues on with an unsolicited tirade of her interests, and we find that we share favorite bands, TV shows, and pop culture in general.

"I love comedians," she says. "I love going to comedy shows and funny people in general--like you!"

Amber is the funny one in my mind though. I like her comments and observations about trivial things. She's that cute sort of accidental funny--unless she knows it.

"Olives are so scary," she says, picking at her salad and dispatching various vegetables like a child. We avoid all topics not entertainment-related, and she manages a five-minute soliloquy about her greatest passion: beach life.

"So why New York though?" I ask. "No beaches *here*. Not a good one anyway."

"Well, I thought New York would be exciting. The city never sleeps, right?" She bounces her head side to side playfully at this. "So I applied to Hunter College with a friend of mine and we both got in."

I balk at this, but say nothing. It just doesn't fit.

"So? What did you think?"

"No bueno."

"You don't like New York?"

"I had fun, but New York isn't for me. I need the beach and warm weather. Plus it's too expensive and the city feels kind of lonely a lot, you know?"

"That's my line! New York can be one of the loneliest cities in the world at times, ironically. And especially if you just moved here." I had felt the same way when I first arrived. I still do now at times. It takes a really large network of friends because in a city of 8 million people you can spend weeks never bumping into anyone you know.

"I can't be alone, not hardly for a minute," Amber says. "Plus there's a lot of weird people and everybody thinks they're so cool."

It strikes me suddenly that Amber is the complete antithesis of Cassan. Cassan would loathe Amber and perhaps vice versa. The "weird" people Amber mentioned are precisely the members of the hipster crowd that Cassan essentially left me to join full-time.

"You probably don't get lonely being a comedian."

"I'm not much of a comedian," I say. "Just something I'm trying out."

"So what did you study in college?"

"English and journalism," I say. Amber reacts to this by nearly spitting out her drink.

"Are you serious? Why didn't you say so?"

"What do you mean?"

"The other night, when I told you I got a job at The Citizen newspaper."

"I thought you said you were going into the business side."

"Well, yeah...but still."

We exchange gentle smiles as the waiter arrives and lays down our entrées.

"So did you ever do anything with your journalism degree."

"Sort of," I say. "I had the copywriting job for five years here. I just left in the spring."

"Oh right. Have you ever thought of being a reporter?"

Somewhere in my sophomore or junior year I had this aspiration of authoring lofty features for magazines and national syndications both online and in print. I envisioned interviewing artists and creative people of all sorts or maybe even becoming a travel writer like Elden but on a much more robust level.

"I've thought about it for sure," I say.

"All I'm saying," Amber continues, "is to let me know if you ever want to try it."

"Why's that?"

"My father's best friend down in Florida works at The Citizen. He got me my job and he said they need a bunch of reporters too. I took the business job because I studied marketing."

We carry on through dinner but skip dessert because Amber says she has a great buzz and that she wants to keep drinking. We pub-hop all around Gramercy, stopping frequently to make out on the streets.

"Are you going to meet up with your friends tonight?"

"Not tonight," she says. She pets my hair. "I texted them to say you passed the test."

"Oh really. What test is that?"

"Well besides being cute and a comedian you are fun and cool and down to Earth."

What I like most about this is that Amber seems to have necessary criteria she needs in relationships too. I mean, we all do, but still--I feel relieved I'm not the only extremely picky jerk.

We make our way back to my apartment and I throw Amber down on the bed without words. I don't even bother turning on lights and so the only illumination is through the windows. I tear off her shirt and she begins kicking away her jeans while trying to unbutton mine, and I shimmy free of them. She's aggressive, and it's obvious she has plenty of experience in the bedroom. Not in the professional Jade sort of way, but rather in an innocently naughty way; the type of girl who is used to getting her man and handling him from there.

We fool around for an hour and then break apart to relax, lying on our backs to talk in the dark. This feels much different than it did with Kate or Jade recently. This has the potential for something real and mutual I think, and I want to give her a real shot. I know I can't keep blowing through relationships so quickly if I expect to find the ideal. Plus, it's tiresome hopping from one woman to the next. There must be some expression on my face betraying these thoughts because Ambers seems to sense this.

"Are you a player," she asks.

"What? Me?" I look back at her with a coy grin. "If anyone is a player it's you."

"Why me?"

"I mean, look at you." She smiles sheepishly and her perfect white teeth sparkle against her tanned skin in the low light. Her button nose seems to levitate with the compliment.

"See. You know just how to talk to a girl."

We lay in silence another moment. Then Amber hoists herself upright in a fast, furious motion.

"I have a great idea. Why don't you move down to Key West with me?"

"What?" I flip my head towards her and we lock eyes. "What do you mean?"

"Just what I said. I think it would be perfect for both of us."

"How so?"

"Well, I'm a little worried about going to Key West where I don't really know anyone. And I can get you a reporter job so we can even commute to work together. You said you wanted to try a new career. It makes sense."

It makes perfect sense to Amber at least. She really can't be alone for a second. Plus she's not tied down to anywhere or anything. Then again, neither am I.

"You're serious."

"Of course I am," she says. "What's the big deal, really?"

I fantasize for a moment about warm weather and pristine white sand and waking up beside a beautiful young girl every day before heading off to an interesting and even meaningful job. Still, this requires much more analysis. I want to run it all through an algorithm like e-Harmony and Monster.com must have.

"You don't think it's a big deal? You're talking about an entirely new life for me."

"For both of us. We could do it together."

"I'm flattered that you even asked," I say. And I mean it. I mean, just look at this girl. How could someone like this be so quick to build a new life around me?

"What if we didn't get along though? I mean, we hardly know each other."

"Then you just go back home if you want. Or stay. It's not like you couldn't manage another wine shop like you said. I'm thinking that you could find an apartment within a week and just stay with me until then."

"When are you leaving?"

"In five days."

"Fuck!"

"Fuck what?"

"That's fast. I don't think I could just up and leave like that."

"You could come down after me sometime. I just thought it would be great to go together."

"I'm not sure." And it's my breathy tone that makes us realize she's got me.

"Why not?" She is moving in for the kill.

"I own this apartment for one thing."

"Name another thing." She rolls on her side to face me fully, propping up her head with one arm. Then she stares at me while awaiting more excuses as her resolve thickens.

"I don't know. Doing standup comedy here. Friends."

"But you said you don't have a lot of friends here and that the comedy was more of a side thing. Plus, I'm sure there is a comedy club in Key West. It doesn't have to be a permanent move."

Amber does make all sound points. Hell, I'm beginning to wonder if anyone has ever known me better aside from Elden. And, OK, fine...Cassan.

"Let me think about it."

"Will you?"

I blow out some air.

"I will."

"Promise?"

"Yeah, I promise. I will."

"It would be so awesome," she says, collapsing back into her pillow. "We would have so much fun together. Hanging out drinking on the beach and meeting new people, and I can come watch you do comedy at the bars. She carries on like a dreamy teenager, a shortsighted Barbie imagining life with her Ken. She presses into me and we connect like two spoons before drifting off to sleep.

✳✳✳

I awake late in the morning and Amber is gone. A note on my pillow explains that she had to run to her college to sign some financial aid documents. I loaf around my apartment for a bit and make an omelet while considering her proposal, and then I call Lutsey.

"What's up playa?" Lutsey says.

"I'm not a player."

"Well you don't have to get all white-sounding on me. So are you ready to do another show? Ian said he would put you onstage again soon."

"Yeah, about that--I actually did an open mic a few days ago."

"Really? How did it go?"

"Terrible."

"Ah, that happens. You gotta take one the chin now and then. You know that."

I proceed to explain what a true disaster it was and how my act even ended in a near fight, but Lutsey refuses to let me get discouraged by any of this. Then I go on to tell him how Amber stayed over last night.

"The Florida girl?"

"Yeah."

"What was that about not being a player?"

"This is different," I say, reminding him about my five-step plan and the grid. And before he can respond, I get another call coming in. It's from Cassan!

"I have to take this," I tell Lutsey. "I'll call you later."

I hesitate a moment as I look at the display that simply reads Cassan. Six letters that have defined my life the last five years and that have led to constant redefinition ever since. I gulp, realizing that the last time I saw or even spoke to her was just before the HRGM party at Hotel Gansavoort. I press talk on the last ring just before the voicemail can kick in.

"Hello?"

"Alan? It's Cassan." The world stops. A million replies instantly dance in my head like insects under a streetlight. I search my feelings quickly, unsure of where my real attitude lies. Am I furious? Mildly angry? Am I happy to hear from her again? Still in love?

"Long time," I manage.

"I know. I wasn't sure how you would feel about me calling, but I wanted to call." I stay silent, so she continues. "Do you hate me?" More silence. "Are you still there."

"I'm here. No, I don't hate you. I'm surprised to hear from you."

"I know. I wanted to call a lot of times before, but…you know."

I wish I had a week to prepare for this call. Not knowing how to handle it, I decide to take the high road for now to avoid any regrets later, and I snap into a higher pitch.

"So how are you? What have you been up to?"

"A lot actually. Some bad, mostly good."

"Such as?"

"I got promoted at work is the main thing. I'm moving to Los Angeles to be a fashion allocation manager."

I don't even know that means, but I know it sounds like something outside of her previous passion.

"What happened to fashion design?" I ask.

"I know. I debated not moving into the business end, but it is a great opportunity and I still stay close to design. Plus, I get to travel internationally and go to all sorts of shows. I'm really excited. But I didn't want to go without telling you."

"Are you with anyone?" I ask suddenly, feeling as though I just yanked aside a curtain to reveal an enormous white elephant.

"Not anymore," she says with an audible sigh. I don't say anything, so she carries on. "It was a rebound. Nothing serious. The truth is, I've had a much harder time getting over us than you might think. I've missed you Alan."

"Did you know this guy before we broke up?" I realize that this question brings things from a casual and friendly level to a nearly jealous boyfriend inquisition and I swallow hard.

"No. Of course not. I met him at a party. Look, I don't want to talk about him now. We literally just broke up and I'm in his apartment now while he is out somewhere. I can't wait to get out of here."

"Sounds familiar," I say, but I keep the tone upbeat and even force a contrived laugh as if I'm beyond such biting remarks. Beyond her statement lay a world of questions naturally. Why would Cassan call me now, fresh off a break up? What could she want from me? Wasn't this boyfriend more serious than she let on if she was living with him? "So," I continue, "are you just going to move straight to Los Angeles then?"

"I think I'll move in with my sister. I wasn't supposed to leave for another month. I just found out about the new job so I'm totally unprepared to just up and move to L.A."

I sit down at my kitchen table and switch the phone to my other ear. I don't know what to say next.

"I do miss you Alan. And I miss our friendship." This jabs at my emotions. More like a sucker punch really.

"Me too," I say, sucking up some pride. I was an utter wreck when she left, in part for imagining all the while that she had simply moved on with the life she *wanted* so easily. Hearing that she got as far as moving in with another man doesn't make me feel better, even if it didn't work out for her.

"I was thinking maybe we could get dinner one night before I go. I mean, if that would be OK with you."

"Yeah, sure. How about tomorrow?"

"Tomorrow is perfect. Just as long as we promise not to throw things at each other."

We both laugh uncomfortably at this and pause. Then some words I don't expect tumble out of my mouth.

"You can live at my place until you go if you like." I can hear Cassan breath deeply on the other end.

"Alan, we can't do that. I think it would be too much for both of us."

"What I mean is, I won't be there."

"Wait--where are you going?"

"To Key West."

And just like that, my subconscious decision emerges. I feel liberated, and I know it's the right move. I realized it was right the moment Amber had proposed it. I need more than just a new relationship and a new career. I have to go deeper. What I need is all this change in the context of different scenery to really replant myself on the grid.

"Key West? Seriously?"

"I'll tell you all about it tomorrow," I say. "I just found out myself." And I doubt Cassan could believe how true this statement really is.

Chapter 15

AMAZING THE POWER OF HUMAN EMOTION, at times a cata-lyst for bliss and at other times so vicious and cruel to the point of attenuating all of the human faculties collectively. My mind is especially dangerous in this regard. I've always been something of an emotional basket case, a poster boy Cancer, always dwelling on memories that I have kept so well preserved in journals since high school. The moment Cassan called yesterday, those daggers of heartache began stabbing me anew. What's more, not even my decision to move to Key West with Amber has helped offset any of this.

Cassan calls me again in the morning and happily agrees to sublet my apartment when I move out, which will be in just four days. I confirmed this with a thrilled Amber who said she would love it if she could help me write jokes on the flight down.

"Do you mind if I bring a few things over this afternoon," Cassan asks. "Toiletries and a few clothes and some work stuff? The rest is already in storage." I agree and we decide to make a full day of it since we are both off from work.

When Cassan arrives we embrace for a moment. Then she begins to look around.

"Doesn't look like anything has changed really. Except I see you have new curtains."

"I can't believe you took the curtains," I say. "That was the worst part of the breakup."

She smiles as she begins to unpack a few bags and then she inquires about my Key West move. I tell her about the job and the girlfriend who is setting me up, explaining carefully that by girlfriend, I just mean that Amber is a friend who happens to be a girl.

"Well, it's kind of weird picturing you in Florida and doing anything besides being a rockstar copywriter to be honest."

"I know. Probably a temporary thing. I just want a change of pace for awhile."

"I totally respect that," she says, looking at me now. Then she moves in and hugs me again and thanks me for letting her stay. "C'mon. Let's go!"

We step out into a beautiful late October day--a Wednesday--and as we walk east, a fresh and steady wind makes music with the fallen leaves. We decide to take lunch at Antique Garage, which is one of our favorite SoHo haunts, before she embarks on a tirade of clothes shopping for her new job in the posh neighborhood of cobblestoned streets and trendy shops that is among the most elite in the world.

"Actually," Cassan says, "Fifth Avenue is the world's most expensive shopping district, followed by Causeway Bay in Hong Kong and then Madison Avenue."

"And then Rodeo Drive?"

"Nope. Then it's Champs Elysees in Paris and 57th Street in New York again."

"Wow. Impressive."

"Yeah well it's pretty much going to be my job to know these things now."

We take a seat by the garage front window at the restaurant, which was in fact a former garage converted into a tiny but chic Turkish restaurant on Mercer Street. When we sit down to eat and sip our first glass of wine of the day, everything sort of slides back in place suddenly--our old rhythm of laughter and goofiness and constant cute moments. It is just as though we were back in college, two carefree fringe hippies, blissfully unaware of the real world and responsibilities and all the different temptations and possibilities life has to offer. I hadn't known the old Cassan even still existed, but I see now she has merely been lying dormant these last few years and that she is--at least temporarily--back with a vengeance.

"Excuse me, kind sir," Cassan says to the waiter. He is a stodgy, stuffy man dressed in a suit and standing submissively by her side.

"Ma'am?"

"I see you've Lamb Kebabs," she says, pointing at her menu.

"Yes Ma'am. Would you like to order that?"

"No, just pointing that out. But thank you." I nearly burst into an audible laughter but hold it in. Cassan can maintain an absolutely straight face when she's kidding so that people have to respect her comments or risk offending a sincere nut. She kicks me under the table as a way to share the clandestine rouse.

"What would you like Ma'am," the waiter prods.

"It's just so hard to decide. I like so many dishes."

"You could order the mezogasha honey," I say, which we both know is fictitious dish I just invented to tempt her laugh. The waiter looks puzzled and Cassan holds off from laughing, kicking me again under the table.

"I could, dear. True. But I'll have the Mediterranean pasta."

"Very good Ms.," the waiter says.

"And could I please get that doused in chicken, beef and shrimp?"

"Ma'am?" The waiter looks positively baffled.

"If you could just douse my pasta with every meat you have please." I can't hold off anymore and I laugh out loud at this. Cassan laughs in turn. The waiter begins to explain that the dish does not come with additional meat options, but she dismisses him, saying "Never mind. Just the dish as is kind sir."

And as the waiter leaves, a sobering reality kicks me in the face: I am still in love with Cassandra. And why wouldn't I be? Nothing has come along since to displace the greatest relationship and only true love I have ever had. We sip wine and talk, but I have trouble listening. Instead I find myself dwelling on the "us" of old, and when it's my turn to talk I switch gears completely on her.

"Do you really miss how we were together," I ask. "When it was good?"

"Of course I do."

"Would you go back to that now if you could?"

"If we could literally go back in time you mean?"

I nod.

"Then yes."

And this is satisfying enough for now so I let it go. We continue to fall back into our old, pure, childish groove though, and I feel increasingly drawn back to her. Beyond just the feelings of longing that had hit me so hard when we broke up; back to when I felt like we ruled the world in our blissful relationship, as though we possessed some secret elixir that all other couples of the world dreamt of.

Cassan insists on paying for lunch as a "thank you" for letting her stay at my apartment for the next month. Now she is ready for some clothes shopping for her move.

The funny thing about Cassan is that she has her own way to shop. I'd seen it before in Harvard Square in Cambridge when we visited Elden a few years ago. She gets absolutely absorbed, running from rack to rack with her own thoughts, forgetting that I am there. She doesn't do this with an air of spoiled pretense, but rather with the awe and innocence of a child on Christmas morning awaking to a mound of unopened presents. As in those older days, I hang in like a dutiful pet for an hour, but it could have been 10 years for all I know. I am just happy to be with her again.

"Are you OK," she says at one point, sensing something is off. And of course something is completely off--the part about my feelings that still exist for her and my burning desire to tell her so. Instead, I take this as a cue for me to step aside for a bit.

"I'm fine. I think I'm going to take a break and grab a beer and check some email. I'll walk up to Bar 89."

"OK. I'll meet you there in like an hour," she says. As soon as I am clear of her sight I light a cigarette, because hey, things are crazy. The sky has grown even more windy and overcast and sinister and I like it. A visible, spooky fog seems to roll in from the east and I swear I can feel the mist as I walk, as though I am actually in a puffy gray cloud. I spot a bum sitting in front of an Agent Provocateur lingerie store and the visual intrigues me, so I take a photo with my phone and decide to decipher the meaning later.

"It costs $1 for a photo opp with me," the bum says. I laugh at this and hand him a ten-dollar bill instead, and then walk back one block from where I just came. When I reach Bar 89, I cozy up to the bar's subtle curve and look up at the gloomy sky through the large skylight ceiling above and order a tall glass of stout beer. There are no emails to check though, and what I really want to do is write my first journal entry in months. I ask the bartender for a pad and pen and he hands me a white paper placemat.

"Will this work?"

"Perfect."

And then I write. I write in a poetic freestyle prose about how the love of my life broke up with me and how I managed not to sulk long at all, but instead invented a new plan to press on with life, mentioning only the words "grid" and "five things." Then I write about how Cassan suddenly re-emerged months later and how suddenly the feelings I had blocked out before have returned. I stop writing. I take a big gulp of my beer and bury my head in my arms over the bar. After a while, I pick my head back up and grab the pen and write: *P.S. I love Cassandra Morgan. Is it is possible that your soulmate doesn't love you? I'm teary-eyed now and I hope the bartender doesn't see me. God I'm stupid.*

I fold up the placemat, stick it in my pocket, pay for my beer and step outside to smoke another cigarette. Just north of me I see the same bum sitting on the same curb. This time I walk over and squat down beside him in my dream-state mindframe.

"What's up?" I say.

"Hey man. Can you spare some change?"

"I just gave you ten dollars before. No more cash."

"Oh sorry man. How are you?" He looks at me with a face that is dark and weathered and thickly creased.

"Hanging in there," I say. Perhaps there should be an almost automatic sense of guilt that I should derive from talking to him this way (as though my life is so terrible) but I can't feel it. The emotional battles of the mind are as brutal as the great wars of mankind, and to this end I feel I warrant as much sympathy as any person in the world right now. I bullet-point my situation with the man in less than a minute and he says he has been there himself and offers me a drink. I don't take a drink though and instead offer him a cigarette, which he declines.

Just then, Cassan shows up.

"Alan?"

"That's her," I say to the man. We bump fists and I wish him luck.

"Making friends?" And I can see she is a bit annoyed with me. Not because of my cavorting with a bum, which is not beyond her to do, but rather for the smoking which she had gotten on me to quit. We had quit together a few years back, but then I picked up the habit again. Still, we are not together now and I think something else is bothering her more so.

"Are you OK," I ask.

"Not really." she says. "I'm done. Let's go back to your place." She walks ahead quickly and I jog a few steps to catch up with her.

"What is it? Your recent breakup?" And then she stops.

"No Alan, not my recent breakup. That meant nothing."

"What then?"

"It's about leaving. Leaving New York. Leaving you too I think."

"Me?" I'm shocked by this sudden sentiment. Especially since this revelation of hers seemed to have come during a shopping spree.

"Well yeah. I still have feelings for you too Alan. I'm not a zombie. I'm going to miss you. And I hope you take better care of yourself after I'm gone."

"So don't go then."

"What?" We are standing just shy of Houston Street where a slew of cabs are racing by in either direction in the early rush hour. The sky has drawn darker too, the days becoming shorter with the advent of winter.

"I mean, maybe we should talk about getting back together. Just talk about it. We never really did."

"I think we both did in our own way plenty. What I said when we broke up still stands. I'd only hurt you if we tried."

"Don't worry about me."

"Yeah right. I know how you can get."

We walk on in silence for a block and turn west onto Bleecker Street, which has always been one of Cassan's favorites. The shops and restaurants look enticing with their neon signs that glow in subtle gestures against the twilight, and the smells of all the world's cuisines seem to congregate and shake hands before wafting on down equally alluring side streets. A decent weeknight crowd begins to fill the sidewalks, and suddenly I break the silence. I tell Cassan how much I do still care for her. She says nothing in return, and we keep walking. Inside of me, old feelings of love begin to swirl with reckless schoolboy abandon, and I know I want her back. I don't want to upset her further just now though, so I try to conceal the extent of my feelings.

Back at my apartment, I strip down to my boxers and put on a t-shirt and get in bed. Neither of us think anything of this. Cassan busies herself with hanging up her new clothes and stashing things away in drawers that were formerly reserved for her and that have remained empty since our breakup. When she is finished, she looks about the room, trying to come up with other tasks to stay occupied. Finally she relents, turns off the lights (save for one on the nightstand) and lies down on the bed beside me. I look at her with bleary eyes and tell her that I am happy that she still cares for me at least.

"Of course I do Alan," she says, staring back. She starts to rub my arm as though to soothe me. Yet she can't know how intense things are for me just now and how choked up I suddenly feel. I want to say more, but I don't know how. I've been afraid all afternoon to push it further, to just tell her that I still love her. And I decide I am afraid no longer.

I get out of bed and stand in the middle of the room, unsure what to say or do. An ocean of sadness engulfs me. I feel like I'm about to cry, but fight it off, and then I see my jeans on the floor. I walk over to them and fish for the placemat that I wrote on earlier, acutely aware of the line that reads, "P.S., I love Cassandra Morgan."

"Here," I say, extending the journal entry to her.

"What's this?"

"Just...here." And then I leave the apartment.

I go outside and sit on the curb, still wearing nothing but my boxers and t-shirt. I start to cry. Upstairs I know that Cassan is reading the postscript, which is a cowardly yet effective way to tell her I love her. It's a dangerous love because it's an old love that I still cling to, and when I look at Cassan I *will her* with all my heart to be the same woman she was--the woman in love with me. A few people walk by and gaze at me with more gusto it seems than they would if I were naked and juggling snakes on a unicycle. The sight of me crying in my boxers on West 4th is somehow a much more unusual spectacle.

After maybe 10 minutes I muster up the courage to go back inside. I knock at my front door and nothing happens. I knock again, and after a few seconds, the door opens very slowly. A rather intense darkness greets me when I step in, and then I realize Cassan is behind the door she just opened, holding a tissue in her hand. Her teary eyes come into focus as mine adjust to the light. She lets go of the door and it closes on its own and we embrace for a while. Somehow, slowly, we shuffle to the bed and lie down. I face the wall and Cassan's arms come around me and rub me and we both cry. I know I must be crying more. I'm soaking the pillow and I can't stop. Even the thought of how much I want to stop makes me cry all the more. She is right here, so immediate to me, clutching me presently, the only man in her world that will ever love her this much and perhaps she knows it. She may not want it this way, but there it is. She loves me too, but not nearly the same way, yet now...almost...maybe. Silence prevails. This is it, I think--this is life.

I explode into a fresh bout of tears. I try to keep it low but I cannot. I've never cried in front of a woman before. Not like this. We snuggle and caress, exchanging soft touches and hard feelings, but we don't kiss. The experience is something cosmic, something dreamy, the likes of which I have never known. Essentially we are just two people openly sharing raw emotion, if only for the sake of releasing some collective valve that has clogged both our lives for months.

"You're a jerk," Cassan says through tears. We both laugh and cry at this remark. It is the only thing either of us says before we launch back into our respective sobbing voids. And this carries on for at least an hour, and somewhere back in my mind I curse Elden for being so right all of the time.

Later, after we have run out of tears, we both agree we need to eat. We dress sloppily and with disheveled faces seek out a nearby restaurant, finally settling on Italian. My dinner is great and Cassan's is terrible, and we laugh at this. We hold hands and stroll down lively MacDougal Street in the night and she asks if I want to go to a comedy club. She even suggests that we could find a place where I can perform so that she can watch me, and I'm ecstatic. The combination of these two gestures by her is touching, and I swallow hard, thinking this may be the closest I will ever come to having a loving woman who knows what I love and who loves to accommodate me out of her pure love for me. I tell her I would rather just walk and talk with her, and we continue to circle the West Village, occasionally stopping at a bar for a drink. The night will be short-lived and I want to savor the moment. We both know the harsh reality--that this is going nowhere. This is Cassan giving me what she knows I want. A last night of being together in the way we once were. She is letting me use her in a sense, and I suppose she is using me in the same way, but neither of us care.

"Tomorrow," she says, "When we wake up, we need to move on."

I say nothing. Instead I take a sip of a pinot noir and nod. From my bar stool, I look beyond her at an older couple walking by, hand-in-hand in street outside.

Chapter 16

One month later.

I'M RIDING MY BICYCLE ALONG ROUTE 1 IN KEY WEST on my commute to work. The morning is sunny and warm, and I inhale the pleasant sea air with pleasure as I peddle. Palm trees and sand line the busy road to my left and boats are docked in the pure blue water just beyond. During our first few days here, Amber and I left our apartment on Duval Street and rode the three miles together to work each morning. Now that she has grown comfortable with the route, she takes the extra time to sleep in since she doesn't have to be at the office until later. I enjoy riding solo anyway. It provides me with time to reflect each morning and to digest and analyze my new life. I was miserable those last few days in New York after seeing Cassan again briefly, and I felt delirious and confused. I lost my appetite and wandered the city aimlessly to respect her wishes and to try to bury my own. I had forgotten myself completely, as well as my plans to continue plotting myself on the grid of experience. Now, with each morning peddle, I can feel myself moving further from Cassan and New York and more towards my new place in life as a reporter for a daily newspaper who lives with an immature--but very fun and hot--Floridian girl.

The morning newsroom is always a bustling, frenzied contrast to my calm commute. Reporters on deadline jog down the halls with notes and coffee in hand. Phones ring without pausing for a stretch. People yell to each other while typing furiously. I walk to my cubicle and dig into my daily morning tasks, which include writing obituaries in a rigorous format and pulling weather and lottery numbers from the "wire." I was told that my predecessor couldn't handle the stress of writing up the obituaries, which I can understand. There is pressure in summing up the lives of three to five people you have never met each day and being absolutely sure to avoid any disrespectful mistakes on deadline. Some might say that a misspelling on a front-page headline is the worst offense imaginable in a newspaper. But I say that short-changing a recently deceased person of an offspring in his or her final shout out is the greater crime. Still, there always seemed to be much more at stake in my deadlines at HRGM, as though advertising was larger than death itself, and so I welcome the comparatively reduced load. My old collegiate studies have rushed back to me with near flawless recollect. AP Style, the inverted pyramid, the Five Ps of a story, journalistic maxims such as getting "good quotes up high" in a story--all of this knowledge that has lay dormant in me is ready to be unleashed. All this for only an 80 percent pay decrease from HRGM, but I can afford it for now.

In the afternoons, I am typically charged with small assignments for the features section. These are mostly human-interest stories centered around local shop owners and artisans or point-of-interest blurbs about Key West. Last week I spent a half a day with a man that owns five cockatoo parrots.

Around 2 p.m., the newsroom's editor Ted Swift calls on me. He is a burly red-haired man with a nevertheless soft, almost effeminate demeanor.

"I have something for you Alan."

"Something good?" I ask, spinning around in my swivel chair.

"I think so. Should be your first full-page feature. I'm assigning a photographer as well." Suddenly I pulse with excitement--the first since I started my new job. I kept it a secret, but I don't want to write news. I want to write features and--who knows--maybe transition to a magazine like the New Yorker eventually where I can cavort with the latest literary giants.

"You'll be covering a children's author who makes fun things for kids out of nature," Ted continues. We both look at each other quietly for a moment. This doesn't strike me as the glamorous piece I was bracing for. "She's well-known on the island and her book has just been published for a regional release."

This moment should call for a bout of laughter, but Ted can't know the greater expectations in my head. What's more, he seems to think this is a real scoop.

"I'm on it," I finally say, trying to look enthused. "Should I go with the photographer?"

"He's on assignment and will probably come by there after you've finished up. But the author, Carol Shefflin, is expecting you now."

✳✳✳

I peddle my bicycle back in the direction of my apartment to the author's house on Elizabeth Street. The feature will not be on deadline today, so I know I can enjoy a short ride home after the interview with Shefflin is over. About 15 minutes later, I arrive at the house. It is a relatively small, but lovely white French Colonial that is obscured by tropical foliage just behind a white picket fence along the road. The neighborhood is quiet, with only a symphony of tropical birdcalls piercing the mid-afternoon air. The front gate is open and I have to duck under overgrown trees as I approach. Getting closer, I can see that the house is old yet well preserved despite the landscaping. There are two floors, each of which feature columns and sweeping verandas, and suddenly a woman calls down to me from the second floor.

"Hello down there," she says in an English accent. "Are you from The Citizen?"

"Yes I am."

"Cheers for coming! Go on around back and find a chair. I'll be right down."

I follow a stone pathway around to the backyard, which I immediately discover to be especially large and lush with foliage for Key West. There is a small patio with two rocking chairs surrounding a little table, and on the table sits a pitcher of lemonade. The job of a reporter is a different one, I think, sitting down and removing a pad and pen from my backpack. What makes it so different is that every assignment is so unique. One moment you might be sitting in the backyard talking to an author of children's books over lemonade. The next, you might be playing cards with firefighters while extracting insight at the station or helping throw fish to dolphins while writing up a blurb about some new tourist attraction. In fact, the job reminds me of my grid theory of life.

"Terribly sorry to keep you," Ms. Shefflin says as she emerges from the back of the house.

"Not at all." I pull out my phone and prepare it for dictation. "Do you mind if I record our conversation?"

"That would be lovely. Go ahead and help yourself to some lemonade." She is dressed in a long, flowery, blue skirt and a white tank top, and her salt-and-pepper hair dangles far down her back in thick braids like tug-of-war rope. I know from my editor that she is 55, and she yet she looks far younger despite the grays.

"Let's start at the beginning," I say. "How did you arrive at the point of writing this book?" And as I talk, I recall from schooling that a reporter should ask questions and then get out of the way. You want to let your subjects do the talking if possible. And right away, I learn that Ms. Shefflin is a talker.

"Well, my original passion was for painting. I was destined to be an artist," she says. I start scribbling notes and look up at her as a signal to keep going. "Of course I started in England and attended university there for art. And once I saw I had a knack for it, I decided to move to Florida--the Keys specifically."

"Why the Keys?"

"I was always drawn to beaches and the sea, and I supposed I could draw on both the tropical landscape and the atmosphere here and develop a niche. I also had a longtime girlfriend who owned a gallery--still does in fact--and I thought the change of scenery would do me proper."

She gestures at our surroundings with her hands to enunciate her point. Meanwhile, I consider whether Ms. Shefflin's girlfriend is also her lover. It's not uncommon for Key West, and my theory would further cement the reason for her move.

"Anyway," Ms. Shefflin continues, "I became quite good at it. I moved slowly, but I amassed enough paintings to start doing shows by the time I turned 30 and I was able to make a rather good living from my art. I continued to paint for another 15 years. Eventually I just grew tired I suppose." I stop taking notes.

"Tired?"

"Yes. You know. Doing the same old thing. I started to think that life is short and there are so many things people can do and I wanted to explore those things. Can you understand that?" I nod vehemently and take a sip of lemonade.

"Completely."

"And I never married, never had kids." She sighs and looks up at the trees and listens to the birds calling for a moment. "I always wanted kids," she continues. "I suppose I just didn't realize how much so until I grew too old to have them. Plus I took to studying horticulture here and spent much of my free time immersing myself in nature as best one can do in Key West. So, I had the idea to start a summer camp that focused on art and nature. And look at this." She again indicates her backyard, which is flat and square. A small brook trickles through one side of her property and there is thick green grass and a dazzling array of trees and plants, most of which I assume she has planted and cultivated herself.

"I still painted a bit in the winter," she continues, "but the camp really took off and it became my focus each summer. I taught kids how to make dream catchers and pine cone bird feeders and how to directly interact with nature physically."

"Physically," I ask, scribbling notes.

"Yes. It became a bit of a wilderness survival camp I suppose. And of course, above all, I taught them to express themselves artistically and to have fun. Here, I'll show you."

Ms. Shefflin pulls out a copy of her book, *Tropical Nature Fun*, and skims the table of contents.

"Here's an easy one," she says finally. "Let us make a horn with just nothing more than blades of grass." She reaches down and plucks a few blades from her lawn, which she informs me is predominantly Bermudagrass. "Here you try."

I put down the lemonade and she drops three blades of the grass into my palms. She holds a page of her book up that illustrates how to do it. I gather the grass to my mouth to form a kazoo-like structure, and she coaches me on how to pinch the ends so that two pieces bow around one straight-standing blade in the middle.

"Now what?"

"Now blow." I nearly laugh at the childish simplicity of this dialogue as I blow into the grass. At first, there is nothing, but after my third try, a flat, duck-whistle type call emits from my mouth and through the blades in a loud thud.

"Excellent!" Ms. Shefflin says. And I know I could be doing much worse things with my time, but honestly, *what am I doing here?*

✳✳✳

When I get home, Amber is already changed and waiting for me like an anxious puppy happy to see its owner.

"Yay! Daddy's home," she says, making fun of our five-year age difference. "Get your suit on. I have the wine and cheese packed." She grabs a Coach bag which she never admitted was a fake, but I overheard her on the phone telling her sister how she got it on Canal Street in New York and how she misses shopping for amazing knock-offs there. She tosses a few copies of Entertainment Weekly in her bag and a bottle of wine and two glasses and when I see this, I nod at her in approval.

"I hope you don't mind, but I invited Hannah and her boyfriend and Juan and that other guy from the rooftop last week."

"Cool," I say. And it's not cool. Not in the sense that I'm not OK with others joining, but rather in the sense that I'm not big on this crew. The same can be said for everyone Amber has come to know. She's the type that has 2,000 Facebook friends. She befriends every person she meets but seldom really gets to know any of them. It's all about photos and status updates and being surrounded by attractive or popular people with Amber I'm learning.

When we first arrived here, the plan was for me to find my own place soon after, but the cottage that Amber's parents had secured for her was large enough for two and she said she wanted me to stay--even if we broke up. This statement had implied two things to me. First, she had already (and carelessly) considered us a couple from the moment I got on the plane in New York. Second, for a very attractive girl of just 22--and given the amount of flirting I have already seen her do--Amber's concept of a relationship is decidedly less engaging than my own. Still, the biggest reason why she did not want me to move was simply for the fact that she cannot be alone. She requires constant companionship and attention and really needs to be back home in Miami with her friends, traipsing down Ocean Drive with drinks in hand and dancing on bars counters. But the secret intelligent side of her--and the need to justify the expensive New York experience--pushed her to put the career first. The bottom line is that Amber is "imprisoned" here in Key West as she puts it. She knows few people besides myself, and nobody that she has felt close to yet. But then, Amber doesn't strike me as the sort that gets terribly close to anyone aside from family and any long-time girlfriends.

So we head out to a rooftop bar on Duval Street, which is something of a tropical Bourbon Street replete with plentiful pubs that are often crowded before noon, and we drink wine and beer while watching the Gulf sunset that Key West is famous for. This has become a routine of sorts--maybe three times a week--and we are always joined by some raucous cast of forgettable, young B characters that Amber rounds up and gossips with about pop culture until the orange sun explodes on the sea horizon.

From there, we resume drinking on Ft. Jeff Beach while lying in the sand, and then by a fire pit. Eventually Amber and I and other couples start making out and the singles slip off quietly into the night.

Lying now next to Amber on the sand under a half moon, I ponder life. Aside from work, my whole existence has taken on the feel of a vacation of an indefinite length. When we first arrived, we were eager tourists, hitting all of the attractions and bars and sampling every beach. We had drunken sex during a tour of the Hemingway House and met more people than I ever met in New York with Cassan. Still, this is not my scene, nor Amber's spring break crowd. Mostly they have been sun-drenched hippies and much older gays and depressed alcoholics.

"Key West is so not hip," Amber says suddenly, rolling over and spooning me.

"Am I right?"

I agree with her as I have agreed with most things she said all through this alternate November world, whether I shared her attitudes or not. I haven't wanted to ruffle any feathers as I have been impossibly tied to her. I was thankful for her offer and the chance to leave with her to usher in the radical upheaval in my life, but already I sense things getting tired for me here. I've begun to miss the hustle and the personalities of New York--the creativity, the comedy, and especially Elden and Lutsey. I even missed the Don and Kevin from the wine shop and Steve from HRGM and Ian, all of whom I had given such short notice to upon quitting my work with them.

"You're right," I tell Amber. "It's not hip for us anyway."

"Do you like the job?" she asks, facing away from me in the spoon position with the soft skin of her thin body pressed against mine.

"To tell you the truth, I don't know. I don't what I like these days, so I'm settling for experience. How about you?"

She shrugs in my arms.

"Same I guess. I just need it for my resume. I need experience too so I can go get a job at the Miami Herald or something back home."

A rare, quiet moment without laughter passes between us. We both try to shatter the silence at the same time. Her by doing the voice of a fictitious person we invented and laughed about while high the other night, and myself by tickling her. The wine runs dry around midnight.

Chapter 17

WHEN I ARRIVE AT THE CITIZEN a few weeks later I learn there has been an accident. A man with liver disease received the amazing news that he had been matched with a donor. He decided to celebrate by partying with a group of friends at the Hog's Breath Saloon on upper Duval around 11 a.m., figuring it was OK to further destroy the bad liver that would soon be removed from his body. Somehow he ended up running too far out into the road and was struck by a car and killed instantly. With our veteran reporters having just clocked out during the slow news hour, my manager Ted calls on me.

"Think you can handle this Alan?"

"Absolutely," I say, summoning my journalistic prowess. I cover the story well and submit it to my editor just before the end of my work day, knowing my first front-page hard news byline will be among the headlines of tomorrow's paper. Next I ride to a bar on the way home to write some comedy, perhaps in part because of the depressing nature of the story I had just spent the day on, but in larger part because I'd been missing writing comedy. I call Amber to say I will be late as I have some stuff to write, which she probably takes to mean work-related writing.

I peddle down to the Southermost Beach Café just a block from the southernmost point in the continental United States, and lock up my bike under a pleasant yet hot 4 p.m. sun. I order a cold beer and buy a pack of cigarettes as well, and then I find a table with an umbrella and a nice view of the sea, isolated from the other patrons. As I watch the soft waves gently lap the beach, I feel something profound that I can't explain. A sudden giddiness--an excitement I haven't felt in some time, something much more fulfilling than having just written my first major news story for publication. As I sip my beer pondering this,

I come to realize that it's the process of writing comedy that I enjoy so much. And the realization of actually liking something is saying a lot for me lately. Life is short. The liver transplant guy this morning reminded me of that. I need to keep this process moving and discover my path before the approaching age of 30 for sure.

I clear my head and grab a pen from my backpack. There are undeveloped comedic thoughts that I have been kicking around on my bicycle commutes, and I gave them slugs like "like condoms ruin intimacy" and "tipping math controversies" along with notes about current events and celebrities I had funny thoughts about.

All spies should be Masochists, I write now. This way if they are caught behind enemy lines, they can't be tortured for information. They won't talk, so the torturer steps up the pain or cuts off a finger. "Ahhh! Now I'm *definitely* not going to tell," the spy yells with pleasure. I take a moment to enjoy this thought before launching into another one:

What's up with the saying that you can run but you can't hide? I'm feeling a comedic high as funny thoughts rush to my pen. I think we've had that saying backwards forever. There's always some terrorist we can't seem to find. That motherfucker's been hiding his ass off! I think the saying should be the other way around. You can hide, but you can't run! I laugh again and write on. What if the terrorist was suddenly spotted by helicopters? There's no way he's going to run away successfully. I smile as I script mock communication between the military:

"Do you see the target Ghost Rider?"

"Confirmed."

"Can you acquire the target?"

"Negative Zulu. He's too fucking fast."

"Roger that Ghost Rider. We'll just wait until he hides."

I keep going for another hour, riffing on all sorts of topics and getting down a month's worth of pent up ruminations. To see it all staring back at me on paper feels good, like a purge, as though a great burden has been lifted from my mind. I realize the waiter hasn't been my way in a while--probably because people have begun to order dinner at this hour--so I go to the bar to order another beer. There are some great Key West postcards on the wall, and I instantly decide to buy a bunch and write a quick note to everyone back home instead of posting an impersonal status update online. I decide to write one to my parents and one to my sister Jen and her husband Dale in San Francisco, and then to Elden, Lutsey, Cassan, Steve, and even to Elmer's Wine Shop. I even write one to Amber with the message "Glad we are here." And as I sit and complete the cards, Amber calls.

"Hello?"

"Are you still at work?"

"No, I left, but I stopped at that beach café on Whitehead to have a beer and write some comedy."

"Really? Thinking of doing some stand-up here finally?"

"Not really. I just want to start writing again for now. Is it dinnertime?"

"Yeah. But how about I just come there? I like those burgers and I haven't heard from anyone about sunset drinks tonight anyway."

"Cool."

✳✳✳

Amber arrives 30 minutes later, just as I had exhausted myself with the writing anyway. There are cheeseburgers and fries and beers for both of us on the table as she walks up.

"Deveroux" I yell, happy to see her after sitting alone for a while. "Wassaaaabeeee!"

"Awww, you already ordered for me! You're the bestest one you know." She sits down and immediately bites into her burger. Then she slugs some beer and looks up at me. "So how'd the writing go?"

"Good thanks. I'm ready for Caroline's." I say this with a smile, knowing I'm years from doing a show at a venue like that, even with some breaks. It's like the Improv and other top clubs in L.A. The day I'm performing on these stages may also be the day I also have my own half-hour special on T.V.

"So you *are* writing to do stand-up then."

"No. Yeah. I don't know."

"Well, you seem to be getting tired of the journalism career if you can call it that."

We exchange smiles and I drink some beer. The setting sun hits us hard so we have to squint and shade our eyes with our hands. A bit of a wind begins to kick up which feels nice in the heat. We sit in silence for while eating, but she is sizing me up the whole time. I've been acting different these last few weeks and she's onto me.

"So I'm glad you're writing! What brings you back to Awesome Alan?"

"Who's that?"

"The comedian you were the first night I met you." Her cell phone buzzes on the table. She picks it up and looks at it quickly then leaves it alone.

"Yeah, well...I guess I'm getting a bit antsy," I say. "I miss the people in New York and such."

Amber reaches over and puts her hands on mine and looks me tenderly in the eye. She really does get it. Despite her party girl demeanor and her passion for the worst TV on the planet, she really can get inside my head.

"You'll make a great wife someday," I tell her.

"Awww. That's sweet babe. Why so?"

"Because you care and pay attention."

"Well maybe, but no marriage until I'm in my mid-30s at least."

"The whole institution of marriage might be over by then," I say. "Dried up like social security."

This might sound unromantic and curt, but she knows I'm referring to a talk we had recently about how traditional marriage and the nuclear family is increasingly going by the wayside. There was a report on TV we watched the other night that said only 60 percent of people under 40 are married or some such thing--down 10 percent from only a decade or two ago.

"We might literally just marry electronic devices soon."

"That's fine," Amber says. I'm equipped to stay single. I'll be even better off because there will be so many more people to hang out with that way."

I laugh, knowing this is all completely true for her. We polish off our beers and order more as the waitress clears our plates. Then I light a cigarette.

"You bought another pack?"

"Yeah. Figured for the writing."

"Nevermind why, just fork one over bitch," she says, reaching for the pack. We both recline and suddenly I feel comfortable enough to talk bigger picture.

"So who is using who the most here? You or me?"

"Ha!" She snaps her head and all that blond hair topples back with it, then she grabs her fresh beer for a drink.

"Both of us equally I think. So it's all good."

"You think?"

"Well, I mean, we have fun together and laugh a lot and have lots of great sex. So that's equal. Then there is me using you to also have someone to be with while I'm stuck here. And then there is you needing to get out of New York for a while to try something totally new like you said. So yeah...I say it's even."

"So you don't view me as long term boyfriend," I ask?

"Why, do you?"

We both take a sip of beer in silence. Then she goes on.

"I don't think either of us do. And I don't think either of us are the safest bets for anyone right now."

I've been agreeing with everything and I know the breakup will be easy like with Kate. Still, I don't like the part about me not being a safe bet.

"I'm not a safe bet?"

"Well," she says, stumbling to explain, "I mean, didn't you say like a few weeks ago how you were trying to date lots of different women to find the perfect one?"

I gulp, recalling for the first time that I did bring that up in a drunken stupor one night at Ft. Jeff.

"I said that, huh? That's just temporary. It's--"

"It's really no big deal. We both sort of said the same thing from day one really. I mean, I always date a lot and need lots of different people in my life. You are like my longest boyfriend and it's been two months. I'm too young for serious dating I think, but I don't know. I have all sorts of theories. Maybe when I date a lot it's like I'm looking for the perfect guy too."

"You mean it's not me?" I say this with a big goofy smile.

She looks at me with concern as if I might be offended by this.

"No, no baby," I say. "I'm *with* you. We're totally on the same page."

She nods slowly. Sincerely. There's relief on her face and I'm sure there's relief on mine.

"I think that we'll be friends well into the future. You can be my Florida girl when I come down for vacation and I can be your New York guy when you get the urge for some Rockefeller holiday spirit."

"I'd like that."

The twilight swoops down on the patio and stars become visible over the sea. Amber reaches over and massages my arm with her hand and playfully rubs my crotch with her foot under the table.

"It's funny that you mention your theory about guys," I say.

"Why's that babe?"

"Because I'm all about theories. I told you about my friend Elden and the conversations we get into."

"Yeah. You mean that relationship-attraction curve thing? I liked that."

"Well there's another one I call the Oblique Triangle Theory."

"Oblique as in long?"

"You know, like a triangle where no angle measures 90 degrees."

"Isn't that like an isosceles triangle or something?"

"No, not really. Just like all the sides are different lengths."

"Like how?"

"Like skewed…a weird motherfucking triangle. It doesn't matter. The point is, there are three points, and each point represents the kind of relationship balance people tend to have when they are not dating or married to a person they love. So you have the girl or guy you are with and dating or whatever--"

"But you don't love her."

"Right. Let's call that point A."

Amber smiles, enjoying the topic.

"So I'm point A?"

I stop and look at her.

"I'm just kidding Alan. I'm clearly point A. I agree. And you are point A for me--as long as point A can still be someone you really like and care about."

"It is!" I slap my head. "I should have said that first. Yes, point A can still be someone awesome like you. Or it can be someone you are no longer into--someone you are with just with for the sake of being with someone, like a crutch or a rebound. Either way, it's the person you are with."

"Got it."

"OK. So then, lower down, and off to the right is point B, which is the person you dream of being with or at least think you would really like to give things a go with. But she is lower down because you are not with her, and she is off to the right because she may be unobtainable, like a reach."

"Oh, I totally have a point B. This guy I went to high school with that I'm still in touch with in Miami."

"Right--perfect. And for me you could say Cassan."

"Oh God. Booo."

"What have you. So anyway, the last point is Point C. And this is someone that you know you can hook up with whenever you want. Maybe it's just a booty call, but maybe you are in the mood for a certain kind of personality or want to share a specific interest or a certain kind of night out with and you can turn to these Point C people."

"Like backups, you mean."

"Like backups. Or like Elden and I call them: shelf girls."

"Shelf girls?"

"Yeah, you know. Like backups you keep on the shelf for use when you need them."

Amber bursts into laugher at this.

"Oh my God. That's so wrong!" she laughs.

"But so right sometimes. And that's Point C. And Point C is at the lowest point and aligned slightly to the right because it's not as steady as point A, but it doesn't stick out as far as point B because you know you can usually get point C when you want. Point B sticks out to the right farther because it might be unobtainable--it's more what you aspire to. And so when you connect the points you get an oblique triangle. A perfect visual for the balance of relationships most single people tend to have. Get it?"

"I get it. And I think it's kind of brilliant. Except I don't see why the triangle has to be oblique."

I flag the waitress who is nearby and ask to borrow her pen. Then I sketch what I'm visioning as best I can on a slightly crumpled napkin for her.

"Here."

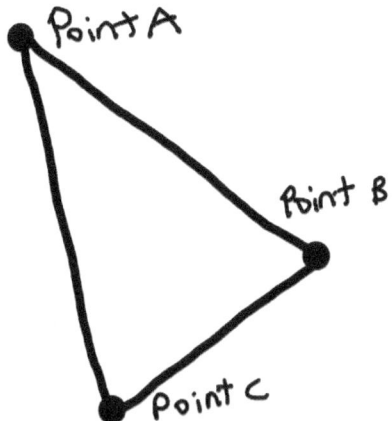

Amber looks at my crude sketch and giggles before grabbing the pen.

"But what I mean is, I think it might be cleaner if you have points A and C lined up because that's what you can get and only Point B juts out, because that's what you can't get or at least what you don't have at the moment." This would make it a nice right triangle. Like this. She draws a little box square around point B and jots down "90 degrees" and then looks up at me with a smile. "There you have it," she says. I present to you the "Right Triangle Relationship Theory."

"Sure, why not."

"So what else? Other theories and such?"

"There's the Three Criterion for what I need from a woman in a relationship: someone who is smart, funny and creative."

"Hmmm." Amber casts a suspicious look my way. "I'm with you on funny for sure, and intelligence might make it. But I would go with attractive over creative. What's creative all about?"

"It's intentionally broad I admit. I'm attractive to creativity. Really I mean anyone who appeals to my interests or who is engaging or interesting to me somehow. It's more than that though. There are at least 15 kinds of humor and I'm picky on the humor front. There are 17 degrees or types of love couples can have. I worked these numbers while high, but they hold true. With humor, I want the goofy or dry variety mixed with smart and wacky. In love, I want the best friends, exciting, passionate sort that rivals the love for any kids we might have."

"That's asking a lot," Amber says. "And that's easy to say now before having a kid. If we had a kid, that kid would be half me biologically, so I can't say who I would love more."

"Well, the kid will be half me too, and it will be *all* us. I think the kids should be something you create with someone because of how much you love that person. And while we will always love our kids, they will go off and lead their own lives. You don't go on living with your kids forever, so that's part of why it's so important to love your partner just as much. That's who you really spend your life with eventually. I don't know. To me, I don't want the marriage to become about the kids. It has to be at least 50-50."

Amber nods pensively.

"So it's not just personality that you dissect left and right."

"What do you mean?"

"I mean, it's not just about the perfect job and the perfect relationship; it's not just about types of humor or types of personality or even types of looks, but rather types of everything. You want the perfect everything. You are like me, but even more so.

"How?"

"I mean like you analyze everything crazy intensely."

"Is that a bad thing?"

"I don't know. Just an observation. But I think if I were dating you for serious I might feel a bit too much pressure in all this. Like I wasn't good enough in some way."

"Don't say that. It would be different."

"Well, you have to admit that we're not the easiest of people to lock down right now."

"Agreed."

We toast our beers and look out on the water. The wind has picked up and stirred the ocean so that the bright blue surface is rippled and choppy.

"Enough of that though," she snaps. "Let's not break us down."

"Totally. Let's just write us off to bad timing and location. I need to get home to New York."

"Agreed. I need to get back to Miami and catch up with family and friends."

She wants to say more, but she doesn't. She probably wants to know how well she passed through my idealistic filter of girlfriend material. And she'd probably come out better than she thinks. I might even regret this one later. But there's something fundamentally off that I can't quite place. Maybe it is summed up in this concept: she can make me feel like the center of the world at times, but if a random guy she met at rooftop walks by, she'd ask him to join us and she would connect with him in her mind just the same. She's complex and shallow all at once.

We drink and talk more about our plans to head back to our respective homes soon. We reflect on the good times in Key West and about the things we won't miss at all. Through it all, her words about my intense analysis of everything in life remain at the fore of my mind. She's right. Maybe the whole grid thing is ridiculous, but I have to figure out what I want somehow.

I try to say so to Amber in roundabout ways, but she shrugs. She wants to invite some people over for the semi finals of a reality dance-themed show and all I can do is shrug back. Seldom can things end between two people without any hurt feelings or resentment. That's the case here. I want to thank her for securing another plot point on my grid, but I can't say that.

Later at night, after everyone leaves our cottage Amber and I go at it with the windows open and the moonlight pouring in. I tell her after, while falling asleep, that I will probably leave in a week, but I want to leave in the morning.

Chapter 18

"**M**Y MAN! MY MOTHAFUCKIN' MAN!" LUTSEY SAYS when he sees me on the doorstep of his apartment, shivering in the cold of an early December night back in New York. "Of course you can stay here. Don't you ever give a brother a heads up though?"

I apologize, explaining how I agreed to sublet my apartment through a website to a young couple after Cassan moved out. The couple only planned to stay for three weeks, but when I called them from the airport tonight I learned that they need the full month they paid for and so I'm homeless for a week.

"Look at you, all tanned and shit. Now we look like brothers--except for that stupid banana watch I told you to lose."

Candice runs into the room like a kid and greets me with a big hug. They have a modest one bedroom on the third floor of a brownstone walk-up in the East 90s, and I'm a little out of breath from lugging my suitcase up the stairs.

"Great to see you!" she says. "And please…stay as long as you like."

"Just as long as you get your ass out by tomorrow morning," Lutsey adds.

I set down my things in a decent-sized living room with exposed brick and a fake fireplace and Candice indicates a large plush couch that will be my bed for a few days.

"It's pretty comfy."

"It has to be," Lutsey says. "I'm forced to sleep on it a lot myself."

"Don't tell me you guys are fighting right now," I say.

"No, it's been all good with us," Candice says. "Right honey?" She turns to Lutsey who nods and then she whips her head back at me with those cool braids of hers flapping in the air and adds, "He's just a bit cocky lately, and plus he farts in his sleep a lot."

Lutsey blushes a bit, and starts waving his finger vigorously.

"C'mon now. A man's got to keep his girl warm at night, don't he?"

I laugh at this and Candice says she's going to fix some drinks.

"How's the business going? I ask.

"It's going great!"

"How so?"

"I put some more animation into the act and I've been focusing on a wider range of topics. And I stopped with the hosting thing. I'm just doing straight stand up now and I'm killing it."

"Wow! That's great man!" This is more the Lutsey I expected when I first met him.

"He's doing real good too, Candice says, emerging from the kitchen with a tray of three vodka drinks over ice. "I think Lutz has been taking a page from your book Alan. He's taken some risks with his style and it's paying off." She puts her arms around Lutsey and reaches in to kiss him on the cheek. "Isn't that right baby?" And I can see that his new energy and success has translated into a much healthier relationship dynamic between the two of them, even though he wouldn't admit this to me. For some reason, Lutsey sees me as free man and has come to live vicariously through my dating escapades.

"So when are you two getting married already?"

Lutsey laughs, as though this question was a playful jab.

"Settle down you freeloader. What about you? Fill us in on Key West and why you are back."

"Aw, you know. That was never meant to be anything long term."

"But you had some fun with that Amber girl I'm sure." Lutsey turns to Candice. "You should have seen this little thing baby. All young and hot and wild. She was Alan's first groupie!"

"Yeah, it was good for a bit. But really I just needed the temporary change."

"How about that reporter thing? Did you give them notice or do they think you're showing up for work tomorrow?"

"I gave them two days notice, and they weren't too happy about it. The job had its moments and I'm glad I tried it, but I don't think journalism is the answer for me."

"At least you tried. You see what I'm saying about this guy Candice? He just won't fuckin' settle. Just keeps shaking things up. I love it!"

"That's right baby. Cheers for that. I don't know about this plan with all the jobs and girls or whatever--it sounds tiring to me--but here's to you anyway."

We clang drinks and I feel a buzz settling in and I also feel kind of mixed about myself suddenly. Granted I'm sticking to my plan to find the ideal girl and the ideal job and there can't be anything wrong with a 20-something exploring both. Still, there is the notion that I'm single and unemployed and I quickly picture some sort of inverted curve on my grid that stretches deep into the southwest quadrant of negativity.

"So what's next?" Lutsey asks. "Back to the stage I hope! I'm ready to resume my mentorship."

"Actually, I started getting the comedy bug toward the end of my stay down there," I say. "I started writing everyday after work and I got a lot of new shit down."

"That's my man! See Candice, Alan Jones can't fight destiny!"

We cheers again, but I go on to confess that my quest for the perfect career--or at least a sampling of a few more--isn't over. Besides, I can't let Lutsey's excitement blind me; I know I'm not going to pay the bills as a stand-up comic. The odds are against it and I'm still a completely unproven novice who has little more than a passion for writing humor and a few new connections in the New York scene. Sure it's the second best scene after L.A. and the only other scene that counts, but everything is still little more than a pipedream.

I tell them about Amber and Key West over more drinks and Lutsey shares his stage stories and eventually we call it a night.

✳✳✳

I awake the next morning alone and disoriented for a moment. The apartment is cold and dark with the blinds still drawn against small cracks of morning light. An alarm clock glows like a beacon at sea across the room, forming the numbers 10:00, which means Candice has already slipped past me for her nursing job at a hospital. I get up and throw on a hat and head out to get breakfast. I also decide to follow up with Steve from HRGM who I have been playing phone tag with to pick his brain about careers. He wants me to come back to copywriting for him, but we do have that sort of connection.

"Steve Beringer," a voice says after one ring.

"Steve, it's Alan."

"Alan! Finally. It's good to hear from you. How are things?"

I smile at his change in tact. He's learned not to get his hopes up or be too pushy with me.

"Things are fine." I tell him I'm looking for the next gig and explain that I'm still not ready to go back to the advertising world just yet.

Steve is quiet on the other end. I have no idea how well he is listening or how much he cares to hear any of this. I even begin thinking that I made a mistake to call him when he suddenly speaks up in a clear, forceful tone.

"Tell you what I can do for you. I have a good friend over at VH1 who is looking for a sharp, creative out-of-the-box guy for a producer position. I don't know what level or anything because he just mentioned this in passing over dinner the other night, but I can have him meet with you if like.

I don't know what I was expecting really, but this is as good a response as any that I could hope for. A producer? Connotations about the title begin swimming around my mind. And it's not like I don't know the job. I've worked with producers on ad campaigns closely before.

"I would really owe you," I say.

"You sure do. I'll make a call and get back to you. And if I get you this gig, you can agree to be a sounding board for me now and then...until you decide to come back to advertising full time that is. Deal?"

"Deal."

We hang up and I nearly skip to a corner bodega to pick up some egg and cheese sandwiches and one thing is clear--it's high time that I get up to Boston to visit Elden. I can't wait to see him in fact. Plus I don't want to impose on Lutsey and Candice all week and there's nothing else to do now anyway.

I make the call and Elden answers on the other end, ecstatic.

"Get up here pronto! How many days can you stay?"

"Three or Four. I'll take an early afternoon train."

"Pack light. I'll pick you up at South Station and I'll have a bike for you."

"A bike? It's winter!"

I forgot that Elden doesn't own a car and gets around Boston by bike or by the T or the rare cab.

"It's not a long ride my man. Half of it is by ferry for two bucks. It'll wake you up from the train ride too."

I don't like it, but I say "yes sir," and start packing as much as I can into an oversized red travel backpack that I've had forever.

Chapter 19

ELDEN IS DRESSED IN RIDICULOUS ATTIRE and looking as giddy as a puppy on the platform of Boston's South Station. If he had a tail, it would be wagging furiously. His wild hair is tucked into a red-and-black-checkered lumberjack hat with long flaps over his ears and he is wearing a puffy black jacket and tan cargo pants that I recognize from our college days. Two bicycles are balanced against him as he bobs his head back and forth with a big, bright smile.

"Alan Jones you nutty bastard!"

There's something in Elden's way of talking that could almost be down-right nerdy, yet he treads this line carefully and instead parlays his demeanor into something fresh and original and cool even. His words are calculated with on-the-fly metaphors, thinly guised intellect, and surprisingly little fluff. His personality wouldn't go over with a lot of women like Amber who would con-sider him weird, but he has enough fans among artistic, hipster and intellectual communities that it is no matter.

"What's the plan?"

"Plan? There's just a series of loosely prescribed actions you anti-Bohemian. We'll ride back to my apartment and drop off your stuff and then I have some women for us in Cambridge and maybe a party there as well."

I fasten on my backpack and gloves and hop on a dirty but effective moun-tain bike and follow Elden. First we peddle over to the New England Aquarium and Elden slows and turns to ask if I want to go inside to see some whales for a bit. The idea strikes me as a bit absurd at the moment and I just nod no. A bike ride in 30-degree temperatures with a heavy backpack is far from ideal and I just want to get to his place.

We catch the Inner Harbor Ferry for just $1.70 each and the motor hums gently as we cruise over the cold, dark water while enjoying a nice view of the Boston skyline. A younger man--a student for sure--recognizes Elden and greets him with a cheerful "Hello Mr. Lewis," and Elden just tips his lumberjack hat by way of reply. We get off at the Charleston Navy Yard and peddle though a brief snowy oasis that is City Square Park en route to Cambridge Street and finally arrive at Elden's place just a few blocks shy of the Harvard Campus.

His apartment is really a sky blue, narrow, three-story Victorian house that has been converted into three separate apartments--one per floor--and Elden has the top floor. I decide to grab a hot shower while he cooks us up some pasta. When I meet him back in the kitchen, we sit at his tiny bistro-style table, and he cracks a bottle of some cheap red wine and serves dinner.

"So I got your photos. Sounds like Key West amounted to little more than a vacation."

"Yeah, but it was nice change of pace." I go on to repeat some of the stories that I shared with Lutsey, such as the rooftop sunsets, the sunny bike commutes to and from work, and odd journalism stories like Carol Shefflin and her nature book. Elden periodically toasts my glass and emits hearty laughs befitting of a genie or some blissful mountain man despite his athletic physique.

"I would have absolutely conquered," he yells. "Haven't been down in Florida since we went with McKinney on that road trip when we peed in bottles the whole way down to make it in 22 hours flat. Remember that?"

And of course I could never forget that. I even spit out some wine in laughter at the recollection. McKinney was this Jamaican guy that lived in our dorm who Elden begged to come with us on our spring break trip to Miami. We were all high the entire trip, including when McKinney and Elden went parasailing and were both questioned by the cops after they way overshot the beach and landed on the roof of a beachfront building.

When we both stop laughing, Elden continues.

"I would have loved to visit you down there if not for proctoring exams and such. So what's next? Still with the job and relationship search?"

"What else is there to do?" I pause, thoughtfully. "You know me. Why don't you just tell me what job I should have? Who I should date and such."

This would seem a simple enough approach to life. Just have someone tell me what's perfect for me. Maybe the socialists have something there after all.

"Don't you know what my response would be to that by now?"

"Honestly, I don't. Tell me."

"You just gotta let it fly man! Must I draw you a map?"

"That'd be nice. So you don't like that I'm trying different things?"

"I love that you're open to anything, but not in that deliberately fashioned manner you are all strict about. The perfect job? The perfect girl? There's no such thing man."

"Why not? You do what you love in life right? But what happens when you don't know what you love? You have to go find out is what I say."

"Yes. But it's how you're going about it. You are set up to fail. How can you have criteria if you say you don't know what you love?"

"I have a foundation," I protest. "I know who I am and roughly what I like. I just need to frame it right."

Elden sits back in his chair and pours some wine and then looks at me in a pleading sort of way. For a moment, a rare silence bobs to the surface between us. I light a cigarette and Elden asks for one because of the wine. Finally he breaks the quiet.

"I want to say something, but I'm not quite sure how. I guess it's like the passage from a philosophy book I read. It goes: "The Buddha was the Buddha because He was Buddha, the Enlightened One, and he who cannot accept this promise will never know more than the shell of Buddhism.'"

"I actually know that one," I say. From our philosophy class at Dartmouth, before I declared English and journalism as dual majors. "Probably where you first heard it."

Elden nods a maybe, and goes on.

"You see what I mean though? This is life and life is beautiful and fleeting and mercurial like some enormous orange waterfall and you can't worry yourself about the particulars so much as getting lost in the mist and awe of it all.

"That sounds like a passive, observational approach to life."

"No, not passive at all. You try to enjoy it, sure, but you kick it in the ass now and then or whip it like a jockey might a horse, to keep it on moooooving brotha, moving through the ebbs and flows. But the idea is that nothing is perfect and so you take that foundation of yours--those things you appreciate and that interest you--and you lay down some other things you *might* like on top of it that come along and see what you see. You can't constantly spoon-feed the journey all the time and you can't keep starting new journeys or you'll never finish a journey and you'll never know how one ends up."

I want to tell him he's wrong, but all he means to say on a philosophical level is carpe diem and to stop worrying about some idealized future, and how can I really argue with that? I knew my approach was different from the start and that's why I'm trying it. But instead of giving him this, I give him something else instead.

"I broke down and cried a few months ago," I say.

"What? When? What happened?"

"When I was with Cassandra. I was crying in my boxers on the street outside my apartment while she was up there reading a love letter of sorts I gave her."

"Wham!" Elden shakes his head a bit in disbelief.

"And so I need to move on obviously, and really that's all I'm trying to do. But I want it to be right."

"I see," says Elden, stroking his chin like an omniscient wizard. "But the thing with that is that is you are probably comparing all these girls to Cassandra, as if Cassandra herself was your criteria for the perfect relationship. And since she didn't like your job, maybe you are doing the same thing with the career search."

And damn Elden for sniffing out the root of things so precisely all the time. I hadn't considered this, but I can't deny it immediately.

"You should be a shrink."

"I am if you say so."

I take a sip of wine and then top off our glasses with the rest of the bottle.

"So let me ask you this. Why exactly did you say I would cry three times within a year?"

"It's nothing complicated, "Elden says. "Just the basic lovesick withdrawal syndrome. I went through it with Marie who was my third and fifth serious girl--remember her?"

"I do. But you can't count her twice."

"Sure I can. Two different times, two fresh and different loves. But the result was the same. Here's this person who is your universe who you invest all of your emotions and being into and then suddenly she's gone and cleared you out and you're wandering around in this great depression as though your soul was broken."

"But I didn't cry when we first broke up. Just later on that curb."

"True--but it was a release that was bound to come."

"And the second cry?"

"The second comes after you've taken inventory of your life. The crying comes after you chase a new life and you give it a go and realize it's not for you either. Maybe you still make comparisons to your old life and find the comparisons bitter because your new lot is entirely worse. Or maybe you simply fear that you may never find true happiness again, no matter who you are with or what you are doing, and so you just break down."

"Is that what happened with you," I ask.

"No, not with me," he says with a grin.

"Whatever. And the third?"

"I'm not really sure about the third cry. I've never gone through it but I've seen it with other people. It's like a third wave, or some such psychological thing. I dunno. I haven't put much thought into it. But I figured you might be a three-timer."

And with that, Elden gets up and clears our plates. I'm ready to wrap this up too, so we both gulp down the rest of our wine and head out just before 9 p.m.

✹✹✹

"So what's first?"

"First we go meet up with some girls I know," Elden says.

We walk a few blocks to another Victorian building and Elden rings the doorbell a few times but nobody answers and there are no girls.

"Are we stood up?"

"Not sure we actually had plans to begin with," he says, shrugging. C'mon!"

From there we walk a few more blocks onto the fringe of the Harvard campus. We turn down a dark side street but there is noise and much light up ahead. A visibly drunken man stumbles past as we get closer.

"This is a party that a girl in my metaphysics workshop told me about."

We arrive at the rock wall perimeter of the party, which is taking place in a small stone house. Despite the cold, there are about 20 people in the yard, filling up beers from a keg and smoking.

"Is this an undergrad party?"

"I guess so," Elden says.

So we simply walk up to the keg and grab cups and start pumping some beer as though we were honored guests. Elden finishes one beer and then pulls out a flask of liquor from his pocket.

"I didn't see you take that!"

"I can't be drinking keg beer all night. A little Jack and Coke for me."

Elden doesn't recognize anyone so we decide to walk into the house through the front door where people seem to be. We open the door to some loud indie music blaring out of cheap speakers and the place is packed. It's hard to make out a word anyone is saying as we squeeze our way past the hall and into the kitchen where there's breathing room, and that's were we see the girl from Elden's class.

"Elden! You made it!"

"Hi lovely, "Elden says, pecking her on the cheek. "This is my undergrad college roommate from Dartmouth, Alan."

We shake hands and she introduces herself as Sara and explains how she is here with a few girlfriends who are scattered about. We get into a conversation about careers and Elden points out that I bailed on advertising.

"What are you doing now?"

"I'm a producer at VH1," I tell her. Elden snaps his head my way surprised.

"I'll tell you later," I say. He smiles, thinking perhaps I'm making this up from scratch to avoid my story. I actually forgot about the pending opportunity myself.

"What show," Sara asks. We shout at each other over the music, so it's easy to avoid much detail.

"I start on Monday so I'll have to tell you then."

Elden asks Sara something about class and I take a peak at some of these Harvard undergrads that are no doubt letting loose with exams being done. It's easy to imagine that Elden and I are at some Dartmouth party now in fact. Nothing has changed, and we have instantly reverted back to our old lack of social graces.

"What's down there?" I signal to a doorframe with just beads for a door leading down to a basement. A few people come and go from it.

"Oh just a few people playing pool," Sara says.

"Let's go!" Elden does one of his happy little jigs. "I've got those drunken pool skills you know."

We walk down into a dank, moldy room that is lit only by a stained glass Budweiser lamp over a small pool table. The green felt on the table is rugged and wet from someone spilling beer. A bunch of young guys stand around the table watching as a tall underclassman with a hat on backwards measures up the 8-ball and sinks it.

Just then, Elden leaps into their group and they jump back, overcome by his energy. He declares that I am his partner and that we have the winners. I rack the balls and they break them and it's on. Nobody wants to get in Elden's way it seems as he bounces from ball to ball, shooting in a flurry. We beat them easily as he polishes off his flask of whiskey.

"Who's next? Bring it!" A few of the guys head upstairs, replaced by a few more. The new crew likely heard about Elden and I get the sense everyone wants to beat us.

The problem for them though, is that as Elden drinks, he gets proportionately better with his pool skills until nobody can come within four balls of beating us. I hold my own, but we are winning game after game because of him.

Two quiet, focused guys--one with a white man's version of an afro and another meek, skinny guy in thick-rimmed glasses--step up to challenge. Elden is drunk now and especially fiery, and he grabs a broomstick and twists off the broom part, and looks them both in the eyes.

"C'mon you charlatans! I'll beat you with just this handle by god!"

And that he does! Elden leaping around the table and nailing each shot without spending more than a second lining them up. He even makes a shot behind his back and another by jumping the cue ball. It's the most impressive display of pool I have ever seen.

We leave the party with Sara and two of her girlfriends sometime after 1 a.m. and head to a diner. The rest of the evening is a blur. All I know is that I wake up on the couch with a raging hangover and without any of the girls with me. Elden, I learn, has all three in bed with him.

Chapter 20

STEVE COMES THROUGH FOR ME AND JUST LIKE THAT, I'M A PRODUCER. Well, an associate producer in television anyway. I'll be responsible for interviewing people and overseeing the editing and scripting of a segment of a new VH1 game show about movie trivia.

"I know you haven't actually produced before, but from Steve I get the sense you'll do fine," my new boss Linus says. I keep thinking how he might resemble Linus from Charlie Brown if Linus was a stocky 30-something. His whole face seems crudely drawn with squiggles except for a pile of blond hair parted down the middle.

We are seated in his office high up on the Viacom building on 6th avenue and I peek out the window behind him at The Rock for a moment as he describes my role. He quickly leafs through my ad portfolio and pretends to glance at a few of my articles that were published in Key West. Then he tosses everything aside and kicks back.

"I hope you know you will be making a fraction of what you made before. Steve told you that our AP positions are freelance without benefits, correct?"

"He did. I saved up a bit and I'll be OK for a while. I just want the experience for now. If I like it, I know I can grow."

"Great! When production wraps, you can push for the next step. Anyway, we're glad to have your creative talent on board, and we look forward to seeing you when we start production."

We shake hands and I collect some documents about the show I will be working on starting just after New Year's in two weeks. My ears pop on the long elevator ride down and I step out onto the crowded street that is just a block west of the dreaded Times Square tourist mob scene. Despite this, I walk around for a bit to scout out the area restaurants and bodegas.

Suddenly I get this excited chill. It's not every day that you land a new job. Granted it's a bit different with me--this is the fourth time in seven months if you count the standup--but it still feels good. And sure, that wasn't much of an interview. Linus conducted the whole meeting as if I was an employee already, and I don't even feel like I've been on a single real interview since I was first hired by HRGM. And as I'm meditating on the concept of interviews, I pass by some posters promoting a strip club, and this gets me thinking. What is the interview process like for strippers? Better yet, how about for porn stars? Are resumes involved? They would have to be right? Otherwise the line for interviews would go around the block. In fact, they wouldn't even call it an interview. They'd just call it intercourse.

"Thanks for your interest Mr. Jones. You seem like a good candidate and I'd love to arrange some intercourse for you to see if you are a good fit. Why don't you come by tomorrow afternoon?"

I smile at this and suddenly a whole new comedy bit starts to develop in my mind, so I decide to flag a cab home to sit down and write some material.

✳✳✳

I write at my desk for an hour and then hit a wall. I gaze out my window at 4th Street, which is already cold and dark at 4:30 p.m. The loss of daylight in late December is the most disheartening thing about winter if you ask me.

Lutsey calls.

"What's up bitchy," he says when I pick up.

"Wow with the hostility!"

"So you better start rehearsing that shit you've been writing. I have a show coming up that's perfect for you and they need another act. They want ten minutes out of you."

"What do you mean out of me? Did you already give them my name? Is this at Liberal Arts?"

"No--something a little bigger. The Strip."

"The Strip? I'm not ready for the Strip! They wouldn't want my novice ass. Did you show them tape of someone else?"

"Relax. It's more of showcase for talent scouts. And it's already set up."

"I don't know man. That's still a lot of pressure for where I'm at."

"It would be more pressure if they were coming to scout you and this was your big chance. But you are just like filler. Plus the crowd will be smaller and mainly just industry types. The killer part is that my friend Rayna will be there. She's a big-time scout and also represents Kylie Fisher and some other big comics. She's bringing some people to give me a look for some sort of show she says.

"Really? That's great man! What kind of show?"

"I don't want to talk about it. I've jinxed these things before. But if you happen to kick ass, that can fast track you too."

"Nice," I say. My tone sounds both positive and negative at the same time. I feel my heart racing a bit. It's not the names that scare me as much as the venue, the Comic Strip Live in the Upper East, where I took Kate to see Lutsey and others the night I met her. It's in that second tier of New York's premier comedy venues and I can picture the likes of Bill Burr and Jim Gaffigan making surprise appearances.

"Ten minutes?"

"Yeah, ten minutes. It's a breeze man. And it's not until after New Year's so you have two weeks to add a few minutes to your set and rehearse. Maybe do a few open mics."

"That's a common theme for me lately. I'm starting a new job in two weeks. I won't have as much time."

"A new job? Since when?"

I explain the VH1 job I just landed and Lutsey considers this with a sigh. "Well, you can do both. You want to do both, right?"

"I think so."

"I know your thing about trying different careers and all, but comedy was always your dream man. You don't want to walk away from a dream for something you never even considered just like that."

I agree and nod my head from my desk. Comedy has always been dream. It's just that the stage has intimidated me in reality. And another thought sickens me suddenly. Maybe I'm just not funny. Not to anyone aside from Cassan anyway. What's the potential upside of this production job? Perhaps more stability with less stress while still enjoying creative work that is showcased on television for the world to see. I'm sure there are downsides, but that's the whole point: to experience and confirm. Maybe I am the next JJ Abrams.

"Of course I'm still into the comedy. I'll do the show damn it!"

After a lonely dinner at home, I feel like getting out of the apartment to think. I walk about 10 blocks to the Strand. The Strand is a New York institution when it comes to book stores with it's long flowing racks of every possible book that puts even online inventories to shame. The place is packed though, and after an hour of browsing and nearly hallucinating under the aroma of old first edition and rare books, I find myself in the welcoming oasis that a small video section provides. The collection of movies is nothing like the books section (it's more of a token section really) but I start thumbing through a rack of classics with no real purpose.

The conversation with Lutsey drifts back to mind. To think that I now have a day job and a night job! I know I should do some research on production, but it's not necessary. They'll tell me what I need to know when I start. It's the comedy that I'm worried about now. I have enough material I think, but you never really know until you whittle it down to what actually works before a live audience. In this sense, a comic is really more like an actor. Even the best comics often have a lot of their material written for them so they can focus on *performing* the material. The writing and the performing are two separate arts really, and to really be great you have to master both like a Louis CK or a George Carlin.

A feminine voice smashes the silence.

"Hey, didn't you work at that wine shop Elmers?"

My head jerks up to see a familiar, cute, young woman in glasses with somewhat pale skin and shaggy brown hair on the other side of the movie rack.

"Sorry," she says, with a smile. "Didn't mean to scare you."

"Ha! I'll never be the same. And yeah, I did work there. I remember you."

"I'm Diane. You gave me movie recommendations one time."

"Right! Casablanca I think I said, right?"

"That's right! But I still haven't seen it. I took your advice on Forgetting Sarah Marshall though and I liked it."

I remember her more clearly. She came for a bottle of white wine now and then after work. She was quiet and always looked tired and stressed.

"So this is where you come after you pick up your wine. You've been seeing other retail stores behind my back?"

"Just on Tuesdays and Fridays."

"And the rest of the nights?"

"I slave away in the office until 11 on those nights. That's Wall Street for ya."

She adjusts her glasses and I notice she is a bit shifty in her stance, but I don't know what to make of it.

"So why don't you give Casablanca a shot tonight. You can't refuse me twice."

"I didn't refuse you the first time. I was planning to get to it. I don't really do black and white very well. Plus it's supposed to be this big romantic movie that I probably shouldn't watch alone while drinking wine."

"I definitely agree with that!"

If I had to put her on the Alan-Elden attraction-personality curve I would place her just to the left of the optimized top of the skewed bell shape. That is, average to cute-looking. That placement on the curve corresponds with a good but not great personality in theory. I've met a few Wall Street women, but none with the personality I go for. Diane seems a bit different. Not because of the wine and movie nights of course, but rather for what seems like a timid demeanor.

"Here it is," she says. "Cassablanca. Humphrey Bogart and Audry Hepburn. Hmm. I definitely know their names."

"Oh my God. Just rent the thing already and watch it tonight. I might even go watch it for the like the 10th time myself now that it's on my mind."

"You want to watch it with me?"

"What, tonight?"

"Sure. Unless you have a girlfriend or someone that wouldn't like that."

"No, actually. I just meant that I don't even know you and it's a work night for you I'm sure."

"No worries. We can be watching with wine in our hands by 8. I just need to be in bed by midnight for work."

I didn't see this coming. I didn't think she would be courageous enough to ask.

"Sure. I'm in. Where is your place?"

"I'm close, but can we do your place?"

"Why my place?"

"Because my TV is terrible. You probably have a nice manly TV. Plus I would feel safer if we were at your place in case you were a stalker or a lunatic. You wouldn't want to chop me up to pieces in your own place. It would be a mess and evidence would be at your doorstep."

I smile at this, surprised by her sneaky wit. "Ok, my place."

If I were going to Diane's apartment I would probably have run home to change or freshen up first. She decides to walk straight back with me though, so there's no time for any of this. I'm thrust into her apparent world of indifference, which I can see in her sweatpants and hoodie, and in her workout sneakers and her faded eyeliner--all those things that Kate and Cassan were so meticulous about.

On the walk, Diane tells me how she has been doing the online dating thing.

"I hate it! Hate it, hate it. It just takes too long. You wink and they wink and then you both share a million emails and then if you finally meet up, they end up being nothing like you expected in bad ways. That's why I said let's just get together tonight to see a movie. I'm just so tired of all the time it takes to hang out with someone."

"That's pretty romantic," I say.

"You know what I mean." We walk in silence a moment before she adds awkwardly, "You know, I thought of asking you out a few times when I was at Elmer's."

"Well, I am far out of your league."

"Yup. Exactly!" She laughs. "I think it was so I could get discounts on wine though. Maybe you'll give me some now?"

I hint at the wackiness that brought me to Elmer's and how that was just a fleeting thing, but none of this matters to her. I mean this in a good way. It's refreshing to meet a woman who doesn't really care what I do. As we talk, this whole thing sort of feels like a date. There's nothing flashy about her, but it feels comfortable.

"Wow! I love this place," Diane says, as I give the brief tour of my apartment. "And your neighborhood is fantastic! This place must cost a fortune."

"Nothing a Wall Street gal can't handle I'm sure."

"I'm a researcher--not where the huge dollars are."

"Do you live alone," I ask. "Roommates?"

"Just a cat."

"I'm sure he keeps clean and doesn't party too hard. So you're a cat lady?"

"Oh my God, not at all. The cat sucks. If I had my way, I'd get a pet skunk."

"What? A skunk?"

"Definitely. They are actually very cute and extremely smart and affectionate. Much more than dogs and cats combined. Of course the scent sacs are removed too."

"So why don't you get one?"

"No building will want them plus there aren't any vets in this state that can treat them properly."

I take her bottle of wine and open it in the kitchen as she checks out some photos on my fridge. There's a photo of me on a boat with my parents and my sister and one of Cassan and I on top of the 230 Fifth rooftop bar. Cassan had stuck the photo there while she was staying at my place. I see Diane looking at it as I unscrew the cork.

"It's an ex-girlfriend. That wouldn't be there if I expected company." She says nothing though and just smiles as I fill up her glass with Chardonnay. For myself I open a separate bottle of red.

"A toast," I say.

"To skunks." I shrug her comment off.

"How about to taking your Casablanca cherry."

We clink glasses and sip.

"I'm not going to hookup or stay over or anything tonight," she says suddenly. And it's a real buzz kill. Not because it was so on my mind necessarily, but more because it is just such an unnecessary statement. I don't know what triggered it--the photo of Cassan?--but this whole night is her doing to begin with.

"Oh no?"

"Just not on a first date."

"So this is officially a first date? As of when?"

"As of the moment we bumped into each other at the Strand." I look into her weary yet hopeful eyes and there is something touching there. She's a real novice when it comes to men and dating, I can see. Probably because nobody outside of her office has seen her since she graduated college.

"I have a big one, you know," I say.

"What?"

"My TV. You were right. 60 inches. Let's watch this movie."

And then I do something neither of us expected. I block her path.

"And no worries about the hooking up thing," I tell her. "I was about to warn you not to get fresh." She smiles nervously and looks away. I know what she wants, so I go on. "But I think the only way to fully enjoy this movie is to kiss first. Get it out of the way...don't you think?" I reach over gently and grab her glasses and remove them slowly. It's a ballsy move, but I know I have this whole thing read perfectly. Plus I don't want to sit there and feel outdone for the next hour and half watching Bogart. And then I lean in and she looks me in the eyes briefly for a moment before reaching in herself. We hold our wine glasses by our sides and grab each other with our free arms and make out. I peck gently at her half-open lips and nibble briefly on her bottom lip, and for a moment we exchange a light tongue and then I stop it.

"Ok. So no more hooking up tonight," I say. "Movie time. You're gonna love this."

Chapter 21

MY HEAD IS THROBBING as I awake with Diane's arms around me. I slowly recall that we went through two full bottles of wine while watching the movie, and we exchanged a series of touching gestures that advanced steadily. After the credits, we erupted into a full-blown make-out session--clothes were shed and so on--and all I really know for sure is that we did not have sex.

Diane is spooning me ferociously now while letting out a cute little snore. I laugh inwardly at this, and at how easily she caved despite her resolution about a hook-up free first date. The alarm clock on my nightstand reads 9 a.m. and I realize that I have to wake her and tell her the news. The poor thing is facing a 15-hour workday with an extreme hangover no doubt. I wriggle out of her grasp so I can spin around to face her and I see she is really lights out. I tap at her a bit and she opens her eyes slowly and stretches.

"What time is it," she asks in moaning, elongated voice.

"I think you, uh...missed work."

"No. I woke up earlier and wrote that I was taking a sick day."

"Really? Wow. I didn't hear you."

She squeezes me tight, and it's an important squeeze. The casual affection shown the morning after a first hookup says a lot. It's a pivotal moment where you awake and either realize you are overjoyed or revolted by the situation and just want the other person out of your apartment. Oddly though, I'm caught in some content middle ground. I completely misread her while working at Elmer's. I took her for an ultra-conservative, money-driven workaholic with nervous social tics and an ostensive apathy towards sex in general. Even her name is a drag. Diane. But these judgments have all been soundly defeated.

"I'm not a morning person at all," she says with a yawn. "Can we go back to sleep?"

"Sure."

"Are you one of us?"

"One of who?"

"Us anti-morning people? Us sleepers? Are you one of us?"

"I don't know," I say. Yet as I close my eyes and sink back into the soft tickle of her hair and the childlike grip of her arms I add, "Maybe I am."

We awake again around noon and decide to walk to a diner. The air outside is colder than we thought though, so we go back inside to bundle up against it. I pack her into a silly hat with a pom-pom and long earflaps and men's ski gloves that are twice the size of her hands so that she looks like cartoon character, then we walk the four blocks to the diner.

Diane is busy trying to make sense of my life when the waiter delivers our food.

"So what are you going to do until your job starts?"

"I'm going to prepare for a show."

"A show?"

"Didn't we talk about this last night?"

"I don't think so."

"I'm sort of doing standup comedy on the side, but I've only been doing it for a few months and I'm not getting paid or anything for it."

"I love going to comedy shows! And I love comedians!"

"Really? Like who?"

"Hmmm. I guess Lewis Black and Jon Stewart and that guy that used to be on Saturday Night Live who did that Broadway Show."

"Colin Quinn?"

"Right! Him."

"So you like cerebral, political comedians?"

"I guess so," she says, digging into her Mexican omelet. And I guess it makes sense.

"What kind of comedy do you do?"

"I guess that's what I'm still learning. I'm more of a writer, so mostly obser-vational stuff like Seinfeld. Coming up with material has always been more fun for me. It's the performing that I have to learn. Style and stage presence is everything I'm learning."

"Well, I'd love to see you do a show. When are you doing one?"

I tell her about my friendship with Lutsey and how I have my biggest show yet coming up in a few weeks, and how I'm going to do some open mics and such to prepare. We finish brunch and I grab the check, despite my dwindling savings and no money coming in currently, and I start to wonder what I'll do this afternoon. Then Diane surprises me with a question.

"So where should we go? Would you be up for Rockefeller Center?"

"Rockefeller Center?"

"I know it's touristy, but I still love it around the holidays. I haven't been in ages."

It's not the destination that I'm thrown by. It's the matter-of-factness of our hanging out. The assumption that whatever happens next will be done by us together, as though we were in some serious relationship. But her company is easy and comfortable and I can't think of anything else I'd rather be doing.

"Sure. Let's go."

We take a cab because it's too cold to walk to the subway, and when we get out Diane grabs my hand.

"Hold up," I say. But it's not because of her hand. "I want to buy some cigarettes." I haven't had one in a few days somehow but I really want one suddenly, and I wonder if this will bother her.

"I didn't know you smoked," she says. "I used to smoke too, but I quit last year."

"I'm weaning off myself I guess."

I buy a pack at a gift shop on Fifth Avenue and when I light up, she gets up close to me.

"Can you blow the smoke in my face?"

"What?"

"I miss it. I know it sounds weird, but I like the smell of cigarette smoke."

"Seriously?"

"Yes." She steps up a bit on her tippy toes and leans in close like she's about to receive communion, and I just start laughing at the ridiculousness of her. So I take a drag and exhale, and she closes her eyes and smiles as the cloud engulfs her.

"Mmmm," she says. "So good! My third favorite smell after fresh cut grass and gasoline."

She takes my free hand again and we push through the crowded little pedestrian street that connects Fifth Avenue to Rockefeller Center. The alley is lined with the iconic Angels blowing trumpets, and I'm floored by how many tourists are here on a weekday afternoon. People bump into me from all sides and I hear snippets of conversation in every language known to mankind. The crazy thing is, I will be working nearby when the VH1 job kicks in. I'm sure I will hate the crowds then, but for now I embrace the holiday vibe, the commotion, and Diane. We get through the alleyway and see the enormous Christmas tree framed by The Rock towering above, and a great clear blue sky above. To our left is the skating rink, which is surrounded by throngs of people pushing in for a view of the ice skaters down below street level, and everywhere is chatter and the smells of roasted nuts and colorful flags and life flourishing.

We grip each other's hands tightly and work our way towards a spot to view the skaters. We laugh at the amateurs wobbling frantically and reaching for others to prop them up, and we marvel at those who seem to dance in smooth choreographic strokes across the ice.

"I love it all," Diane says. She looks at me suddenly with a big, cheerful smile, and she pecks me on the mouth with our lips closed before her eyes revisit the ice.

"Have you been here before," I ask.

"Twice I think. I was always younger though. We grew up in Connecticut and we took the train in around this time as a family. I always forget how beautiful it is."

I explain how I'm from Connecticut too, but not the part she is from. She in turn tells me how she attended the University of Connecticut for her BA and then again for graduate business school, and how she has never really known much of the world outside of Connecticut and New York City where she moved upon graduation. For my part, I shudder to think that someone could have no experience with travel outside the country or to the West Coast or even out of the Tri-State area.

I start to tell her about one of the jokes I will have in my comedy routine--the bit about gay travel as a category along with ski travel and such. It was a hit with Ian back in the spring I recall, but Diane looks at me for the first time with a bit of contempt.

"Alan!" that's terrible.

"What's so terrible? You have ski travel and adventure travel and gay travel--that's how it appears on travel websites. So all I'm really doing is pointing out how gay travel seems sort of incongruous with the other travel types." She doesn't get it and I knew she wouldn't and maybe the whole thing was set up as a test I knew she would fail. Either way, I don't care. And I think something else is at play here: the stuff Elden and I got into recently about my need to see past the Three Criterion and how I need to stick some of these relationships out and give things a chance.

So I up the ante. I tell Diane about the Attraction-Personality curve, which she dislikes as well. She confesses a strong politically correct sensitivity, but she admits that politically incorrect humor is part and parcel of stand-up comedy.

A little girl next to us drops her pretzel and I say out loud, "Wow, that's soooo embarrassing." The girl looks up at me confused and saddened, and Diane scolds me playfully. And I continue my tirade of goofy, immature humor as we go. Through it all, Diane scratches her head in caution or confusion and keeps asking if I'm making fun of her. Her responses are the exact opposite of what I got from Cassan when we were going well, but I shrug it off with determination to be more open.

We walk up Fifth Ave. past FAO Schwartz and across 59th past the Plaza Hotel and past the horse draw carriages where I attempt to discuss time travel with a huge brown stallion as Diane smirks and giggles. Then we head back down Broadway hand-in-hand as I continue to let her see the real me while I exploit the real her as best I can. Yet by the time my barrage is done and the sun has begun dropping on this shortest day of the year, Diane's random kisses continue and our fingers naturally interlock as we swing our arms against the multitudes of passersby.

Chapter 22

Two weeks later.

"HAVE ANY OF YOU ACTUALLY READ THE INSTRUCTIONS ON A CONDOM BOX?" I ask this of the small open mic audience at StandUp NY Comedy Club where I'm practicing for my show. I pull out a box I brought for this joke and begin reading the instructions verbatim. "Wash hands, as well as penis and vaginal area *before* and after sex."

Diane is seated with Lutsey at a table about 20 feet away stage right, and she smiles at me. I stop and breathe, keeping my pacing in mind for this new joke.

"What if you are hooking up for the first time and you suddenly go at it all passionately. You'd have to be Don Quixote to get through these instructions without ruining the mood or sounding like a doosh. Also, you have to assume you are definitely having sex without offending her. You'd have be like, "OK baby. Now before we actually have sex, what I need for you to do is to go into the bathroom and wash your vaginal area. I'll be over here scrubbing my penis and balls. Then I figure we can sort of reconvene by the bed in a few minutes. How does that sound?"

This gets a mediocre response from the 20 or so people here. I spot Diane laughing behind a covered mouth, but that's probably shock since she hasn't seen me do comedy before.

A light above the audience flickers, indicating that I have just a minute left. So from the condom bit, I segue smoothly into the bit I thought of after the VH1 interview about porn stars: The idea that resumes must be involved, otherwise the line for the "interviews" would span blocks.

"I'm looking for an entry level position," I say, imitating a job candidate.

"No shit. Who isn't?"

And from there I wrap up and jump off stage to a decent applause.

"Alan, that was awesome!" Diane says.

"Not too vulgar for you?"

"It's fine."

It's nice to hear, but I'm much more interested in Lutsey's feedback. He pulls me in for a hug.

"Getting there man. You ready for this showcase?"

"Really? You mean I sound like an actual comic up there?"

"You are improving quickly. It takes most comics several years to sound that legit onstage."

With this, Lutsey tells Diane it was nice to meet her and he excuses himself. He has to get back to Candice for some family event. Diane and I decide to stay for another drink to respect the other amateurs, but this proves painful. A few of them just stop in the middle of their act and walk offstage out of nervousness. Another guy just tells jokes that are ripped off from the old *Truly Tasteless Jokes* books without any style or voicing or transitions.

Eventually we slip out of there with Diane insisting on finding buffalo wings. The cold is a freshening change from the dank and overheated comedy room, and Diane takes my hand and buries her head against my shoulder as we walk.

After just a few blocks we hit the jackpot--a two-story restaurant advertising 30 different flavors of wings. We sit at a small booth by the window and order some beer and then Diane asks me about my new job.

"It's fine," I say. "I am interviewing actors and we are getting the rights to movie clips that contestants will be quizzed on.

"That's so cool!"

She takes my hand and rubs it thoughtfully.

"Do you believe in love?" And this throws me on edge immediately.

"What? Where did that come from?" *And are you crazy*, I add in my mind. This particular non sequitur borders on mental instability.

"I don't know. But do you?"

In my mind I quickly consider how serious I might be about this "one criteria" girl who I would never have gone this far with in the past. She's smart, but the humor is par and there are no creative or artistic aspects.

"Of course I believe in love. Why wouldn't I?"

"I mean, lasting love that stays powerful between a couple until they grow old and die."

"Yikes," I say, grabbing for my beer. "I think there are so many kinds of love, and if it's the right kind between the right people then sure."

"What do you mean by the right kind?"

So I try to explain this to her. The last time I counted (which happened shortly after my breakup with Cassan) there were 17 forms of love. It's the sort of list a man can come up with only when love-sick and drunk, having fallen into that abysmal, woeful despair beyond all immediate consultation and repair.

"I bet you can't name five," she says.

I admit the list isn't fresh in my mind, but I quickly spout a bunch off.

"Well, you've got love that is passionate, supportive, comforting, platonic, familial, tender, lustful, nostalgic, whimsical, compromising, innocent, passive, aggressive, passive-aggressive and more."

"Shouldn't love between two people be all of those things?"

"Sometimes it is. Usually it is a combination of many of these things. But to answer your original question, I think people need to feel the right way about each other and to the same degree. They need to demonstrate it at just the right levels I think. Some people are turned off by overbearing love, others need intense love splashed in their face at all times for instance."

Then I consider that I'm spouting off pure shit. Regardless, Diane takes a second to digest it, grabbing at my hand again under the table as she always does. She really is a good listener--I give her that.

"Wow, you really have thought this through."

"I think everything through more than you would know."

"OK, so can I ask you something else?"

"Go for it."

"What's going on with us? Like, are you sincerely interested?"

It's a sort of a taboo question for several reasons. First and foremost, it displays a lack of confidence that is always a turnoff. It gets the other person thinking unnecessarily about why he or she shouldn't be with you after all. What's more, it also messes with the head of the person this is said to, as though they were missing something or were about to be broken up with. So I go back to that soul searching and dig for an answer. Fortunately, what I find is that I do like her. For the life of me, I don't know why--but there it is. Before I can reply though, Diane beats me to it.

"The reason I'm asking," she says, "is that I have some news. My boss pulled me into her office today and offered me a big promotion that would require me to move to London next week."

I don't know what to say to this, so I offer what should be the first natural response between two people who are fairly new to each other.

"Wow. Congratulations. Next week though? That's fucking fast!"

Diane eeks out a wry smile in return.

"I know."

"Are you excited? Do you want this?"

"Yes. I thought they'd offer it next month, but things came up."

"Did you already accept it?"

"No. The thing is, I like you Alan. So the timing couldn't be worse. I could say no to it because I might have the same opportunity again in a year or two if I passed now, but there's something else."

"What?" I can't imagine what, so my question sounds demanding.

"It's my mother. I told you how she is sick and needs expensive treatments and this would give me the chance to help her cover it all."

I barely recall this, but it resonates fully now. "Except you wouldn't be with her. Or would she move with you?"

"No, she would stay here. She needs her specialists she travels to here in the city. But if I don't go, she would still get the treatments and she would just owe more later is all. Plus I can still take this opportunity next year. So really, the tiebreaker for me comes down to how you see us. I mean, how much potential you see in us."

"Wow." It's all I can say, and it sums up how I feel. "I still can't believe they're only giving you a week to move there. That's really short notice for such a big move."

"I know. That part sucks."

I take another sip of beer and decide to tell her exactly what I'm thinking.

"To be completely honest, I hadn't thought too much about things with us on a high level yet. This has all started out of nowhere and I'm enjoying it and having fun with you and I like you. If you're telling me that your decision to move to London depends on whether I think we could possibly end up engaged or something down the road, I'd like to ask if I could get back to you on that. I know that's not a very romantic response, but I need to think.

"How much time do you need?"

"When do you need to tell them by?"

"Two days max--Saturday. I might even leave as early as Monday if I say yes so I can get settled."

"Can I sleep on it? Is that fair? I don't want to sound like I'm putting it off. I also have that comedy showcase in two days and this is a lot to weigh, you know?"

She nods gently, and this time I take her hand and I ask her if she wants to come outside so I can smoke a cigarette and blow the smoke in her face. She smiles at this and we do just that.

Chapter 23

IT'S THE NIGHT OF MY BIGGEST SHOW YET, the comedy showcase for agents, scouts, and--most notably--Lutsey's powerhouse industry friend Rayna who is in from L.A. The show is much more important for Lutsey though, because apparently he will be auditioning for a new comedy talk show on cable. This is why Rayna flew out with several other colleagues. Lutsey doesn't like the pressure anymore than I do, so we decided to set up a dinner beforehand with our girls to distract us. We are seated at an amazing Brazilian barbeque restaurant on 49th St.

The elephant in the room for me is Diane, who I have yet to give my answer to. She's smart and easy to be with and I enjoy her company, but after lying in bed dwelling on things last night I realize this: She's has a good personality, but just not the personality I seek. I enjoy her company mainly because she enjoys mine so much, but it's more of a one-way street. She doesn't move me to the level of fun and passion and energy that I need--like I had with Cassan. It's closer than I expected though, I have to admit. I would have never considered a girl like Diane before, so that's saying something I guess. Maybe my Three Criterion aren't as accurate and necessary as before. Perhaps I can bend the rules and maybe happiness can't be bred. I mean, Diane really has little of what I seek on paper and yet I do like her. Not enough to commit to her so intensely and so quickly though. I don't think we have enough of a foundation for her to change her life, and so the biggest problem I have now is how to tell her so. It's been a while since I felt bad about breaking something off.

We flip our coasters on the dinner table to the green side, which means we are a go for a bonanza of 15 kinds of meats that waiters come around and slice onto plates. The girls order Caipirinha, which is a strong blend of Brazilian liquor made from raw sugar cane, sugar, and limes over ice. Lutsey and I opt for water, citing the need to stay sharp for the show. I'm working up a little beer buzz though.

"Are you feeling good, Alan," Candice asks.

"Baby, don't be messing with Alan's head like that."

"I'm just asking."

"I'm fine I say."

"He did a great show the other night," Diane says. "Lutsey saw it too."

What nobody knows is that I also snuck off on my own last night for another tune-up. I did an open mic at Ha! for a small audience and it was total shit. Granted, I only did the show to work out some kinks, but the audience will always get to you. I stopped a few times and looked at my notes and said a bunch of rookie things like, "that wasn't supposed to go like that" or "whoops, my bad," and I was met with a few jeers and heckles.

"Don't forget," Lutsey says, "Right after the show Alan and I are getting drinks with Ian and Rayna. Sorry ya'll, it's a business meeting for just us four."

"Is Rayna an agent or a comedy scout? I'm confused," I say.

"She's both. She's been a scout for a few networks and film directors, but she's also representing a few big comics like Kylie Fisher that she discovered."

"So is she scouting Alan too?"

I want to shush Diane her for intervening and making it about me like some over-proud mother. I'm curious about the answer though.

"She's not here for Alan, but I told her all about him so she'll be paying attention. Plus we are meeting after the show like I said."

"I see. But could Alan get discovered for TV shows or movies or something?"

"I'm not ready for any of that," I snap at Diane, trying to get her to back down a bit, but Lutsey doesn't mind.

"Why not man? The whole meeting can be huge. Actually, the meeting with Rayna after the show is just as important as your set. It's like an audition. Scouts want to see your act and that you can connect with the crowd, but they also want to see that you are a natural character offstage in real life. They like smart comics who are always on and just as funny in conversation as they are on stage. At least that's what Rayna told me."

"Rayna? Just her name sounds intimidating," I say.

"No worries. She's very cool and down to Earth."

"Tell me about this girl," I ask.

"What do you want to know? She's from Colorado and sharp and doesn't take any shit. She's tall, wavy brown hair. Curves in all the right places."

"So what should I talk about with her?"

"Just be you. Go with the flow man. You'll be fine."

✳✳✳

After dessert we take a cab over to The Strip on 82nd St. for the show. Lutsey and I go backstage, leaving Diane and Candice in line to get seated. There's a bar inside and as we walk past it, Lutsey spots Rayna, along with some other comics huddled around her.

"Hey baby!"

"Lutsey!" She jumps up and hugs him. "How are you darlin'?"

"Never better. Rayna, this is Alan Jones."

She has this larger-than-life presence about her, sort of like a rock star. She radiates this aura of social energy and this has nothing to do with her cute looks or her big chest set on top of a curvy but athletic, wonderful body. Her rugged brown hair flops out in casual yet calculated loops beneath a black hat with a silver star on it. She wears a matching silver shirt over nice denim jeans and tall suede cowboy boots.

"Of course he is. I've heard a lot about you Alan."

"Same-zies," is all I can muster, but she smiles and repeats the word.

"So you are going up tonight, right?"

"That's what Lutsey tells me."

I find myself drawn to her face, which is the slightest bit freckly and beset by big blue-green eyes like swimming pools that nearly throw me into a trance. Her lips are full and her cheeks are delicate and I'm attracted to her.

"So I see you like my hat," she says, just as she catches me peaking at her cleavage.

"Completely. Big and firm. You wear it well." I've decided to let the dogs of flirtation run. "I like it all. Is this going to be a problem?"

She laughs again and points a thumb at me to Lutsey.

"Where did you find this guy?"

"His old company booked me to perform at a launch party last spring. It was for a campaign he created."

"Ugh. I hate advertising--glad you got out," she tells me.

"What do you hate?"

"Just in my dealings with the industry on a professional basis."

"Aw, Rayna, our first fight!"

Her and Lutsey laugh at this and I feel good about this introduction, even if the flirtation route is cheating a bit.

"So I'm looking forward to meeting up with you guys for some drinks after the show."

"Me too."

She blows a kiss to Lutsey and I and leaves to go sit with her colleagues.

Lutsey had told me earlier in the week to keep my act fairly clean. Blue comedy (dirty comedy with lots of swearing) doesn't translate well to sitcoms and other things that scouts might be looking to cast for, and you don't want to blow your chance at some break because you relied on cursing. With these last thoughts, he gives me a bear hug and we head backstage.

Most of the comics know Lutsey and are on great terms with him in the green room. He walks me over to the emcee, Billy Thorngate, who I've never heard of. He's a tall guy with wacky thick hair like Conan O'Brien, but otherwise intensely ordinary features. He's nice and smiles wide as we are introduced and shake hands.

"Nice to meet you. Where are you from?

"Connecticut originally, but here in the city since college."

"Any credits you want me to list when I introduce you? All they have here is "a rising comic making the rounds throughout New York."

"I'm still pretty green, so you can leave that."

"Are you doing the ATM bit tonight?" Lutsey asks me.

"Yeah, why?"

"See if you can work in that he's a frustrated New Yorker," Lutsey tells Billy. Then he turns to me. "Frustrated is sort of a theme for most of your bits so far right?"

"Good point."

"You're up first, FYI," Billy says. I frown at this, but I can't complain. I'm in a room of major talent tonight and I'm the most inexperienced comic here, so it's to be expected. "Anyway, I hope you have a great set tonight."

And just then the lights dim and music plays as a deep voice comes over the speakers welcoming everyone to the "world famous Comic Strip Live," and Billy pounds our fists and runs on stage. Just like that. Normally I'd be terrified and feeling horribly inadequate, but I have a nice little buzz going and feel good for some reason. Maybe because I know where I stand on Diane. Maybe it's how things just went over with Rayna. Or perhaps it's Lutsey who is reaching over and plucking me suddenly like a kid. Either way, it feels good to consider how far I've come in this standup comedy thing, and I'm thinking clearly and ready to go.

After a few jokes about where people are from and a general warming up of the crowd, Billy announces me as "a frustrated New Yorker" to a big applause and I jog out to the stage full of adrenaline.

The lights are shining brightly in my face and I shield my eyes a bit to see that the room is packed to a point of possible fire violations. The club holds about 200 people and 200 are here tonight. Of course, they are here to see Jalen Moore and above all Seth Reed, America's hottest new comic and I hope Lutsey as well. So for Alan Jones, the pressure is off.

"What up?" I ask, adjusting the mic stand. Everyone claps and yells and I wait for the noise to trickle down to a few whistles. One cute college girl in the front screams "hi" to me, which makes her friends laugh.

"No, cutie. I wish I was though," I say. "Wait for it." Then there are a few laughs.

I see Rayna and three other people seated in the front row off to my right. She is whispering to one of them while a third is jotting notes. And the thought occurs to me suddenly that I should go off script a bit to let them see how I can interact with the crowd spontaneously. It's a dangerous play for me right now at my biggest show to date, but I feel sort of invincible and suddenly I'm going for it.

"So I heard some of you are from out of town?"

About half the room applauds.

"Where from?"

"Canada," some drunken guys yell from the back.

"Canada! America's hat," I say, which was on a t-shirt that I saw somewhere.

"Kansas," another person yells.

"Kansas? I was in Kansas," I say, which isn't true. "They call soda 'pop' there right? That's just stupid. I stopped at this gas station in the middle of nowhere--which pretty much sums up Kansas--and asked where they keep the soda. The guy stared at me like I was crazy and finally he said, 'you must be from out of town.' So I looked around at all the barren fields and said, 'I didn't realize I was in town.'"

The crowd voices their approval and that goes a long way for my confidence as I launch into my routine.

"So I was up in the ER recently and they put me in one of those robes with the hole in the ass. You guys know what I mean right? Those easy access robes. What's up with that? Shouldn't the hole be around the heart or something? I can't imagine the ER is loaded with ass injuries. It seems a bit perverted. I'm surprised they don't have little circular cutouts around the nipples and maybe a clear window with a zipper over the groin area."

From there, I transition into all the "frustration humor" as Lutsey calls it. I do the thing about the lost family looking for directions and move into the bit about frustrating things such as waiting in line for people at ATM machines.

"What takes people so long? Just push the button for the amount of money you want. Shouldn't it just be that simple? But no! This piece of shit is up there rolling over his 401K, he's taking out a home equity loan..."

The audience likes all of this. Then I do the bit about condoms and pull out my condom box and read the instructions and all, and I see Rayna and company laughing.

I start wrapping things up with a goofy bit about commercial jingles where all the melody is stripped out of them. Then I segue into my close--the bit I thought of a year ago about the old McDonald's jingle and tagline that went, "we love to see you smile."

"Are you telling me the McDonald's Corporation gives a shit whether you or not you're smiling as you're ten deep in line," I ask the crowd. "I can't imagine two guys mopping the floor after a busy Saturday night being all sweet thinking about us.

"Man, thank God this shift is done. I'm shot."

"Yeah but it was worth it. I mean, did you see all those muthafuckas smiling?"

I get a solid applause--the likes of which I've never known, not even in advertising campaign parties. Then I promptly exit the stage and head back to the green room.

"You killed it yo!" Lutsey yells at me.

"You think it was just the alcohol applauding me back there?"

"Nah man. Plus they just started drinking. That was your best show by far! You were natural and yourself and, most important, they connected with you!"

I sit with Lutsey watching the next few acts and I can tell he is the one who is a bit flushed for a change. He is growing quiet and distant with each minute and I can tell he is more thinking over his act than he is paying attention to the other comics. I start to feel nervous for him. Finally he is introduced and he slaps my knee and says, "See you on the other side of fame." Then he runs out and takes the stage to a big applause.

Lutsey has a real seasoned act and style on stage and everyone seems to know it. I really enjoy watching him work. He digs into online self-help medical care, and he talks about paranoia and how fatigue is a side affect of everything, even sex. All of his jokes are spot on, quick and powerful with solid punch lines. And what's more, I see how he tells stories that reveal a character of sorts, which is basically who he really is. It's that authenticity he was talking about that makes him so likeable. My style isn't nearly as authentic.

Lutsey drops a final joke about his pathetic savings account and exits to a standing ovation. He slaps a bunch of hands on his way over to me and pats me on the shoulder.

"You rocked that!" I say.

"Thanks. C'mon. Let's hit the bar. There's just one act left."

We settle in at the bar and Lutsey orders us both a Jack and Coke on him and we break down my act piece by piece. He refuses to discuss his act, and as always, he assumes this proud father role over my short comedy career. Other comics come by to say hello and before I know it, the show is over and all the patrons are filtering out past us. Candace and Diane come over and give Lutsey and I kisses respectively, and I order Diane a glass of her favorite Chardonnay.

✳✳✳

About ten minutes pass, and finally Rayna finishes saying her goodbyes to half the club and walks over to join us.

"Hi boys. Lutsey--they loved it. We'll talk later but I think you got it." Lutsey pounds the bar with the good news. I give him a hug and rub his head furiously. "And Alan, that was a professional set--newbie or not. Impressive! Are we still up for our little pow-wow?"

"Sure thing," I say, sucking the last bit of color from the ice cubes in my drink. I turn to Diane and kiss her again and tell her I will see her tomorrow. There's a world of expectation in her eyes and it crushes me for a moment. She looks up at Rayna and smiles and says good night to everyone and then leaves with Candace as planned. I watch her go for a moment, feeling a pang of guilt, but when I look back to Rayna and Lutsey this thought is completely replaced with excitement.

"I know a great little place with the ambience we need just a few blocks up," I say. "I know the owner and he'll hook us up."

I'm referring to Auction House on 89th. Cassan was great friends with the owner a few years back. We walk up 2nd Ave. and I sneak in a cigarette just before we arrive. The Auction House is small and dimly lit with candles and there's red velvet everywhere. The walls are lined with renaissance paintings and gilded mirrors, and soft jazz issues from hidden speakers all around us.

We sit on plush, elaborate couches around a small table and a staff member runs us over some red sangria. I sit like a third wheel for a while as Rayna and Lutsey discuss his set and the likelihood of him landing this TV show. I'm proud of Lutsey who is positively beaming.

"So, tell me about yourself Alan," Rayna says, turning to me after a while. Her tone is casual and harmless enough, but I know from Lutsey that it's a loaded audition question. "What are you into?"

I appreciate the question and launch into an unscripted, heavily buzzed monologue.

"What can I say? Life is constantly humorous to me. I've been into standup since I was six or maybe seven minutes old in the ER, but I was detoured by the advertising career out of Dartmouth."

I interject some pointed facts about myself--how I'm into comedy and literature and, above all, adventure and exploration of life. I explain my quest to find the perfect career and relationship and my five plot points and even mumble something about the curve and the triangle theory and it all sounds just zany enough to keep Rayna smiling and engaged all at once.

"You say you date a lot? What was the worst date?"

I consider the time I walked out on Jade while we were cooking together in her kitchen, but I realize I can't explain that without sounding like an asshole. "Nothing interesting. I was set up through a friend on blind date a few months ago. I had trouble getting in the mood to engage her, and what came out was a sea of banalities like, 'have you been here before? Nope. Do you like seafood? Yep.' That sort of thing. She obviously wasn't in much a mood either, and we both inwardly cursed our matchmaker. The date hadn't lasted 10 minutes and I was thoroughly bored. I went to the bathroom right after we got our wine and when I came back she was gone."

Rayna laughs at this. "Aww, you poor thing."

"No, really--it was brilliant! We both wanted to go and she just left and spared us both. I actually *wanted* to date her after that move."

Rayna asks for my opinions on a few celebrities and then prods me to share a funny story. The last time someone in the industry (Ian) asked me for a story I went with the time I got community service for wreckless driving and ended up working at the aquarium. So I decide to retell that one. Lutsey loves it from the moment I start, yelling "oh yeah, tell her that shit! This is mad funny Rayna."

I talk slowly but in an animated way and Rayna is loving it. Lutsey drains his sangria while laughing along as though he's never heard this.

"You're like my color commentator," I say to him. "Get it?"

Lutsey laughs and gives me drink a cheers. "You just get on with your story cracker."

"The thing is," I say, "they thought we were both marine biology students donating our time, and they would have never given us those jobs if they knew better. They put me in charge of the touch tank, which is where I had to pull these sea creatures out of tank like horseshoe crabs and educate everyone."

"Ha ha! And you didn't know shit," Lutsey yells.

"Exactly! I reach in to grab a crab and it's all snapping at me and pinching me and I drop it. If it looked blue I'd say things like, 'this is North American Blue Crab,' and anything I could to get through the day."

I start cracking myself up as I go.

"The funniest part--they had my friend Andy upstairs feeding the sharks and the seals. Sometimes they gave us megaphones and all these people would congregate to listen to us talk about stingrays in a tank."

Rayna gazes on me as I finish the story, listening to how I talk rather than what I'm actually saying. She's not laughing as much as smiling. This is something deeper, and I keep gazing deeply back. There's some unspoken connection that's palpable, and Lutsey brings this up himself when the two of us hit the bathroom at the same time.

"You are crazy in with Rayna," he says.

We don't say much more. None us do. We all decide to head home a little after midnight. Lutsey catches the first cab and I'm standing on the street for Rayna trying to flag another one.

"I'd like to talk to you about representation," she says, her eyes fixed on mine. "I don't usually take on new comics, but I think you have a shot at this. What do you think?"

"Send me the papers," I say.

A cab pulls over and I open the door for her. Before she gets in, she turns and says, "Can you write up a list some of those things you look for in a relationship and some things you hate? Maybe add a little color to each bullet point. I think that could be the basis for a good bit or something more. I want to share it with my partner in L.A. so he has some idea of why I want to roll the dice."

"You're giving me homework?"

"Yeah. Plus I get to see you more often this way. Let's meet again tomorrow for dinner and get this all done. I'll get your number from Lutsey and call you. Oh...one more thing. I don't usually mix business with pleasure."

She starts to sit, but suddenly pops back up and backs out of the cab, looking a bit tipsy. She leans in and kisses me. I kiss her back, slowly at first. And then we really go at it there on the street with the cabbie waiting.

"Not usually anyway," she says. "See you tomorrow."

I shut her door for her and watch as her cab shoots off. Perhaps I'll regret this kiss later, but certainly not now. Plus, it's good business!

Chapter 24

I HAD ALREADY WRITTEN THE SELF-PORTRAIT LETTER that Rayna wanted from me a year ago. I recall the day vividly. I sat down with a half-pint of vodka after a fight with Cassan and began jotting down some of my ideal wants and needs regarding women, along with some other thoughts about careers and humorous ruminations.

I want to read the letter now, but I'm running a bit late for work. I'm supposed help out with this shoot we are doing for the movie trivia show even though it's Sunday. Still, I can't help but sit at my kitchen table for a moment to read at least the beginning part of the letter:

Top three attributes I seek in woman:

1. Creative—Someone who is out of the norm a bit and highly creative and interesting; a hanger-on in the arts or one or more creative fields; ideally someone who not only appreciate these things but also contributes to some of them. Leads to engaging and interesting conversation.

2. Witty—A woman who is not only smart but extremely social and almost too lively; someone who can color any points or humor with snippets of brilliance; bizarre but intellectual inanities and a good knowledge of a vast array of fields like a Renaissance person.

3. Funny—Someone who is witty and wacky and goofy and always on with a great sense of humor that jives well with mine.

My phone rings. Diane is calling to say she is going to drop off some bagels and coffee for me in the middle of her Sunday morning jog, which I keep refusing to join her on, especially here in freezing cold January. She wants to have our serious talk of course, which I say we will do tonight. I tell her I have to get in the shower now, but that I'll leave the door open for her. Diane is gone when I get out of the shower, but my breakfast is there.

✳✳✳

A few hours later I'm staring at a monitor in the edit room at VH1 watching the same stupid video clip for the hundredth time. A video editor and the lead producer of the show--who is all stressed about wrapping this thing before her deadline tonight--surround me. And really, there's no need for me to be here. I worked to bring them the content that is now before them, and it's their job to make it sing. But the producer either values my opinions or is just hoping I'll spout out some random gem to help her get through this in time. I've actually enjoyed writing for TV so far--as much as I can, given the strict guidelines I have to work within. It's not like writing standup material where I can take things in any direction.

We finish at 4 p.m., and I head out into the cold, windy twilight, bundled fiercely in a thick gray overcoat and scarf over jeans, a v-neck sweater and collared shirt beneath that. I start walking while looking for a cab and Diane calls.

"Hi. Thanks for breakfast this morning," I say.

"Alan, we have to talk."

"Aren't we doing that now?"

"No. Seriously. Be serious for a minute."

All Cassan had to do was say "extension 207," our mutual code for getting serious. I smile thinking how much we respected it and how we reserved it for rare and vital uses. One time I said extension 207 when I didn't really need it and Cassan didn't talk to me for the rest of the night. That shit floors me.

"I'm listening."

"You never seemed totally firm, and you are always talking about what's ideal and perfect, and none of those things seemed to really describe me."

"What do you mean? Where's this coming from?"

"Well, I've been thinking too the last few days, and I agree we would be rushing it. And then I found that letter on your kitchen table about the perfect things you are looking for in a woman.

"Shit. That wasn't meant for you."

"Obviously."

"What I mean is that I put that together for Rayna."

"Wow. Is that any better? I got the sense you were into her."

"What? No! She asked me to write down some things as a bio of sorts. She's going to represent me like an agent."

She pauses.

"I don't know Alan. Why would she ask for what you seek in relationship?"

"Because we were talking about it last night and she needs to get a sense of my personality offstage to share with her colleagues. I guess it's important to them.

"Ok. So you do feel that way then?"

"I mean, I wrote that a year ago and I feel like I don't agree with most of it anymore."

"The thing is--those things you wrote, what you are looking for in your perfect relationship partner--those things aren't me. Not at all."

"Look, that stuff is not important to me anymore. It's basically like a sketch of a character I used to be and one that I am creating to give to Rayna. She wants to send it back to her team in L.A. since they haven't met me and she wants to sign me now. Tonight. It's not like I'm looking to marry a comedienne. And besides, I do like hanging out with you and you're smart and witty we totally get along."

I don't know why I'm suddenly defending this relationship and myself. Yesterday I would have been thrilled for Diane to break up with me without realizing I was about to break up with her. That way I would come across as the good guy. Perfect!

"I'll call you back. I have to take this call coming in," she says. And then she clicks off.

Just as I hang up and flag a cab, Lutsey sends me a text asking me to stop by Bar Nine in Hell's Kitchen where he is having a beer and doing some work. I text back that I'm on my way.

***

"What's up kid?" Lutsey says when I arrive minutes later. "Damn that was some fast response."

"I was in Midtown and getting in a cab."

"Sit down," he says, his eyes beaming. He ushers me to a seat at a table where a bottle of Veuve Cliquot is uncorked and a bunch of champagne flutes stand.

"What are we celebrating?"

"I got it!"

"The show!?"

"Yip! My own talk show man! A half-hour show with guests and break-downs of videos and shit. Sort of like Tosh.O meets Fallon."

"Holy shit! Congratulations!" I don't know what to say. I toast his glass and we throw back some champagne. "So you made it!"

"Well, it's a big step anyway."

"No, you made it. Even if the show got cancelled in the first five minutes. That's like every comic's dream!"

"Is it your dream?"

I hesitate.

"I didn't think so," he says. "But you're right. For me it is a dream. It's like finally all those years of working these clubs and squeezing out a living has paid off. I'm fired up son!"

Lutsey is positively beaming, and why wouldn't he be? He doesn't have all the details because Rayna just gave him the news over phone for now.

"Does it shoot in New York?"

"Yeah. Thank God! Could you imagine me driving a car and pumping gas and shit?"

I can't get over it. I'm thrilled for Lutsey and for being a part of the celebration.

"I couldn't have done it without you," he adds after a moment.

"Me? What do you mean? That's what I should be saying to you."

"Just being around your passion man. The way you have been going after things. It just lit a fire under me, you know?"

"Thanks for saying that. I'm glad if I helped at all. But I'm the one who owes you."

"Fuck you! You owe me nothing bitch. And by the way, don't forget you are going out with Rayna tonight. She said she's gonna fly you out to L.A. and get you on some big stages."

"Yeah, well, I wonder how much that has to do with my talent vs. her wanting to hook up."

"You hooked up with Rayna? I knew it man! Candace just lost a bet."

"Just for a bit on the street after you left."

"Look at you, sleeping your way to the top."

"Bad idea you think?"

"Maybe. Either way she's taking you for a ride. Maybe it's a great thing all around."

✳✳✳

I call Diane when I get back to my apartment and she answers in a somber tone.

"I thought you were going to call me back," I say.

"I wanted to think some more. But I do want to talk."

"Um...okaaaay." I take off my coat and sit down on the couch. "Let me have it."

"I'm taking that job and moving to London."

I pull the phone away from my ear and look at it. My emotions are mixed, but I know this is the best outcome. It is so done in my mind already that I want to move on and tell her the news about Lutsey and even about myself getting representation. After all, I might have stumbled into the dream situation. Not only a shot a possible dream career, but also a shot to date a woman in Rayna who is optimized on the personality-attraction curve and who possesses the *Three Criterion*. A woman my self-portrait letter describes--someone who is witty, funny and creative, and somebody who is not only in the comedy business but knows comedy inside and out and can help make it my business. Someone interesting and fun and energetic. In fact, I may be plotted perfectly on the grid of life suddenly.

"Alan, are you still there?" I hear Diane's voice issuing faintly from the phone and I put my ear back to it.

"Yeah. You know what? I think that's best. Best for you that is. Luckily we just got started and I don't want to get in the way of this huge opportunity for you and what it can do for you and also for your mother."

"You're not upset at all?"

"I'm upset, sure. I want to be happy. I want you to be happy. Luckily we weren't together long enough for it to hurt as much as it would have."

She doesn't like this reply, and I know it's pretty weak. I can sense frustration or maybe anger over the airwaves.

"Fine."

"When do you leave?"

"In two days."

"Do you need help packing?"

"No. I've already called the movers. It's all taken care of. Listen, I have to go. I have a lot of things to tie up quickly."

"Listen Diane--"

"Let it go Alan. Good luck to you and the comedy thing and finding the perfect girl."

She hangs up with that.

✳✳✳

I barely recognize Rayna when she arrives to meet me at Sushi Samba for dinner. She's shed her Colorado country girl flair. Instead she's dressed to kill in a black dress that sensuously hugs her body, illustrating her wonderful curves from head to toe. The black contrasts with her hair nicely, making it look blondish.

"What's up rock star," I yell over the noise in the restaurant's bar area. "You look great." We kiss cheeks.

"Thanks. What's good here besides me?"

"Everything. It's one of my local favorites."

"Looks like everyone's favorite," she says.

The bartender comes over and presents some warm sake and pours it for us.

"I took the liberty since I was a few minutes early," I tell her.

"Yummy."

"So is this real? You really want to represent a lowly green comic?"

"Why not? I've done it before. It's good to diversify a portfolio." She cracks her neck and sips her sake. "You never know when you might stumble upon the next big thing."

I sip some sake too, processing this quietly.

"It had nothing to do with that kiss last night," she adds abruptly.

"Nothing?" I'm glad to hear this.

"Well, nearly nothing. Lutsey was a much a bigger factor--as was your act that I saw of course. Can we slip outside for a cigarette?"

"You smoke? I didn't see that last night."

"I like to have one or two with some wine and good company. Call it celebratory cigarette."

We put our coats back on and tell the hostess that we will be right back and step out into the cold. The sun is well down and 7th Ave has resigned to nighttime. I look over at Rayna, whose sleekness is suddenly destroyed by her furry hat and thick scarf and puffy coat.

"You don't look so dangerous like that," I laugh.

"Me? Who said I was dangerous?"

"Well, cutthroat maybe? Or intense."

"You're just saying that because that's what you imagine a successful agent has to be like. But really, I'm just a social butterfly who loves good humor."

A passing cab blares its horn, which angers Rayna to a surprising degree.

"Stop honking your fucking horn sir," she yells at him as he comes to a stop. "Don't you see the signs that say don't honk?"

All I can do is laugh at this.

"Really? Are you serious with that?"

"Sorry. I've been hiding the fact that New York isn't my favorite place.

When we sit back down for dinner we talk about my background and then hers. She attended the University of Colorado at Boulder where she studied communications and knew everyone on campus. Her connections and her social skills opened some doors for her in L.A. where she dreamed of getting into entertainment on the business side. She started as a comedy scout and made a name for herself with some big finds like Kylie Fisher. This led to her becoming an agent in addition to a scout only two yeas ago at the age of 25.

"Would you believe they're paying me close to 200 to see who will make me laugh the most?"

I nearly spit out a spicy tuna roll when she says this.

"Is it a young person's game or are you just that perfect or that lucky?"

"A combination of all three. From what I hear, it was the same for you in advertising."

I nod while chewing. Her phone rings and she takes the call without apologies.

"What did he say? What? No, I'll call him and deal with it. Stay in Vegas tonight and I call you in the morning."

She hangs up and looks at me. "That was Kylie. Some dispute over a show he's supposed to do tomorrow night." She looks off blankly. Then she snaps back to me in a different gear. "Do you have any material on Japanese restaurants? Just curious. I haven't heard anybody do anything about them."

"No, just the stuff about Chinese restaurants I told you about. The mythological cuisines, the duck sauce, the fact that you've never heard a commercial jingle for a Chinese restaurant and what that might sound like."

"Sing it," she says.

"No."

"C'mon. I wanna hear one."

"I'm eating." She reaches at me to grab my chopsticks away and I pull back giggling with my mouth full and then she throws a piece of edamame at me.

"I'm sure Larry David could go to town on Japanese restaurants."

"Oh definitely," I say. "He did touch on them a little bit. Even shot an episode of Curb at Sushi Mambo on Bleecker Street."

We decide to walk off our dinner despite the mid-20s temperature, so we stroll down 10 relatively short and scenic blocks, following Bleecker over to the heart of Greenwich Village where the bars are always lively. We walk past the Red Lion, and I asked Rayna if she feels like dancing and she responds, "totally." So we dip in on a whim and starting moving to a decent rock band among the NYU undergrads while holding vodka drinks in our hands. Outside, the cold air is a relief suddenly. There is a stretch limo and I quickly negotiate with the driver who has an hour to kill.

"How about $20 bucks just to take us to the East Village," I say.

"Get in."

Rayna and I jump in the back and there are several bottles of liquor we have all to ourselves.

"Can we drink that," she asks. But as she looks over at me, I'm already pouring us drinks.

"How the fuck are we in a limo right now? This is ridiculous."

"You're ridiculous," I say, for no reason. I realize I'm pretty buzzed and I know she is too.

"No sir. Take it back or I tear up your contract."

"Hey I never saw any contract."

"Oh my God--we totally didn't get around to the contract yet! Let's talk at the next bar. Where are we going?"

"To the Merc Bar," I decide suddenly. "We can talk and it's chill there at this time." I roll down the partition to tell the driver where to go and then I open the sunroof to stand and stick my head out. Rayna stands up too and we cheers a few people with our glasses of vodka and she screams at New York. Then she turns to me and we start making out.

"What's not to love about this town," I say. I pluck her tits for no reason and she smiles drunkenly.

We look impressive stepping out of the limo on a Sunday night, but it's nothing out of place on this chic, cobblestoned street lined with expensive, world-class galleries and boutiques. The Merc bar is a notoriously dark lounge with a Niagra Falls theme and it can be romantic when less crowded as it is now. We nestle into a plush couch and exchange a few drunken witticisms that come out more like slurs.

"So is there a lot to talk about with the contract?"

"Not at all. Not now anyway," she says. "All I really need to say is that I sent your stuff to my colleagues as a formality and you just need to fly out to our offices in L.A. next week some time to sign off on the legalese. Then I can start coaching and preparing you for the L.A. scene and start booking you."

"The L.A. scene, huh?"

"Of course."

I balk visibly at this and stare down at my drink.

"You'll still live in New York and I'll be booking you in New York most of the time," she adds. "But to fast track you, we have to get you doing shows in L.A. too where I am. This way I can get you seen by more people who matter and create a bigger buzz for you."

"I get it. I just hadn't thought about it at all. So you want me to be a bit of a jetsetter and do the west coast-east coast thing?"

"Yes. Are you good with that? That's what you want, right?"

She puts her arms around me, and she stares at me with those seductive, lovely eyes in a way that no man can refuse, and it's easily apparent how so many comics have signed with her. At the same time, I'm taken aback at her lack of professionalism, even if she is drunk. Her advances might articulate what a long shot I am at making her money as a client. Would she be so reckless with bona fide talent? I don't really care at the moment.

"Of course that's what I want," I finally say. "And what do you want?"

"Just the best for you, which will be the best for me. And if it's not too much trouble, I think maybe I want you too."

Chapter 25

Four months later.

M Y VISION OF LIFE AS LATTICEWORK with its infinite points of intersection between relationships and careers and my exploration of them
has become tiresome. Somewhere on one of my countless flights between New
York and Los Angeles these last several months, I have begun to crave stability.
I've become a jet-set, bi-coastal guy with all the travel covered by my girlfriend
and manager Rayna and her agency. She usually books me for shows in the
second-tier Hollywood clubs on Friday and Saturday nights. When production
on the movie trivia show finally wrapped in late March, Rayna offered to put
me up at her place for a while.

Romance aside (and really, there has been less romance than business),
the whole point of the back and forth as Rayna explained it is that I am
preparing for the largest comedy showcase there is--Montreal's Just for
Laughs festival in July. My first real rehearsal is coming tomorrow when I
am going to be the featured performer at the Improv in L.A. It's a Thursday
night, but impressive nonetheless. For the most part I have been thankful
for everything she has done for me, pushing me along like no other green
comic could ever dream of. Still, there are those nights when I'm not up
for it, when a little angel appears on my shoulder and tells me this is not
the path; that this is not what I want. Even the Devil on my other shoulder
seems perplexed.

"What do I want?" I ask the Devil.

"I don't know man," the Devil says after some time, his pitchforked tail
tucked between his stupid devil legs. "But not this."

✳✳✳

We are at our favorite bar--Red Rock in West Hollywood (which is just blocks from Rayna's townhouse)--having drinks with Kylie Fisher who just got back from a series of shows in the southeast. There is also a writer for a late night show and the actor Hayden Fox at our table. Rayna doesn't represent either of those two, and it's unclear how she even befriended them. In her typical too-cool style she just mentioned to me that we were meeting up with some of her friends, and sure enough they are Hollywood successes--especially Hayden. And as much as Rayna and I enjoy a chronic battle of wits, I have quickly grown to dislike the whole Hollywood thing. I've come to see with Rayna that there are no casual get-togethers and that everything is somehow business. There's a grand pretention to the whole Hollywood scene with the constant need to be meeting up with industry people and gossiping as though we were TMZ staff on camera. Just once I'd love to have a laid-back teacher or a tech guy or a scientist or something at our table. And I know that L.A. is crawling with plenty of down-to-Earth people and that I'm only exposed to Hollywood types thanks to Rayna, but it just feels like out here, the whole universe depends on who you are seen with and what your next project will be. Lutsey had warned me about this and I totally get it now.

"I'm telling you Rayna, that hotel was for shit," Kylie says. "But I loved the cookies. Two fresh cookies they give you when you check in and I must have eaten 10 of them. I kept going back to the front desk and telling them I didn't get my cookies, each time using a different accent just to make them laugh so they would give me the frigging cookies."

This reminds me of the hilarious comic Bill Burr and his bit about how pissed and embarrassed he was to be offered a cookie by another man at a Doubletree Hotel. The whole emasculation he felt by the question irked him. "The sad part is," Burr said, "I would have loved a cookie! Ohh I would have loooooved one! But I say when. Not you!" I bring this up to Kylie, but he just nods and engages the table in another topic. It's obvious to me he doesn't like me. Or rather, he doesn't like how I'm getting a golden ticket in the industry for reasons he assumes are completely related to me hooking up with Rayna.

I excuse myself to step out for a cigarette, which is fairly well looked down upon in this town to the extent that nobody ever joins me. Even Rayna only smokes in New York. A line has actually formed to get into Red Rock since we arrived, and people in line look at me wondering who I might be. Surely they saw that I keep with some somewhat famous company through the windows. I ignore them though and call Lutsey to confirm that he is coming in for my show tomorrow. He had insisted on this all week. As always, he picks up right away.

"My man. You ready for tomorrow?"

"I guess. When are you getting here?"

"I land at 4 p.m. your time," he says.

"Are you going up?"

"Hell no. This is your moment. I'm just flying out for moral support. Although Rayna says she might get me up Sunday night to promote my show. My PR manager suggested it. Did I tell you I have a PR manager now?!"

"That's really cool man. I appreciate it you coming. And, no--I didn't know about the PR manager. When does the show start again?"

"June first. They said the guests are going to be some major actor and a rock star for the debut. Don't worry, you'll have front row seats."

"Can't wait. Listen, I have to run back inside this bar we're at. Give me a call when you land. We'll grab a quick drink before my show."

When I go back inside, I see everyone has slipped out except for Rayna who is sitting alone texting.

"Where is everyone?"

"They were going to that party, remember? They said to say goodbye."

"I didn't know Kylie was going too."

"No, he left for something else. You have to stop smoking out here," she says with her head still down typing.

I say nothing and sip my drink. I know she is about to go any minute too because she has to entertain some clients tonight. Finally she puts down her phone and looks at me.

"What's the matter babe? You seem distant tonight. I had to tell Hayden and Pete that you are normally the life of the party and that you must just be nervous about the show."

This annoys me some, because the implication is that I made her look bad. What's more, she barely included me in any conversations or even looked my way. She's such a fanatic about her job and the industry that whenever we go out with her Hollywood friends (which is all the time), she's always engaging them in industry news that I know little about and care for even less...except regarding comedians.

"Just jitters I guess. This is a big fucking deal. Or so you've been saying."

She reaches over and rubs my cheeks.

"I'm sorry babe. I know. But this is the first of many, and I just thought if I treated it casually tonight you wouldn't get so worked up."

"That's a great line, I have to say. Very diplomatic."

"What do you mean?"

"Nothing."

"Alan? What is it?"

Her phone rings.

"I have to get this," she says. "Just a second."

So I keep sipping my vodka and soda as she takes a call from someone she is meeting up with tomorrow. I don't even know what her plans are, and I don't really care. When she hangs up, I feel like ripping into her a bit, but I don't. We haven't really fought about anything high level yet, even though there's been this silent crescendo of animosity I have towards her job and the person she is when in work mode. Of course, that's also what makes her the best at what she does, and that's what put me here in West Hollywood, ready to be featured at the Improv tomorrow.

"Sorry again," she says after hanging up. She takes my hands, and at the same time, she leaps back into the Rayna that I like--or rather the Rayna that I should like given how well she meets all the girlfriend criteria I dreamt up. She massages my palm while looking at me with those intoxicating, beautiful eyes, and she speaks to me in that way she has of making a person feel like they are the only person in the world. God, I'm dating a schizo!

"You are amazing," she says.

"Go on," I say. "Be both manager and girlfriend."

She laughs.

"You are crazy smart and creative and you can do anything. You are as witty and funny as anyone I know and you are beautiful and soon to be a star."

"I guess I'll accept that," I say playfully. Neither of us has said much about any feelings we might have. Part of it is her awkwardness about relationships. She has had little experience with a boyfriend because of her extremely driven, workaholic mindset since college. Then there is the fact that we haven't really spent much quality time alone together with my weekend-only visits and her industry friends always with us.

The hand massage is all I get. Just as quickly as Rayna turns on the charm and attention, she turns it off, snapping back into her Hollywood industry self.

"OK, I have to run babe. We are meeting for sushi at Nobu before the House of Blues. C'mon, I'll drive you home," she says, standing up. But I'm not ready to go. I have a solid, wonderful buzz, and that's the only good thing I have left before this show. Once I'm home, I'll only be lying in bed alone and thinking about the show and working myself up into a nervous, self-doubting fever.

"I'm going to have another drink first and go over my act."

"Fine--but just one more so you're sharp tomorrow. And don't rethink your material at this stage because it's good. If anything, just focus on transitions and voice and being yourself."

"Impressive," I say. Her manager skills can be nearly as good as her agent skills.

"Thanks. I'll be back late knowing these clients, so we'll both sleep in and then I'll work my magic and have you in world-class form by show time tomorrow."

"Sounds perfect."

"Night babe." She reaches down and kisses me and then heads out the door with her phone to her ear.

✳✳✳

Red Rock is getting too crowded and I want to be alone with my thoughts like I used to be riding my bike in Key West. What a calm, wonderful time that was. So I decide to walk up Sunset Boulevard a little closer to home where I know an unassuming, divvy bar with an upstairs that I can have to myself. I want to write or just think or something--anything that involves being in a quiet bar alone. So I hit the bar and order a Jack and Coke and go upstairs. Sure enough, there is just this small room with a few tables and nobody else up there despite the great street view.

I begin by writing down my entire act for tomorrow night just to reassure myself that I know it by heart. As I go through the bits, I start to lose myself in the humor and slip into this dream state where I'm watching some professional comic idol of mine telling my jokes as I laugh inwardly with a huge smile on my face. I run downstairs to refill my drink, then right back at it. The material takes on this wonderfully surrealistic quality like the circular paint daubs of Van Gogh's starry night, and I feel like a conductor waving my fingers over the words that sing to me in ways that are suddenly every bit as artistic as they are hilarious. I feel the liquor course smoothly through my veins in rhythm with the humor, and I feel so suddenly on top of the world like never before. I wrote this material and it is the funniest material every written, and I realize that all of this is the culmination of a process that began the day I was born. Jokes crafted from 27 years of experience in this crazy, mad, funny, bizarre, silly life, and all finally coming together in a grand score of comedy that is my act. I don't even think about the performance. It's the work on paper before me that I am most proud of, even if the presentation of these words on stage tomorrow is what will determine my success and perhaps fame one day. I certainly do not care about the fame either though. It's the material I love.

I finish going through my routine, deciding it is brilliant, and then horrible, and then brilliant again, and eventually I settle on the fact that it is what it is: something I enjoy. Instead I'm more interested in writing new material without concerns for how it will come across on stage in my style--whatever my style is--but rather just writing comedy in it's purest form. Just getting funny thoughts and connections down on paper. I laugh aloud as I do this and feel better in the process. This is what I am best at! I know this now (or did I know this before?). I am a comedy writer first and foremost and only. Not a comedian. Not a professional stand up anyway. I fact, where was the need for my grid and the exploration of so many different careers when the very thing I am passionate about is what I have been doing all along!

A waitress comes up and delivers me another Jack and Coke.

"On the house," she says.

"Tell the house thanks!"

She leaves me alone again and I put my pen down. I start to dwell on the other dimension of the latticework--the part about relationships. I have a clear new perspective that ironically comes via drunkenness at times. Rayna and I? Something is off in a big way. Maybe my whole approach to optimization is off. Hell, the world is off, save for writing comedy and Elden and Lutsey and my family. The world hasn't really been on since I was with Cassan. Cassan, who I had all but forgotten in recent months and who is actually here in L.A. somewhere now! The thought of that is utterly surreal to me. And I don't mean that the perfect woman is out there as that old grid might suggest. Everyone will always be off in some way, I know. Even Cassan never really fit my criteria. I realize that now. But even then I was too busy thinking of what was wrong and what could be and analyzing everything to death. I set the system up for failure. Rayna fits all criteria and yet I barely like the girl. Sure there are always things people look for in others, but maybe there is also some intangible component that is every bit as elusive as happiness. Maybe that component *is* happiness. Simple stated and simple felt. Is it that simple?

I am tired and dizzy and want to go home suddenly. I polish off the rest of my drink and gather my things and head out.

The crazy thing about alcohol, I realize while walking onto the street, is that you can drink so much of it. That doesn't work with most other drinks. One Pepsi is just about right. If I drink another two or three, that's pushing it. After that, the process of drinking more would be slow and painful, like torture. But with alcohol, most guys I know have three or four drinks just to prepare for some real drinking. I don't know how many drinks I had tonight, but I think I just surpassed my old college record of 20, including beer, shots, and liquor drinks. I'm invisible, as they say in Mexico when you reach that point, and I find myself jerking down Sunset Boulevard all uncoordinated as though I'm on a unicycle. When I reach the gate of Rayna's townhouse, a police office comes over to me.

"Where do you live?" he says.

"Right here."

"OK, glad you got home safe."

"Thank you very much officer," I slur.

I stumble up the steps to her front door and have some trouble with the key as the cop watches from down below. I want to confuse him and just run. When he catches me he'll learn I do in fact have the key and that I've done nothing wrong. The frustration he would feel makes me laugh. Finally the door opens to a dark living room. I close the door and feel my way to the couch and when my legs hit it, I topple down hard. The world is spinning in and out of alignment.

Chapter 26

I HEAR RAYNA YELLING FOR ME in the hallway backstage at the Improv, but I slipped into a vacant room so I could be alone for a moment to breathe. Rayna had spent the whole afternoon nursing my hangover with every known home remedy, scolding me for getting drunk last night all the while. She had me fairly recovered, but it's show time, and suddenly I'm more nervous than ever before.

I'm pacing around the room, rehearsing the act in my head. Suddenly the door slams open to reveal Rayna again, her eyes fixed on me in a cold stare.

"What are you doing? What is this?"

"I'm fine. I just needed a moment alone before I go on. Am I on?"

"Jay has a few minutes left."

She's referring to the opening comic who is warming the crowd up for me. I can feel my heart pounding a bit and I tell her so.

"It's adrenaline. That is the rush that comics crave," she says.

But I'm not a comic. Not in the professional standup sense. I knew it in Key West with Amber. I've known since last May when Cassan broke up with me at that French bistro before I began this maddening, singsong journey of mine, and I began to accept it, I think, on every trip back and forth from New York to L.A. these last four months.

"I'm not a comedian," I say, avoiding her stare.

"What? Alan, you're just nervous. You're—"

"No!" I demand. "You don't get it. You couldn't get it or you don't want to get it, but you've turned a blind eye to it along, and I've been doing the same. I'm just not a comic."

"What are you saying? Are you trying to say you won't go on?"

"I'll go on," I say. "I owe everyone here that much. I owe you that much. But then I'm done."

"Alan. You have to calm down. I get it. It's your biggest show ever. The nerves always creep in."

"It's always going to be my biggest show ever. And I'm going to hate the feeling that comes with all of them. I'm not cut out for this."

"What are you saying? Comedy is your greatest passion."

"I love comedy, yes. I love to watch it. I love to laugh with friends...with anyone. Most of all, I love to laugh to myself as I write it. But performing it onstage--the anxiety of acting it out--it's just not what I enjoy. It's not your fault or mine. I gave it a try. And I've learned it's just not something I want to do anymore. I just don't like it. In fact, this whole thing with us doesn't feel right."

We stare at each other in silence. She must think I'm a quitter. This whole thing has felt more like business than romance since we first made out in New York and she must know that.

"Well, I'm not sure where this is all coming from all of sudden, but we need to talk about it later babe. For now, you have to get in the right mindset to give a good show."

I'm taken aback that she is not more curious about my feelings regarding *us*. Can't she know I'm hinting at a breakup?

I look at her big eyes framed by that black hat and sloppy brown hair, and then down at those tall cowboy boots of hers. I am no longer drawn to her, and I can see her aura of happiness is just that--an aura. If you permeate it you will find a woman vehemently pursuing her own concepts of perfection and attempting to surround herself with these images, paying little regard to any actual connections she might make. I bear no ill will toward her for any of this. None of this is her fault really. It's just who she is. Rather, I cringe at the notion of myself forcing self-actualization.

The door busts open again and we both turn to see Lutsey in the doorway. He had phoned that he would be late, so this is the first I've seen of him.

"Lutz," I say, utterly thankful to see him.

"There you kids are!" Then Lutsey addresses me specifically. "Are you ready to rock this brother?"

I nod yes in a way that implies no, but I do feel instantly better by his mere presence.

"I'm fine," I say finally. "How much time."

And as Rayna starts to answer, we all hear my name announced outside the hall on the other side of the curtain where a few hundred people are ready for jokes.

"You got this man."

"Call me Ishmael."

"That's the spirit!" He runs over and slaps my back. I look over at Rayna and feel a bit bad for her suddenly for no particular reason and for 100 reasons all at once, and I reach in and kiss her.

"I'll be fine I tell her. You'll be fine."

She doesn't seem to hear any of this. She smiles and she wishes me luck as I run out the door and through the curtain to applause.

✳✳✳

There is no standing ovation as I'm still an unknown quantity. The crowd knows I'm the headline act tonight, and I can see the expectation on the faces of people in the first few rows outside of the spotlight. They give a warm applause and I know many are scouts looking for a few more fresh acts for the Montreal festival. They are here to see something new, something exciting. And then, as I adjust the microphone and wait for the clapping to subside, I notice one familiar face at a table off to the left. Cassan.

"Thank you, thank you," I say. "Who the hell are you people? I do know one person over there. Hi Cassandra."

She looks absolutely flustered and waves back. And I give a breathy laugh into the mic and say, "I used to have sex with that girl." The crowd turns their heads to look at Cassan, who is a good sport about this. She waves a dainty hand at the crowd as if to imply that I'm just a goof talking nonsense and she goes back to sipping her drink silently. And really, this provides a good launching point for my routine.

"When it comes to sex," I say, walking about the stage, "it's much better to be the fuckor than the fuckee. You know how guys talk with their friends. They're like: 'You know Jenny from accounting? Yeah. I fucked her. That's right.'

"Girls will do it to. They're like: 'Oh my God. Did you just fuck Steve? You did, didn't you! Go Michelle!'

"But what's the first thing you say when something goes horribly wrong? 'I'm fucked. I'm getting totally fucked on this. Unbelievable.'"

I get a good reception and I look to my left where Rayna and Lutsey are standing out of view from the audience smiling. Next I do the bit about annoying things--the ATMs, and bodegas being treated like casinos--and then I do my relatively older joke about screen names.

"I tried to get an email account and every screen name I typed was taken. I got frustrated and typed 'eat monkey, taste monkey,' and even that was taken! I got a message suggesting I go with 'eatmonkeytastemonkey54.' So apparently, there are 53 other eat monkey, taste monkeys out there."

My act runs 25 minutes and when the lights flash to indicate I need to wrap it up, I feel I huge sigh of relief. I had a good run--a great run considering how long I've been at it--but sadly this standup thing has missed the mark. I bow to a clapping audience, including Cassan, who I look over and wink at before exiting the stage.

✳✳✳

Cassan is seated at the bar near the club's entrance waiting for me. When she sees me, she stands and we swallow each other in a huge hug.

"Oh my God. That was awesome!"

"How the hell did you know I was here?!"

"I saw your name in Time Out and had to come. Seems like you're doing great."

"I'm OK," I say. "How about you?" We both sit down at the bar and I order a scotch and I order Cassan her favorite--Grey Goose and soda--without asking her.

"Well, the fashion career isn't as glamorous or fulfilling as I used to dream, and I'm between relationships now, so I've been better." She bobs her head sarcastically. "But I see things more clearly these days. And one thing I see is that I should have supported you more on this comedy thing when we were together. And in everything else really."

Rather than cut her off to explain how that was likely the last show I'll ever do, I just nod along with thoughtful eye contact. I can feel my body warm and tingle all over at just the gist of what she is saying, even if the words are a blur.

Our drinks arrive and I quickly sip at mine in silence, which Cassan takes as her queue to keep talking.

"So I know we sort of made up back in New York, but I deserve to take some shit from you for who I was when we dated, especially at the end. You were never in the wrong. I just wanted you to know that. Anyway, I just want to say that I'm sorry...for everything. I've made some mistakes and thought I wanted things I didn't really want. Maybe that's just part of being young, but I should have known better."

It's almost as if she had been spying on my brain the last year. I quietly keep sipping my drink. She continues talking cautiously.

"Also...I...I just want to say that I will always love you. I want you to know that. I know I said differently when we broke up but I didn't mean it. I didn't know what I was saying."

"Why did you leave me again?" I ask. For the first time I think I know, and yet I want to hear her say it.

"I guess somewhere I got blinded from the fact that I love you. I wanted to force you to become something that I didn't even want you to be. I have been trying to change since we broke up. Even before we did. You have no idea how hard I've tried. I dated people that weren't for me. I pursued things that didn't interest me.

"Same here--*believe me*."

"Really?"

"There's a former girlfriend of mine over there, with the cowboy hat on." I nod towards Rayna who can be easily be seen watching the show off to the side of the stage from our angle."

"You dated her?"

"Yeah."

Cassan smiles at this for some reason. Wiping a tear from her eye.

"Interesting. When did you break up?"

"Just before I walked out on stage. Same with the standup comedy thing."

"Oh," Cassan says. There's a look of bewilderment on her a face.

"Change is overrated," I continue. "Everyone promotes the importance of change all the time, but I don't know why. I was so happy with you and I just never stopped and focused on that. I got distracted thinking about these ideals of mine and you picked up on that. I just didn't know you were going through the same thing. I was angry with you for going through exactly what I was.

Cassan nods her head, piercing my world with her blue, soggy eyes. "So what are you saying?"

I take a deep breath and finish my drink. Then I place down a twenty for the drinks and pull Cassan by her wrists towards a side door with an exit sign. The door opens to an alleyway with a stoop that is illuminated by an overhead streetlamp. I slump down on it and indicate for her to sit down beside me, which she does.

"Look, Cassan. You know I still love you. I always will. You were perfect I thought in many ways, but I wondered if I was just in love with the *idea* of you. And that night in New York I fell in love with you all over again. And just seeing you now--it's happening again. I never wanted to lose you and I still don't." I want to say more, but she cuts me off.

"I still love you too Alan."

Cassan throws her arms around me and we kiss long and hard. It's the sort of kissing that attempts to match the passion. We twist and reposition ourselves and kiss softly at first then hard as though we are speaking of our love through our kisses. This continues for what feels like days. Blissful days.

Eventually we pull back, eyes drooling with love and happiness. We look at each other and kiss again. Cassan begins to cry and I suddenly being crying too. The true, prophesied cry decreed by Elden the Seer; A great and holistic release constructed from the deepest reaches of everything that I am and that I believe in and feel. It is perhaps, a purging in a sense, of all my idiocy in my quest for the ideal and the countless blown opportunities along the way. For all the people I may have hurt and let down up to this moment. I cry joyfully for us, and sadly for letting down Diane and Rayna and Kate and Jade and Amber. There is crying for letting Lutsey and Steve down, and for my abrupt departure from VH1 and my journalism career, for my wine management career, and for a thousand careers and relationships that I have never known and never will know, because the one thing I do know is that we live but once and there's only time to enjoy what we can. Above all there is crying for finally knowing what I want and for knowing that I have it.

Chapter 27

"I HAVE AN OFFER FOR YOU," LUTSEY SAYS the next morning some 30,000 feet in the air. I turn from my window seat view of the scattered clouds and look at him. "Nothing Earth shattering or anything. I mean, it's pretty damn obvious actually."

"What's that," I ask. I stretch in my seat and maneuver for more legroom for the remaining five hours of flight time back to New York.

"Come write for me and my show." Lutsey stops there a moment to gauge my initial reaction. Receiving none, he continues. "I mean, why not man? You said it yourself. You don't want to do standup anymore, but you still love to write material, so there it is.

"There it is," I say.

"Yeah man, it would be great for both of us. Hanging out, writing together, both doing what we enjoy. Making decent money too."

I'm half surprised he didn't mention it before, even when he thought I was going to make it doing standup. And he's right: it is a great idea.

"Sounds solid. I was wondering if maybe I go back to advertising though," I say. "I enjoyed it enough and did well."

Lutsey shakes his head.

"I still think you can make it in comedy man. Even just writing it."

"Thanks. And I owe most of that to you. But maybe it's time to stop jumping from thing to thing."

"But this isn't a jump man. Comedy writing is what you really wanted all along. It's pretty much what you've been doing all along. Am I wrong?"

I consider this as I pour a ginger ale in my plastic water cup over ice.

"No, you're not wrong. Do you even think I can do it though? I mean, writing for other people?"

"Hell yes," Lutsey says. "Of course you can. And it's not writing for strangers--it's writing for *me*. You've been doing it in a way since I met you."

It's an inspired little comment, but as soon as he stops talking, Lutsey cracks open a bag of potato chips and crunches into one. This makes me laugh.

"I'll think about it," I say. He scowls. "I will," I protest.

"Cool. Not to press it or nothing, but I need an answer by like tomorrow."

"Tomorrow?"

"Yeah, before they fill the last staff writing spot. The show starts next week kid. I have major pull, but I can't just have you come on any damn time you want. I can sell this if I have a few days before we start taping."

"It's your show isn't it?"

"True. But it's my *first* show. I can't get all prima donna on them by making demands for extra staff writers before I even get on air. You know?"

"Fine. Tomorrow afternoon. Let me just see about Cassan first."

After the L.A. show, Cassan and I went out to dinner and discussed her moving back in with me in New York. We couldn't keep our hands off of each other at dinner and then at her place where I slept, agreeing that we are both more in love now than ever before. She's all I can think about.

"I'm supposed to research flights and moving companies for her as soon as I can."

Lutsey nods. And then I wonder if I'm being a bit of a jerk because it seems my whole life has suddenly been cast aside in getting Cassan back.

"Do you think Rayna will be ok?" It's the first I've even really thought of her since yesterday.

"She wasn't too happy about it, but she'll be fine."

Before we left the comedy club, I ran back stage to thank Rayna for everything--for the opportunity and for believing in me and for our time together. I meant every word of it, but she just shrugged and said good luck.

After a while, we both nod off to sleep and when we finally arrive at LaGuardia, we jump in cabs and speed off into the comfortable New York night. It's only 10 p.m. when I arrive at my apartment, but with the jet lag and mental strain of the weekend I just drop my bags and plop down on my bed and crash.

✳✳✳

It's late Monday morning when I awake to the sun brightening the maroon curtains that Cassan left intact when she borrowed my apartment last. I must have slept 12 hours. I hop on the computer and do the research I promised her over breakfast and then my phone rings. Elden.

"I'll paint a picture," he begins to say in lieu of a proper greeting. "The air is a bit breezy but warm and wonderful and people are in bars partying already. I'm sure you love New York in the late spring like I do. It's really quite tenable... concur?"

"Damn you. Why don't you ever let me know you are coming? I could have been in L.A. or something."

"Well then I'd have to just hang with my lady friend instead. The world would still spin. So are we going out?"

"Where are you?"

"Penn Station."

"It's Sunday."

"Wrong. It's Cinco de Mayo. I bet you haven't even noticed in your fluxed state."

"Fluxed state?"

"You know, swooning over Cassan and the whole L.A. weekend you texted about. And in any case, who needs to define what days of the week are for having fun?"

I could never say no to Elden, I know.

"You have a party lined up I take it."

"Nice take," Elden says, probably with that huge, cartoony smile. "Yeah, Lower East Side. Friend of a friend. Are you in?"

"Of course I'm in!"

"Wham!" I can picture him doing a little jig on the other end of the phone in front of a bewildered crowd of strangers.

"Not like I have work tomorrow anyway. I'm glad you're here man."

"I know. Lutsey called with some details and I grabbed the next train."

"I'm glad he did."

"And he wants to surprise you by showing up," Elden says. He tacks this part on late as though he were fighting it back.

"You ruined his surprise."

"Not at all. *Just don't tell him.* It's a pointless surprise anyway."

I tell Elden to come straight over (which was his plan regardless, having a key and all) and I whip up some sandwiches for lunch along with glasses of water and wine as I breakdown my entire weekend for him. He grins at times as though this were all part of a grand plan he concocted.

"Not bad for a year."

And by this he means the all my stupid struggles--self-inflicted and otherwise--and arriving on my feet for the most part. The fight with Cassan in that French bistro seemed liked only minutes ago, along with Elden's declaration that I would cry three times this year.

"I've only cried twice really," I say. "Twice in utter sincerity anyway."

"I stand corrected then. Gladly."

✳✳✳

The clock strikes 5 p.m. and the perfect weather combined with a wine buzz has us both itching to hit the holiday happy hour.

We take a five-minute cab ride to a dumpy looking three-story brick apartment on Rivington. Elden presses the intercom button and somebody buzzes us in without saying a word. We walk the three flights up a dreary staircase and we can clearly hear the noise of a party issuing from a red door to our left. Elden nods for me to follow and he opens it without knocking. Immediately we are thrust into a crowded living room comprised of about 30 people clamoring over hip-hop music. There are large abstract paintings on the wall and a makeshift bar in the corner of the room that supports a few bottles of vodka and tequila and many bottles of Mexican beer. There are also streamers spewed about the walls in a noble attempt to preserve the Cinco de Mayo vibe. Just behind the bar is a glass sliding door that appears to open out onto a large rooftop area where a few people can be seen talking in several small circles.

"Just got a text from Lutsey," Elden says. "He'll be here in ten."

I like that Lutsey and Elden are getting closer. It's always great when you introduce two of your friends and they click. Not sure why. Maybe it's part selfish--the idea that you have two human beings that gravitate towards you and want to join your alliance. And here you have my two closest friends bonding over the common need to celebrate what only they would know to be my post early-life crisis. I can't help but feel much lighter and relaxed. There never was a crisis at all perhaps. It's as though someone sat on a Whoopee Cushion and a year's worth of angst suddenly hissed out and all of the stress and anxiety and sadness has been displaced by good friends, a good woman, a renewed positive attitude and the realization that the world is once again mine to enjoy.

Elden takes my arm and pulls me to the bar.

"Dos cervecas por favor," he says with an unabashed disregard for hipness to a stoic male bartender. Of course, with Elden's zealous tone and demeanor, even the smuggest hipster can't help but appreciate him.

"Sure thing man. Here you go."

The bartender cracks two Coronas and hands them over and we clang our glasses.

"To the three of us gentlemen. Enlightened from doing what mooooooves us," Elden says, and then we chug our beer.

A moment later, a tall girl with a sombrero comes over and kisses Elden.

"There you are darlin'," he says. "Where were you?"

"I was there Elden. Now I'm here. Like you." She smiles and Elden smiles back and steals her hat for himself.

"Atta girl. Just like I taught you."

Elden turns to me, and the girl turns in succession.

"Alan, I present the Generally Accepted Lewis Principle of Location"

We all laugh at this nonsense and I'm introduced to the girl who I now realize is the very same that Elden met at the HRGM Advertising party at Hotel Gansavoort last spring.

"There's my people!" And this familiar voice hurdles over half the room towards us. We all turn to see Lutsey pushing his way over in a sleek black shirt and slightly askew Yankees hat. And as I promised Elden, I feign surprise.

"Lutsey! Holy shit! What are you doing here?"

We hug it out and Lutsey is beaming.

"Candice here too?"

"Fuck yeah!" she yells, moving in behind him. And it's great to see this couple elevated together like never before. I can tell Lutsey's new show has done for him what Cassan has done for me. We've been given a rebirth of sorts, and that new joy has trickled down into Lutsey's love life. The sight of them happy together fills me with warmth, and suddenly I'm compelled to tell Lutsey what I knew the moment he brought it up on the plane earlier. So as soon as he reaches me I pull him in closer as if to whisper.

"About your show. I'm all in. If I can still do it."

He drops his jaw and his face lights up.

"My man! Of course you can still do it! And damn good thing, cuz I already told them yes for you this morning."

"You did?!"

"We both knew you would take it, especially with you being back with your girl and all. You good with that?"

"I'm great with that," I say, and I mean it.

Elden hands Lutsey a beer and pats our backs and raises his glass.

"To Ishmael."

"Here, here!"

"What's Ishmael?" the girl asks. Elden attempts to explain that whole mess of joke as Lutsey heads for the bathroom, and I excuse myself to smoke and check out the roof patio scene for a moment.

I open the slider and the warm, breezy, fresh May air charms my soul. I walk to an edge away from everyone, but decide against the cigarette and instead take a long drag of clear blue sky. I feel amazing. And in an unexpected instant, my eyes suddenly tear up a bit. At first I wonder if it's the breeze, but no--I'm tearing up, damn it. Tearing, I know, for the big lovely rolling picture of life that has so suddenly been realized. I'm 28-year-old comedy writer for a show starring my idol and now close friend Lutsey Lampkin and I'm love with Cassan.

I see the slider open from the apartment and one of the girls from inside appears in the doorway. The odd thing is that I recognize her. Megan, I think. She's a small, freckly brunette production assistant from VH1 that I worked with briefly. I remember her as being fun and goofy. She lights a cigarette and spots me with the same vague sense of recognition and yells over to me.

"Mind if I join you?"

"It's a free world," I say, hoping she doesn't catch my watery eyes in the booming sunlight. She can't though, and she begins tiptoeing towards me around the skylights and pipes that emanate from the rooftop. She trips a bit as she draws close and her skirt flaps up in the breeze à la Marilyn Monroe. And as she approaches, I know indeed that it is a free world with a great infinitesimal number of possibilities like stars under a dark Key West sky. And I can date this girl and it might be great, but even the thought of departing my current grid point in life disgusts me. Nothing--nobody I could ever imagine would make me happier than I am now no matter how perfect they might seem. And as this girl stops before me and says hello, I wipe at my eyes a bit more. Eyes watery from happiness, I know, but that doesn't count now, does it Elden?

About the Author

Jeffrey Allen amassed seven W2s in a single year shortly after graduating college, which helped spawn the idea of the Perfect Everything. He has experience in stand-up comedy, newspaper reporting, and a litany of creative and professional ventures. He maintains a renaissance passion for writing and plans to author novels in several genres.

Mr. Allen was born in Greenwich, Connecticut, and currently resides part-time in the West Village of Manhattan.

www.ingramcontent.com/pod-product-compliance
Lightning Source LLC
Chambersburg PA
CBHW020607180626
46810CB00007B/2679